But the LORD was not in the wind: and after the wind an earthquake: but the LORD was not in the earthquake. And after the earthquake a fire: but the LORD was not in the fire: and after the fire a still small voice.

—I KINGS 19:11–12

Can't find heaven, I don't care where they go.

—SKIP JAMES, "HARD TIME KILLING FLOOR BLUES"

my dreams out in
the street

my dreams out in the street

KIM ADDONIZIO

Simon & Schuster

New York London Toronto Sydney

SIMON & SCHUSTER
Rockefeller Center
1230 Avenue of the Americas
New York, NY 10020

SIMON & SCHUSTER and colophon are registered trademarks
of Simon & Schuster, Inc.

For information about special discounts for bulk purchases,
please contact Simon & Schuster Special Sales at
1-800-456-6798 or business@simonandschuster.com.

Book design by Ellen R. Sasahara

Manufactured in the United States of America

10 9 8 7 6 5 4 3 2 1

Library of Congress Cataloging-in-Publication Data

Addonizio, Kim.
   My dreams out in the street / Kim Addonizio.
      p. cm.
   1. Homeless women—California—San Francisco—Fiction.
   2. San Francisco (Calif.)—Fiction. 3. Domestic fiction. I. Title.

PS3551.D3997M9 2007
813'.54—dc22

                              2007009569

ISBN-13: 978-0-7432-9773-8

for Steve Vender

1. On the San Francisco Muni bus, Rita sat facing a woman in a purple and yellow clown costume with billowy sleeves, and huge white shoes that took up half the aisle between her seat and Rita's; the clown's little girl picked up a Snickers wrapper from the floor and was about to put it in her mouth when the clown slapped her. The child wailed, the wrapper clenched tight in her fist, while her mother tried to pry her fingers open. Rita couldn't stand to watch. She got off at the next stop, several blocks early, and arrived at the shelter just after ten P.M.

The shelter's big double doors were locked up tight. Rita knocked and knocked, but nobody even came to the other side of the doors. She stood for a couple of minutes, waiting, listening for footsteps or the sound of a kid acting up or someone dropping coins in the pay phone. But it was eerily quiet in there, as though everyone were asleep already, or dead.

Whatever they are, she thought, they're inside. Safe in their bunks, inside four walls and a roof, and I'm shit out of luck once again, which is the story of my life and will forever be the story of Rita Louise Jackson.

She sat down on the cement stoop. Someone had drawn a narrow, blue chalk heart on it and, next to that, a gun with a long barrel, pointing at the heart. It was signed TALISA '97. Rita listened to the wind rattling the dry tops of the eucalyptus trees bordering the parking lot and felt afraid of whatever was roaming the earth. A spirit, a demon, following her, judging her for the bad things she'd done.

On the bus, she had felt frayed and depleted, her head buzzing, motes of dust in the air swirling like gnats in the fluorescent lights. She hated being on the bus at night. Those lights were brutal—all the ugliness of people's faces coming clear, with sharper edges than in daylight. The face of the woman clown had been pinched and mean. Rita had felt the slap like it was her own face.

She'd imagined getting to the shelter in time, crawling into the bottom bunk that had been hers for the past week, falling asleep before lights-out. Now she forced herself to shift gears. Hell, it was early. No one should have to call it a night at ten o'clock. Old people, maybe. Sick people, and little kids who belonged in bed soon after supper. *Now say your prayers, honey, and I'll tuck you in.* When she was little, Rita had prayed for a doll that drank from a bottle and wet its diaper, for a bicycle with streamers, for her mother to be happy. Her mother was often sad or angry, closing her bedroom door, in bed watching TV surrounded by magazines and cigarette packs and pills that had gotten lost in the blankets. Rita had prayed not to be, as her mother put it, such an ungrateful little pain in the ass. After her mother's death, Rita had prayed for her mother's immortal soul, hoping it was in a place where prayers could do it some good. Maybe the clown on the bus would be nice to her girl later, saying, *I'm sorry, baby, I lost my temper.* Rita pictured the girl curled up under a pink blanket with a pattern of blue horses on it, her arm cradling a stuffed animal, and wanted to cry because she wasn't that little girl and the shelter doors were locked and her bunk would be empty, all because of a bitch in a clown suit.

All right. Next move.

She headed toward the splash of light that was a café. Outside, at one of the wrought-iron tables, a girl in a long flowered dress and combat boots sat across from a boy with thin blond hair and a clean black T-shirt and boots that matched the girl's, and they were both smoking and gesturing with their hands, talking excitedly. She hated to interrupt them, but no one else at the tables had a cigarette in evidence.

"Hey," Rita said to the girl. "Sorry to bother you. Spare a cig?"

The girl looked about her own age. Rita wanted to ask the girl how she'd worked out her life so she wasn't alone and homeless at twenty-four, how she'd worked it out to be sitting in a café with a boy who looked like he was sensitive and sweet.

That could be me and Jimmy. We could be sitting there, having a fine time.

"A cig," the girl repeated, a little disbelieving, like Rita had asked for her dress or something equally outrageous.

Rita shrugged. "If you can spare one," she said.

Jimmy was her husband, and he was who knows where now. They had once had an apartment and everything, but they had sort of slipped down. They'd been evicted and were in a hotel room for a couple of months. Then he walked out after a fight, and Rita went looking for him but she got lost for a few days behind heroin, and when she made her way back to the hotel, their room wasn't their room anymore. That was in July. It was November now.

The girl flicked her eyes at Rita, granted her a half-smile and a Merit Ultra Light, and turned back to her date.

"Thanks," Rita said to the girl's profile. "Appreciate it," she said and moved away toward the corner before she lit up.

A cigarette was always the first move when a problem

presented itself. A few deep drags and no matter what was wrong she was in control, having a smoke, a little time-out from not knowing what came next. She walked down Waller Street, turned on Clayton, back to Haight Street. The next move was obviously a drink. Having a drink was also a good time-out. After that she wasn't sure. Maybe she would try to make some money. Maybe she'd just get drunk. The rest of the night would have to sort itself out.

I don't care what I do, long as I'm away from Terrance.

After Jimmy wasn't at the hotel, she had spent a few days sleeping on the streets and visiting the places they used to go. She'd gone back to their old apartment on Jones Street. She'd gone every place she could think of they had been, but he wasn't ever at any of those places. Then Terrance came along with his two-bedroom apartment, a settlement from a car accident that left him with a metal plate in his brain and a kitchen stocked with alcohol. He had cable TV with a million channels. All he seemed to want, most of the time, was someone to listen to him while he rambled on about the state of the country under Clinton and the son of a bitch who'd run him down while he was peaceably standing at a bus stop. He gave her money when she asked. She took over paying his bills, which since the accident he had been unable to decipher, and buying needed household items. Every few days, she made the rounds of the places where she and Jimmy used to go. Terrance never tried anything sexually with her, but recently he had started, in his inept fashion, to get violent. This usually happened in the midst of some argument he started and carried on one-sidedly, until he turned to her, saying, "Don't you see what I mean?" followed by a wild swing that usually didn't land. When, a week ago, he had tried to make a particularly forceful point by attempting to push her face onto an electric burner on the stove, she had gone to the shelter.

A bus stood at the corner of Haight and Clayton, pointed toward downtown. She decided to get a drink on Market Street. She slid into a plastic seat halfway back and closed her eyes against the glare of the lights and the bus driver's knowing, contemptuous look. He could tell she wasn't just a club-goer, in her tight black skirt and silver tank top, headed to meet a group of friends or maybe a boyfriend. He could tell that she was something else. Somone less than he was, who didn't deserve respect, who men could handle like a bar of soap, leaving themselves clean and satisfied and her disappearing down to nothing. She couldn't stay at the shelter forever. She needed to make some money, and this was the fastest way she knew. She hated how the men touched her, but it was like hating the small blotch of the birthmark on her cheek; it was a flaw she couldn't do much about. She always covered the birthmark with makeup, and she tried not to think about what she had been doing with various men for the past week.

She opened her eyes to slits to see if the bus driver was checking her out in the rearview; he met her eyes and smiled in a way she recognized. She pulled her black nylon bag onto her lap and turned toward the window. The reflection of her face floated there, pale and anxious. She leaned her forehead against the glass, looking instead into the city at night, the storefronts and restaurants, the bright neon bars where people were gathered. She could feel the indifference of those people, like some kind of particles in the air. The particles got into her skin and settled inside her with her other burdens.

Around two A.M., she got let off back in the Haight by a

man in a panel bakery truck. The truck had wire racks filled with soft, fragrant rolls and cellophane-wrapped loaves of bread, but the man had smelled like meat—like raw hamburger. His face was the shape and color of an uncooked patty, flushed pink, his mouth a tiny effeminate bow. For a five-minute blow job in the back of the truck, he had given her eighteen dollars, a loaf of day-old rye, and a free pass to a movie at the Landmark Cinema of her choice.

The first time Rita had sex for money, she'd run away from her latest foster family in San Jose and hitchhiked to San Francisco. She took the cable car to the top of Powell Street and went into the Fairmont, because it was so glamourous—a stretch limo with smoked glass windows was parked out front. She sat in the lobby watching everyone, admiring the big vases of flowers and feeling self-conscious in her jeans and sweater. Nobody paid her any attention for a long time, but then a blond man in a gray suit offered to buy her a drink. She told him she was only seventeen, and then he just came out and offered her fifty dollars, *to go somewhere with me*. She knew what he meant by how he looked at her. She'd run off with a backpack of clothes and thirty-four dollars, so the fifty was hard to resist. And the man seemed nice; he had green eyes and smiled in a way that said he'd like to be her friend.

Rita followed him down the street to an office building, along a hallway, and into a bathroom where he pulled down her jeans and fucked her quickly over the toilet. Then he left, saying he had to go get his wallet. She waited several minutes until it sank in that he wasn't coming back, and then she walked back down the hall, past a desk where she felt the eyes of the receptionist burning into her with total knowledge and recognition of the bad thing she had just done.

The next time a man looked at her that way and offered her some money, she said, *Pay me first.* It wasn't as bad when she got paid; she was worth something, she wasn't getting ripped off like the first time. It was wrong and it was ugly but it was easy to fall into when she hit a wall.

Plus, by then she had discovered heroin. It helped to be high—to deal with the men, and life in general.

When I met Jimmy, I thought all that was over.

She could taste the lubricant from the condom the man in the bakery truck had worn.

Haight Street ended at Golden Gate Park. The park was scary at night—the blackness of trees and bushes, the small sounds coming from animals she couldn't see. She scanned the shapes of shopping carts and prone bodies, the neighborhood homeless camped out on the wide stretch of grass. Her throat felt dry and raw, and she wished she'd gotten some more alcohol before it was too late. She wasn't drunk enough to feel safe. She should have filled her flask when she had the chance. The fear rose in her, fear of the darkness, of the next few hours and the hours after that, and she tried to push it away.

The breeze was wet, filled with fog, silvery in a narrow path laid down by a streetlight. There was an old wino named Charles, who usually got his meals at the shelter, who she knew slept here. She went to find him, walking in a wide arc to avoid the other homeless in case anyone was awake. A car took the curve of street to her left, and a few bars of Whitney Houston's singing soared over her and Dopplered off while she stopped and stood still, feeling like a rabbit on the roadside. Then she walked farther in.

Charles was on the hillside, down close to the pond. He lay flat on his back next to his cart. His dog, Sally, a scraggly terrier, was curled against him. Rita slipped a rolled-up pea coat out from under Charles's head. Neither of them moved. They were both probably drunk; she'd often seen Charles feed Sally a Styrofoam cup of beer. Thinking of beer made her thirstier than she already was. She lay down a little ways from Charles, under his coat, and fell into an exhausted sleep.

*

"Rita, Rita, talk to me," Charles said.

He was leaning over her. His long white beard, yellowed with strings of tobacco spittle, was the first thing she saw. His morning breath was in her face. In her dream, she had been petting a huge animal that looked sort of like one of the buffaloes that lived at the other end of the park, but also like a giant roach. Then she dreamed about her mother, lying dead in the bathtub in their old apartment in San Jose. It was a familiar dream. In real life her mother hadn't been killed in the tub, but in her own bed, by a man named Karl Hauptmann. Karl Hauptmann had starting coming around a few months after Rita's father left. Her father had sold coupons door-to-door for Golden West Photography—*Professional Full Color Portraits Only 99 Cents*—and was gone from home for long stretches, until, when Rita was twelve, he just stopped coming home at all. Karl had made her mother happy at first, but it didn't take long before they were yelling at each other more than kissing and dancing around the living room.

Rita knew it was her own fault that Karl killed her mother. First of all, she had told her mother what Karl had done to her one day after school, and her mother and Karl had a really bad fight. And second of all, Rita had stood outside the bedroom door listening to them, instead of calling the cops or trying to stop him somehow. Just stood there paralyzed and afraid, while things broke and her mother screamed, *Get out,* and Karl yelled, *Fucking bitch,* referring to Rita or her mother or both. The phone was shut off again, so Rita would have had to go next door to Mrs. Morales to use hers, and Mrs. Morales might not let her; it depended on her mood. So Rita stood there until Karl came slamming out of the room and shoved her aside and kept going. And that was how things went from bad to terrible, and how her mother ended by lying there with her throat cut, and Rita ran away and came back and landed in foster care, and Karl went to prison and was still sitting on death row where Rita hoped they were going to fry him one of these days.

Charles shook her gently, his hand on her shoulder.

"Rise and shinola," Charles said. "Time to get a move on."

Around them and farther up the hill, people were sitting up and scratching their heads, rolling up sleeping bags or blankets or ponchos, lighting cigarettes and joints. Sometimes the police left them alone, but right now there was a campaign to clean up the park. They'd be rousted from one place and move to another, sometimes getting jailed for a night or having their carts taken away. The park was okay, as long as you got up early and sauntered down into the neighborhood for a while. People sat in doorways on Haight Street or on the steps of the Free Clinic or on the sidewalk, leaning back against a brick wall, and after the police made their sweep they would circle back and hang around the park all day, drinking and smoking and talking.

Sometimes during the day, Rita went to the other end of the park, to the Arboretum. The summer tourists were gone. She would walk along the paths looking at desert plants or trees from New Zealand or sit by the lake watching the turtles sunning and the swans circling side by side. Or she would go

over to the small redwood forest and sit on a log bench, look-
ing at the lilies and the light coming down through the tops of
the trees.

"What's up with you?" Charles said. "You on the streets
again?"

"Missed the shelter curfew." She sat up, shivering.

"I prefer the great outdoors." He straightened, threw out
his arms. "Fresh air," he said.

Charles didn't smell very fresh. He smelled like a Port-A-
John that hadn't been serviced in a while. Rita moved
slightly so she wasn't downwind.

In the shelter, some people had jobs and were trying to
save for a place of their own. It took a lot: first month, last
month, security deposit—and everything had gone sky-high
because of the dot-com boom. People ironed their clothes at
night and put them on hangers at the ends of their bunks
and went off every morning to work. Others were headed
the other way, from apartments that had burned up or
houses they couldn't pay for, and they were scared that this
was just the beginning of their troubles. When the kids did
crayon drawings, they all drew houses: boxes with two win-
dows and a door, like eyes and a mouth, with bright flowers
in the yard. The drawings were up on all the walls and made
Rita think of store windows full of things you could look at
and wish for but never have.

At night, she would lie on her bunk behind the faded
flowered sheet she'd hung from the bed above her, listening
to people talk in their sleep, to kids coughing, to a loose win-
dow jiggling in its frame at the slightest wind. She didn't
sleep very well. She thought about Jimmy, and Terrance
blasted out of his mind on Wild Turkey or tequila, and that
piece of shit Karl Hauptmann. She thought of how she was
supposed to believe in herself more. This was according to

the counselor, Sheryl. Sheryl had told Rita to say to herself every night, over and over, *I am a good person, I deserve to be loved.* But after saying it a few times Rita got to thinking about other things instead.

What I have to do, she thought now, watching Sally frantically scratching behind one ear, is get some more money together and get my own place.

If I could just find Jimmy, everything would be all right.

Charles was whistling in between drags off his cigarette; it made Rita's head ache. She looked at his Safeway cart, filled with pots and pans and other kitchen junk. She checked the front of her underwear for her plastic Baggie of folded bills, making sure it was still tucked there. The morning was foggy, but she wanted her sunglasses. She didn't like people being able to look in her eyes. She put them on and the fog darkened a couple of shades, so it seemed almost like it was still night. People were shadowy, the tree trunks black.

She took out a sweater and jeans and fresh underwear, changed her underwear under the skirt and pulled the jeans up before removing the skirt. She combed her fingers through her hair a few times. It needed to be washed. She sniffed at an underarm and it smelled like sweat and the baby powder deodorant she used and Charles's coat.

I'll get a hotel room tonight. I'll start figuring things out. I'm twenty-five soon. That's a quarter of a century already. Time to get my act together.

Step one, no more shelter.

The tune Charles was whistling was "Zip-A-Dee-Doo-Dah." Rita's father used to sing that. There was a funny word in the song that used to make her laugh. Satisfactual. *Everything is satisfactual.* The mornings would be sunny, he'd be frying eggs. She could smell them, sizzling in butter. She stood on a red kitchen chair to help cook, gently working the spatula underneath so the yolk wouldn't break and spread all over. Later, she would help him in the garden, weeding and picking off snails and dropping them in a blue plastic bucket of beer. So they would die happy, her father said. She'd pull up carrots and pick mint leaves for tea and fill a white mixing bowl with the sweet strawberries that peeked out from under their leaves; she would pluck them and eat as many as she put in the bowl.

Charles was squatting beside Sally, rubbing her behind the ears. "Hey, darling," he crooned. "Hey, honey darling." He had a pink bald spot on his head the size of a sand dollar and long hair past his shoulders. He'd been a longshoreman once, working on the docks in Oakland. He said. Everybody made up stories, so who knew. Everybody lied to and used everybody else, and women in clown suits slapped their kids silly for nothing and then looked at you with hate in their eyes like it was your fault, and you wanted to pull the kid away from all that, but instead you got off the bus and missed curfew. It hurt her head even more, thinking about how life was, how people were. Sometimes they surprised you, though. One more pearl of fucking wisdom from Sheryl, the counselor. Sheryl was younger than Rita, and she was actually only an intern, an earnest, overweight girl in expensive jeans and sweaters. "I'll help you figure it out," Sheryl had said. "You're not alone in this." But two days ago she'd left to go back to some college down the Peninsula, without even saying goodbye.

"Time for breakfast," Charles said. "Wanna come?"

"No thanks," Rita said.

Charles sang, "The beer I had for breakfast wasn't bad, so I had one for dessert."

"Dessert doesn't go with breakfast."

"The hell it doesn't," Charles said. "Later, then. Good luck, baby girl." He piled the pea coat and a military green rain poncho and a rolled sleeping bag on top of his shopping cart of junk. Rita wondered what he did with that stuff. Pots and pans and muffin tins and rusty steel graters and slotted spoons, and no kitchen. It was crazy. He went rattling off toward Haight Street with Sally leashed at his side.

Rita's left hip and shoulder ached. She stretched a little, but it didn't help.

Just about everyone who'd been in the park a few minutes before had melted away like ghosts. There was only the fog and the trees, the grass worn to bare dirt in several spots, damp McDonald's wrappers and rings of cigarette butts and drained bottles of Night Train and Thunderbird. A police car slid around the corner. She started walking fast away from it.

*

The Blue Door Deli was part of Rita's daytime rounds, one place she and Jimmy had gone sometimes. She ordered tea, swirled the Lipton's bag, and stirred in two packets of sugar. EAT OUT MORE OFTEN, it said on the packets. Rita always thought that was funny. HAVE ORAL SEX MORE OFTEN. Men never wanted to do that. They wanted to put it in your mouth, but most of them didn't want to get their own mouths anywhere near you, except your breasts. They wanted a doll, a dead person. Usually, Rita knew how to go inside herself so she barely noticed them. But sometimes she had to pay attention to follow what they wanted. Or else she'd start thinking about Jimmy leaving, which always brought her back—from floating somewhere beyond the moon, her head on Jimmy's chest and one hand playing with the few fine hairs on it, crash-landing back into reality. Then she'd smell their skin and their bad breath and hear their nasty words, and she'd feel panicked and trapped.

Late last night, after she'd been locked out from the shelter, she'd found herself in a hotel room in the Mission, her skirt pushed up, lying under a drunk black man who couldn't get hard. He kept rubbing himself and trying to push it in, but his penis, damp and wormy, slid away each time. Blues was playing on a little clock radio beside the bed. Somebody singing with a slide guitar, and then a harmonica part. That called up a picture of Jimmy, sitting on their bed in the apartment on Jones Street playing his harmonica, and suddenly she was breathing too fast, trying to get enough air, but her throat was shut tight like there was a wad of gum lodged there and she couldn't get the air to go past it into her lungs. Then she was hitting and shoving at the sweating body above her.

"What's up," he said, rolling away. It wasn't quite a question. Like he wasn't surprised, and didn't really care.

She was already standing, grabbing her bag. The hall was empty, except for a rat exploring a red plastic dish drainer. The rat looked up as she passed, looking like it had something to say to her, but she didn't wait to find out what. She ran down the stairs and into the street. She kept going for a couple of blocks, then went into a bar, into the bathroom at the back, washed and put on clean underwear and threw up, then washed her face again. She'd had a few shots of Canadian Club by then and no dinner. She ordered a vodka cranberry at the bar and ate two bags of pretzel sticks. After that she walked for a while down Mission Street, and the man in the bakery truck stopped and offered her a ride.

In the Blue Door, she nursed her tea at a corner table, watching the room. People came in for coffee to go, for croissants and muffins. A slim, olive-skinned man in a gray suit and a Jerry Garcia tie, holding open the *New York Times,* smiled at her and she lowered her eyes. Maybe he was just being friendly. She couldn't tell. The rule of thumb was simple: With the rare exception, men will try to fuck you, or fuck you up, or both. She had learned this when she was a girl, and nothing since had contradicted it.

The owner of the Blue Door was a big, scary-looking man, six feet and over two hundred pounds, and Rita knew for a fact he was gay. He used to own the deli with his boyfriend, who would talk to Jimmy about blues musicians they both knew of. The boyfriend was a skinny man in a wheelchair with red hair and sores on his face, and he looked half dead, but he always perked up once the music conversation got going. Rita could never quite keep straight the names of the people they talked about. There seemed to be a lot of Little Someones. Little Walter was one she remembered. And Sonny Boy Williamson. There were a lot of Sonny Someones, and Blind Somebodys, too. There had been two Sonny Boy Williamsons.

She was sad now that the boyfriend wasn't there—he had gone into a hospice around the time Jimmy disappeared, and then he must have died. At least she could have talked to somebody who had known Jimmy, who knew who Rita was. She was still Jimmy's wife, even though she didn't have the ring anymore, or the blue and white paper that said "Marriage Certificate, State of California, County of San Francisco." It had their names on it—Rita Louise Jackson and James John D'Angelo—joined in marriage on November 30, 1994, in the presence of Matthew Chumley and Diane Johnson, and it was signed by the justice of the peace above the words, "Signature of Person Solemnizing Marriage," certifying what had happened three years ago and was supposed to last forever. Rita had looked at the marriage certificate a lot after that terrible day when she got back to their hotel and Jimmy wasn't there. The manager had saved it for her with a few other possessions. Then it got lost, somehow. Like everything else precious.

"Fags and foreigners," a skinhead boy at the counter said, looking at the man with the Jerry Garcia tie. "That's what's ruining America." He said it quietly, though, and not like he was mad about it. He looked at his companion, a big, overweight girl whose hair, like his, was shaved to a shadow on her skull.

"That's exactly it, Slam," his girlfriend said, nodding a little too vigorously, so that for a second she looked like one of those dolls with their heads that wobbled on springs. Rita felt sorry for her. She could imagine the girl in high school, sitting alone in the cafeteria hunched over two pieces of cake on her lunch tray, ignored by the rest of the kids.

"Why don't you two get on your way," the owner said.

"Sure, man," the boy said. "But only because we feel like it. It's a free country, right?"

"Right, Slam," the girl said. Nod, nod.

"At least it was last time I checked," Slam said.

They walked to the door. Rita watched them go without being obvious about it. You didn't want a skinhead to notice you, because skinheads would mess you up for no good reason except their own hate. Rita would never walk past a group of them; it was better to cross the street or just go back the way you came. Outside, on the sidewalk, the boy turned to the window and gave a Nazi salute, and then they clomped off arm in arm in their heavy black boots.

"Stupid kids," the owner said. Rita smiled at him, but he didn't notice. She wondered if he remembered Jimmy, but she didn't want to ask him, in case he said, *Jimmy who? No*, he would say, *I don't remember any guy like that. Dark hair, Saint*

*Christopher medal, played the harmonica? Nah. Do you know how
many people come in and out of here every day?*

She set the tea bag on a napkin on the table, put a couple of
sugar packets and the Styrofoam cup into her bag, and left.

In front of a closed liquor store, she tore a piece of card-
board off an empty box from a pile, then asked people pass-
ing for a pen until a young woman with a baby in a back
carrier stopped. Hungry, Please Help, Rita wrote on the card-
board. The baby grabbed at its mother's hair and then stuffed
its fist in its mouth, drooling, watching while she wrote. The
mother gave Rita a dollar and wished her luck.

She sat down in front of the store with her sign. It was a
good spot; the bus stop was right there. People were more
likely to give you money if they had to look at you for a while,
rather than if they were just walking past. They'd stand gazing
down the street where the bus would be coming and then
glance around, catching Rita in their gaze and moving their
eyes away, trying to pretend that she was the same thing as a
milk crate or a trash container. They'd step off the curb and
look down the street again or turn their backs to her, but usu-
ally if they had to stand there long enough they'd turn around
again. Finally somebody might finger the change in their
pocket or reach into their purse. Usually they'd wait until
the bus was coming, then hurry over and drop something into
the cup.

At eleven, a man showed up to unlock the padlock on the
iron gate across the store. As he slid the gate open, Rita felt
the rasping sound of the metal inside her head. She moved
to the next doorway for a while, but now the street was fill-
ing up and a steady stream of people separated her from the
ones waiting at the bus stop, and hardly anyone noticed her.
She dumped the cup of money into her purse without
counting it and headed back toward the park. Charles would

probably be there, and maybe a few other people that knew her, people who, like Charles, ate at the shelter sometimes. They weren't her friends, but they were more likely to look at her and see a person, not a beggar on the street or a piece of ass. Her head was starting to really throb now, and she remembered she'd woken with a headache, that Charles's whistling had set it off. She'd have to spend some money on Tylenol.

I better find Jimmy soon.

She wondered if he'd take her back.

★

At the Piazza di Spagna, south of Market Street, the lunch rush had begun. Every table was full, and several parties were waiting at the bar, drinking white wine and sparkling water and martinis and Cosmopolitans, and the sound of all their voices rose into the large airy space above their heads and mingled with the clinking silverware and glasses being set on trays and chairs being hitched closer together. Jimmy came from the clatter and yelling of the kitchen, out through the swinging doors and into the dining room, carrying orders of Fettuccine Alfredo and Spaghetti Carbonara. He liked it best when it was busy like this, when he didn't even have time to think, just move from one table to another and back to the kitchen, carrying plates and baskets of bread and bottles of wine he would hold out to customers, then open and pour a little and stand waiting while they tasted it. He knew by now how to taste wine. You swirled a little in the glass to release the flavor, then sniffed, then took a sip. He didn't really drink wine, he preferred beer or Jim Beam, but he knew tasting it was something you should know how to do.

He set down the pasta orders in front of two women who looked somewhere in their thirties, pretty women with short straight shiny hair and soft blouses, small leather purses slung over their chairs. They'd been leaning in close to each other, talking, and now they sat up straight and waited for him to go.

"Careful, the plates are hot," he said. "Anything else I can bring you ladies?"

"Ladies," one said. "I thought ladies were old women. Blue-rinsed hair and heavy rouge. Do you have to call us ladies?"

Jimmy felt his face flush in anger. He forced himself to take a long breath, a technique he'd been trying lately. He'd gotten it from a self-help book, *Don't Let Your Moods Rule You,* that he'd found in a Borders bag someone had left beside their chair. Ordinarily he'd have turned it in, but he'd been in a mood of deep depression that day and decided to take it home. Besides depression, the other mood he'd always had trouble with was an immediate desire to hit someone when they looked at him sideways.

Then he realized that the woman wasn't making fun of him. She was flirting; she smiled, a frank smile that said she liked how he looked.

He had just been promoted to waiter a couple of weeks before. He had started off as a lowly dishwasher, a miserable month of scalding water and endless plates scraped into the compactor. After he made busboy, he spent only two days bussing tables; his boss seemed to notice Jimmy for the first time since he'd hired him and gave him this job. Jimmy was nervous about making a mistake that would send him back to the kitchen permanently.

"Would you two beautiful young women like me to bring you anything else?" he said, and smiled back.

"How hot are these plates anyway?" the flirtatious one said. "Are they as hot as Tom Cruise?"

"Oh, please," her friend said. "Tom Cruise is a Scientologist."

"I'll have another glass of Chardonnay," the first one said.

He turned and walked toward the bar. "What do you think," he heard her say to her friend, "briefs or boxers?" He was tempted to look back over his shoulder, to let her know he'd heard. Better not, though. He wanted to be professional. His job was to serve the customers, not flirt with them. There was a fine line between being friendly and overdoing it. She might decide to get offended if he said or did the wrong thing.

"Loach," he said to Chelsea, the bartender.

"Sit tight," she said. "I'm jamming here."

DeLoach was the house Chardonnay. If they asked for Chardonnay, you gave them a choice of that, or three others. If they wanted a drink you asked if they preferred it up or on the rocks. If they wanted to order something that wasn't exactly the way it came on the menu, you told them the chef would be happy to accommodate them. You took the food back if they didn't want it, even if they didn't have a particular reason. You smiled when you first approached the table and told them your name—his name here was James—and asked if you could get them something from the bar. Jimmy had picked it all up quickly, watching and listening. He was good at keeping track of things in his head, like who ordered what and who was ready for another drink or the check. He would get into a rhythm as he worked, and the time would fly by.

He loved totaling his tips at the end of his shift, leaving his job with the concrete, daily evidence that he had earned something for his efforts. The only trouble with having cash in his pocket was that he tended to spend it pretty quickly,

usually on drinks somewhere. When he worked until clos-
ing, he would head to the Kilowatt on Sixteenth Street to
unwind. The lunch shift was better, because then it was
early enough to go downtown afterward to the old boxing
gym—he'd wrap his hands and put on gloves, hit the heavy
bag, the speed bag. Or he would run over to Dolores Park,
past the tennis players and homeless people and gay couples
on blankets on the grass, past the Frisbee players and stoned
conga drummers. Then he'd go home to his studio apart-
ment in the Mission, but it always felt too early to be there,
sitting inside alone while things were happening in the
world. So it would be the Kilowatt again, drinking shots and
beers and shooting pool, or Café du Nord on Market Street
where they sometimes had blues bands. He'd get drunk and
stop at a taqueria on the way home, the food cheap and
steaming and delicious, thick chips fried in lard, spiced meat
and beans and tortillas to soak up the alcohol in his blood.
Eat it fast from a red plastic basket under the bright light,
pitiless on white tiles streaked dirty from mopping. Then
climb three flights, sit on the couch, and play harmonica in
front of the TV, the sound off, the images flickering into his
brain.

Twice, he'd met women and gone home with them.
Women were always coming on to him. If he wanted to, it
wasn't that hard to find somebody. He would roll off them
and think about Rita. How he had walked out on her that
night after telling her she was dragging him down. Into
heroin and self-pity and her pain that no matter what he
said or did could not be solved. He left her at the hotel and
stayed on his friend Chumley's couch, and the next day he
and Chumley spent drinking with a friend of Chumley's
named Rudy, and that night Rudy had the brilliant idea to
rob someone as the three of them came reeling out of the

Blue Lamp at closing. Instead of talking Rudy out of it or just walking away, Jimmy had let his mood rule him—a mood comprised of emptiness, rage, and regret that led to mentally popping what he thought of as the Fuckidol pill. As in, fuck it all and let the shit fly. The guy was in an expensive suit and looked like an easy target, but there their fortune ended. Unfortunately, the guy had a scream to wake the dead, which he demonstrated right after Rudy took his wallet, and also unfortunately, a patrol car they were too high to notice happened to be sitting right across the street. The cops had laughed at them when they arrested them.

Jimmy tried to call Rita from jail when he got his phone calls. But there was no phone in their room, and he could never get an answer at the front desk, which was manned by a young coked-up East Indian who spent his time talking on his own phone, one of the cell phones that were popping up all over the city along with the big SUVs. The desk clerk, when Jimmy finally reached him, told Jimmy that Rita had been and gone, that there were a couple of boxes of Jimmy's things he was welcome to come and get.

Rudy went off to state prison for a year, while Jimmy and Chumley got three months in jail as accessories. When Jimmy got out, he told himself he would find Rita as soon as he got a job, an apartment. But now he'd gotten the job and apartment and somehow he still couldn't look for her. Maybe she was better off without him. Maybe, instead of helping her, he would just be pulled down by her again. He was free now, from jail and from Rita, from the burden of their relationship.

He was so fucking free he felt hopeless.

"Wake up, James." Chelsea set a full glass of wine on the chrome bar. A full glass at Piazza di Spagna took up exactly half the glass. "Sorry it was so long coming," she said.

Jimmy realized he'd been daydreaming and felt a sicken-
ing rush of adrenaline at the thought he might have fallen
behind. He picked up the wine and hurried to the table and
set it down, hardly glancing at the women, then walked fast
toward the kitchen again.

*

Rita could remember some things like they'd happened just
the day before, like there was only the small space of a night
between then and what was happening now. Riding in a red
van down Mission Street after they got married, Rita leaning
out the window and yelling the news at strangers. The cedar
smell of the cabin in Tahoe where they had spent the two
nights of their honeymoon, staying in bed or walking
around with blankets on because it was cold and drafty and
the heater didn't work very well. Jimmy naked on the couch
in their tiny apartment on Jones Street, playing something
slow and sad on his harmonica, or the fast shuffle that began
and ended with the long, two-note sound of a train whistle
that always got the dog upstairs howling. He had a leather
pouch where he kept all his harmonicas in different keys.
His tattoo and scars and the two dark freckles close together,
one a little bigger than the other, right near his navel. How
he'd shoot up (only once in a while, though; she was the one
who couldn't let it alone), belt looped around his bicep, the
end held in his teeth, pulling it tight, the blue veins rising to
the surface under his skin.

Just thinking about that made her long for a needle, and
for the thick dreamy rush of pleasure as the drug washed
into her and everything was fine, just fine, perfect exactly
like it was, nothing to hassle about. But she had sworn she
wouldn't anymore, because she blamed it for her losing sight

of Jimmy. She couldn't wait in their hotel room for him to cool off and come back after their fight, she had to go out and get high, and then one thing had led to another, the way it did. When she got back and found him gone, she had quit in penance. She had even started going to church again, something she hadn't done since she was a little girl. She went to services at St. Matthew's in the Mission or just ducked into an empty one and sat in the back and prayed. *Just bring him back. I'm sorry. I know it was my fault he left, I know I messed up again. I won't do junk anymore or whine about money or anything if you just help me find him.*

Now anxiety was with her all the time, even when she got drunk; when she slept, her dreams were full of vague problems she worried over, trying to fix whatever it was, not able to figure out what was wrong. Her dreams were inhabited by specters. Or wolves. They looked like dogs but they were wild. She would be running from them, and then come up against the dread certainty that there was something worse up ahead, and she'd stop cold in her tracks, and the fear would drill into her.

She was drunk now, sitting back against a tree in Golden Gate Park and trying to fix her nail polish. She'd picked up a pint of Gilbey's Vodka and some Cranberry Juice Cocktail along with the Tylenol. Her red polish was chipped and she went over it slowly with fresh polish, trying to keep the tiny brush steady, but she kept getting it on her fingers. She bit her nails down to the quick unless she had polish on. When she was little, her mother had brushed on some clear, evil-smelling stuff to keep her from doing it. Her mother was constantly slapping Rita's hands away from her mouth.

Most of the people who'd slept in the park the night before were back, stretched out or sitting in small groups scattered over the grass. A boy with greasy blond hair and a goatee was hunched over a guitar, swiping at the strings occasionally to produce an out-of-tune chord. Dogs with bandannas for collars wandered around, nosing the loose trash. A black man with wild dreadlocks sprouting from his head stood nearby, muttering something that occasionally rose to an audible "*Jesus Christ* our *Sav*ior" among other fervent religious remarks.

Rita closed her eyes, drifting. She saw purple flowers blooming behind the dark of her lids, getting larger and then smaller, like they were breathing. She saw narrow halls, and an endless series of rooms without any doors, just rectangular spaces with shadowy shapes moving around inside them. Jimmy's face appeared for a second and then sank into blackness. "And *God* shall have *mercy* on your *soul*," she heard.

Rita had seen God once. She was seven years old, lying in some yellow grass in front of the house in Reno, looking up at the sky. She had on shorts and a sleeveless top, and the grass was prickly on her arms and legs. She had been kind of in love with God then; she was planning on becoming a nun. She had gone to church every Sunday with her friend Claire and Claire's mother and father and two sisters. Rita liked the coolness inside Our Lady of Sorrows, the air hushed and clean, the rows of pews oily and dark. Colored light was caught in the leaded panes of the stained-glass windows. She especially liked the white statue of Our Lady with her downcast eyes and gentle smile and her arms held out like she would hug you if you got close enough, if you climbed up into the alcove where she stood surrounded by fresh flowers.

As Rita lay in the front yard, she was repeating the words of the Hail Mary, which she'd just learned. She didn't understand the part that went, *Blessed is the fruit of thy womb, Jesus.* Baby Jesus couldn't be a fruit, so it must mean something else. Maybe Jesus was a womb, whatever that was. She said the prayer over and over, watching the clouds form and then spread out and dissolve, letting her eyes go unfocused.

Then she saw him, looking down at her from a cloud. He looked a little like Santa Claus with his white hair and beard, but the beard was shorter and his cheeks weren't round and red like Santa's, and he wasn't smiling. He just gazed down at her, serious but not sad. Rita knew it wasn't a cloud in the shape of a face, but a real face. She gazed back, feeling calm and quiet. She didn't know how long she looked at him. Nearby noises—a squirrel in the leaves, cards snapping in the spokes of a passing bike, a door scraping shut—seemed like they were happening in her head instead of outside her. That was how she described it to herself later, but she knew that didn't quite explain what it had felt like. After a while she grew tired and closed her eyes for a long instant. When she opened them, he was gone.

She jumped up and ran into the house. Her father was on the road somewhere. Her mother was sitting on the couch cross-legged in cutoffs and a bra, watching TV, drinking a glass of beer, and eating from a box of Cheez-Its. She seemed absorbed in the TV even though the vertical hold was broken so that the picture was weird, the top and bottom reversed, a black band running across the middle. At the bottom of the screen, a man's and woman's eyes closed, and at the top their mouths merged in a kiss and then drew back. Their noses were somewhere in the black part.

"What's up," her mother said, in a tone of voice that said nothing had better be up because she was busy watching a busted TV and having her beer and Cheez-Its.

"I just had to pee," Rita said, and went past her into the bathroom. She decided not to tell her parents, or even Claire, about seeing God. It was her first time having a secret, and she liked the feeling of knowing something nobody else did. But later, after Rita and her mother moved away and there was no one to take her to church anymore, she started to doubt that she had seen anything but a cloud after all.

Lately, Rita thought that maybe, all those years ago, God had been calling her. He had shown her a sign and she was supposed to act on it somehow, but she had failed to do whatever it was he wanted. He didn't call again. Instead he began to test her, like he had tested Job in the Bible. Over the years, God had continued to test and test. Sometimes, she wasn't sure she believed in him and she hated people who were certain, because she wasn't. And sometimes she just hated God for what he had let happen to her and to her mother.

She opened her eyes before any images of what had happened came into her head.

"And his *wrath* shall *come down upon* thee," the self-appointed preacher was telling his burned-out and drunken congregation.

"Amen," somebody said.

"Shut up," somebody else said. "I'm trying to enjoy the *day* without your *bull*shit."

"Amen to that, brother," the first voice said.

This sign of an attentive audience seemed to inspire the preacher. "*Sinners*," he shouted. "The *Lord* will make the *rain* of your land *powder* and *dust*; from *heaven* it shall come down upon you until you are *destroyed*."

A rock the size of a fist flew past Rita and hit the preacher square in the back between his shoulder blades. He whirled around and looked at her.

"*Harlot*!" he cried.

"I didn't throw it," Rita said.

He advanced on her anyway. No one around her seemed inclined to move to help her. The boy with the guitar was slumped all the way over it, his eyes closed. A couple of men passing a pint bottle smiled at her. They weren't going to do anything but watch the show.

The preacher stood over her. His eyeballs were yellow. He smelled of some kind of sweet cologne and faintly of old shit.

"And your dead body shall be food for all the birds of the air, and for the beasts of the earth; and there shall be no one to frighten them away," he said. He was speaking quietly, barely above a whisper.

"Yeah, so," Rita said, trying not to show him she was afraid.

He wore heavy scuffed cowboy boots; on one of them, the sole flapped open. Rita could see his dusty foot and twisted toenails as he raised that one and kicked her in the face with it. For a second, everything stopped, and then her jaw seemed to come unhinged, slammed sideways, a white pain through nerves and bone. She jerked her hands up as he tried to kick her again, but he was off balance and fell abruptly backward, and she brought her left palm to her face and held it there as he crawled toward her and grabbed her throat—he was crazy, his eyes looked down into himself at some other event he was experiencing—his thumbs pressed into her windpipe. She gagged. She heard shouting and then a rushing sound and then she passed out.

*

Rita's bag was gone, and also the vodka she'd been pouring into her Styrofoam cup to mix with the cranberry. The bottle of juice lay on its side, half-full. There was blood in her mouth. She took a swig of juice to clear it, afraid some of her teeth were loose and she was going to swallow them. She felt them with her finger and they were all there. She licked her bottom lip and touched her face and could not focus on what was happening, on why her bag was gone and she was sitting under a tree feeling like her face had been dislocated. Finally, she checked the front of her jeans to make sure her money was still there. She wanted to take some more Tylenol for the pain in her head and thought of getting some from her bag. It took her a second to remember again that her bag had been taken.

No Tylenol and no change of clothes. Also no California ID stating that her name was Rita Louise Jackson, that she resided at 1764 Jones Street, San Francisco, California, 94102 (that was true in April, but not anymore). Sex: F, Hair: Blnd, Eyes: Bl. Ht: 5-05, Wt: 110, DOB: 12-18-72. There was a picture of her staring into the camera. She looked like a deer about to be shot, alert and wary, having no idea of what was about to happen. She could see the picture of herself clearly in her head, that person carried away with the rest of her past, tossed in the trash somewhere.

And no sunglasses. The day had gotten bright. She shaded her eyes with her hand and looked at the scene before her. Someone had rigged up a kind of tent using a few blankets, hanging them over a low tree limb and holding down the corners with rocks. A small dog in a red sweater was licking itself rapidly and obsessively. A fat man in a too-small T-shirt lay spread-eagled on the grass nearby, snoring softly, his exposed brown stomach rising and falling. The two men who had been passing the bottle earlier were still there, so she went over to them.

"Hey," she said. "Did you see that guy that kicked me?"

"He was one crazy dude," one of the men said.

"He stole my bag," Rita said. "My ID and everything. Did you see where he went?"

She waited, but the men just looked at her. One scratched his nose with his pinky, then inserted it into a nostril. The other blinked his reddened eyelids rapidly, like he was trying to get out a speck. They both gave off the odor of cheap wine left open too long. The one who had picked his nose now scratched at his crotch, stained a darker shade than the rest of his bright green pants.

The one in the green pants said, "Wasn't him. Some other guy pulled him off you and he ran away. Must have been that second guy who took your stuff."

"Well," Rita said. "Did you see where *he* went?"

Green Pants smiled. "He went to heaven," he said.

"Hah, that's a good one," his companion said.

" 'Course, that would be nigger heaven," Green Pants said.

"What's nigger heaven? Hey, what's nigger heaven?" his friend wanted to know, but Green Pants didn't answer.

"I guess you're not going to help me," Rita said.

"I guess you got that right," Green Pants said. "Unless you want a little of this in your hidey hole." He moved his hand to his stained crotch again, cupping it suggestively.

"Hidey hole! That's a good one. That's a damn good one. Man, you come up with some funny shit." His friend couldn't get over it. "Hidey hole," he said again. "Get that little girl right in her hidey hole."

Rita turned and walked away from them, their laughter following her. The air felt heavy, like she was trying to walk across the bottom of an Olympic-sized swimming pool. Even if she got to the other end, there wouldn't be any silver ladder leading up to a sunny patio with deck chairs and umbrella drinks and fashion magazines to read. At the other end, there would be a cement wall, and she would have to turn and slog back the way she came, getting more and more tired.

She headed down Haight Street. It was crowded with shoppers and kids hanging out on the corners and people asking for spare change. You saw every kind of person in the Haight: couples pushing strollers, and young girls with pink and purple hair and rings in their noses, and thin black men with stuff spread out on the sidewalk they were trying to sell, stuff nobody wanted like old paperbacks and broken toasters and rags of clothes they'd picked out of Dumpsters. The stores sold recycled clothing, or expensive party clothes made of leather and vinyl, thigh-high boots with spiked heels, boas and long gloves and wigs. You could get a slice or a burrito and wash it down with Budweiser, or you could sit and have a plate of grilled shrimp and wine if you had real money. You could get ice cream from Ben and Jerry's on the corner of Haight and Ashbury, the corner the hippies had made famous. You could get hash pipes and bongs and posters and T-shirts, espresso and art supplies and fabric and books, and tattoos and piercings anywhere on your body that you wanted. It was constant activity, everyone hungry to buy or to sell, or to be looked at, everyone stoned on drugs or shopping or talking fast, and no place to rest, really rest. As she walked, she checked the corner trash receptacles in case the man who'd stolen her bag had rifled and then tossed it. The receptacles overflowed with trash, but her bag wasn't in any of them that she could see.

She ducked into a drugstore and went into an empty aisle, reached down the front of her jeans and pulled out some bills. She bought some Tylenol and nail polish remover and a pair of sunglasses with blue plastic frames she put on as soon as the girl rang her up. At the bus stop, she hung around, waiting for someone to drop a transfer or offer her one. She got on the Number 7 and fell into a seat.

Tonight I'll get a room. I'll check into a hotel, put my money down, and get my key, and I'll walk into a room and shut the door and then I can cry all I want.

But it turned out she had to cry right there, quietly, keeping her face aimed toward the bus window and away from the other passengers, while the city blurred by.

*

"Five card draw, nothing wild," Chumley said, looking around the table at Jimmy and the other players. "Ante up, you chumps." He flipped cards from the deck and sailed them expertly in front of each player. Everyone chipped a quarter to the middle. Everyone had a small pile of bills and change, a beer bottle, and a cigarette going in an ashtray beside him. Chumley was also hitting off a pint of peach schnapps he refused to pass around, not that anyone wanted it.

"Well, well," Chumley said, fanning his cards out and peeking at his hand. It was hard to tell if he was sad or elated about what he saw. He snapped his cards closed, set them down, and took another drink of schnapps.

Chumley lived with his mother in the Sunset District, in a gray stucco two-bedroom house across the street from grass-covered sand dunes, beyond which was the ocean. On Tuesday nights, his mother went out for bridge, and Chumley hosted a poker game in her dining room.

Nothing had changed in the months since Jimmy had spent the night on the basement couch. The same fat little dachshund still slept on the corner of the same flowered sofa, and the same wind rattled the shelf of plants set against the window above the kitchen sink. Chumley looked the same, too. It was like being in a time warp, Jimmy thought, like nothing that had happened since then had really happened. The last time he'd seen Chumley was in July, in a courtroom at 850 Bryant, when they were about to be sentenced; they had both ended up in San Bruno, but in different wings. Yesterday, coming from the lunch shift at the restaurant, Jimmy had spotted Chumley attaching a cherry red 1968 Mustang to the winch of an enormous black tow truck that had SUNSET SERVICE lettered in yellow on its doors.

"Hey, Jimbo," Chumley had called. "I thought you died or left town."

"Hey, man," Jimmy said. He was glad to see Chumley, even though he hadn't especially wanted to call him. They'd known each other since they were kids in Trenton. They had smoked their first joint together in the bathroom of some fancy hotel in Philadelphia where Chumley's mother was playing in a bridge tournament. Later, they'd cruised the streets of Trenton in Chumley's dented Nova, buzzed on pot and cough medicine, looking for girls. They'd sparred together at the gym and stood together through a few bar fights. After high school, Chumley had continued to live at home, and would have stayed in Trenton forever if his mother hadn't moved. Almost nobody left Trenton, especially not for San Francisco, but Chumley's mother had some kind of obsession about the Golden Gate Bridge, and when Chumley's father died she headed straight for it and Chumley came along.

"Jimmy's bet," Chumley said.

"Buck," Jimmy said. The limit was a dollar.

Everybody else tossed a dollar at the pile.

"How many cards you want, Jimbo?" Chumley said.

Jimmy slid one over, and Chumley gave him another from the deck.

"Drake," Chumley said. Drake was a skinny, bucktoothed mechanic who had an annoying habit of noisily drawing in his breath between his teeth, then working up some saliva and making little wet kissing sounds with his tongue.

"Three," Drake said.

"Good luck, dude," Chumley said. "You're gonna need it. Stan*lee*," he said. "Stan the Man."

Stan stared hard at his cards. "Five," he said finally.

"You can't pull five," Chumley said.

"I know, dickhead," Stan said, "I was just kidding."

"Sorry, Stan," Chumley said.

"Don't you know humor when you hear it?" Stanley said.

"Hey, I'm sorry," Chumley said again, and laughed hard, like he was just now getting how hilarious Stan's joke was.

"Just gimme two," Stan said. Stan was a jeweler. He was fifty-four years old and had a rent-controlled space next to a dry cleaner's, where he fixed watches and resized rings and occasionally sold something to the rare customer. Jimmy had learned this from Chumley earlier, before Stan and Drake had showed up. "Check this out," Chumley had said, displaying a silver death's head ring on his right pinky. "And this," he said, jiggling a chain-link bracelet on his wrist. "Cool, huh. You should fall by his shop, man. Plus he's always got killer weed."

"Okay," Chumley said, "Stan the Man gets two big ones."

Stan was packing a wooden pipe with pot from a Baggie next to his ashtray. A Carlton 100 was burning out in the ashtray, untouched. He flipped a lid closed on the pipe, tilted it vertically, and lit it with a blue Bic. Stan looked like a guy from the forties, sharp-toed shoes and a checkered sports jacket and a neat gray brush cut when he took off his fedora. The kind of guy Jimmy's grandmother would have called dapper.

Also, according to Chumley, Stan had spent several years in prison. For what, Chumley didn't know. Looking at him, Jimmy tried to guess, but after drugs, rape, assault, robbery, murder, forgery, and child-molesting—none of which seemed right somehow, except drugs—he ran out of ideas. It was impossible to tell, anyway. Guys who had done time looked just like anyone else, only more definite. At least that's how it seemed to Jimmy. Like there was more of them inside their skin and they were aware of just where they ended and the world began.

"Here, man," Stan said, his voice tight from holding in the smoke, and passed it to Jimmy.

"It's to you," Chumley told Jimmy.

Jimmy pushed a dollar toward the pile and toked on the pipe.

"I'm out," Drake said sadly and sucked in his breath. "Fold." He leaned back on two legs of his chair, and almost fell over.

"Me, too," Stan said. "I'm not having any luck tonight."

"Looks like it's me and you, Jimbo," Chumley said. "I'll see your ass." He dropped a five on the pile and slid back four ones.

Jimmy smiled. "How about I raise your ass," he said, and put another dollar in.

Chumley shook his head. He looked at Jimmy, then at his own cards. Reluctantly, he pushed one more dollar to the pile.

Jimmy laid down his cards. Three jacks and two sevens. "Full house," he said. "Dickhead."

"All I got's two pair," Chumley said. "Give me some of that weed."

Jimmy reached for the money on the table with both hands, pulling it toward him. He had a nice little streak going; he'd won three of the last five hands. He felt pleased with himself and the evening. He was winning and he was slightly stoned and everyone was having a good time. He had a moment of nostalgia for high school, when he and Chumley and their buddies Rick and Pedro would stay up all night at the apartment on Broad Street, playing cards and drinking, while Chumley's mother sat on the couch watching TV and sipping vodka martinis and finally passing out, then waking up in the middle of the night and heading back to the bedroom. Chumley's father was a guard at the state prison and would come in at dawn and sometimes join the game. The dachshund had been a puppy then, and Chumley's mother had been, not exactly young looking, but not so bad looking, either.

SILENCE LABOR PENITENCE was the motto over the entrance to the New Jersey State Prison.

It was a shame how everything had to keep going.

Time warp, Jimmy thought, trying to remember what he'd meant by it before, what that thought exactly was. He realized he was pretty drunk. Everything's fine, he thought.

"I won again," he said aloud. But it was the middle of the next hand already, and he didn't have anything.

"You're the man, Jimbo," Chumley said.

*

At four A.M., Jimmy and Chumley were sitting on Ocean Beach, watching the waves, viscous and oily-looking, slide over the sand. Low clouds came down to the water. The waves carried in a yellow foamy substance, like soapsuds or dirty snow, and left it trembling in the wind when they pulled back, hissing. The cold got in through Jimmy's unlined leather jacket, and he shivered uncontrollably, his teeth chattering. Before the game broke up, Stan had laid out lines of coke for everyone. He also unwrapped from a cloth and laid on the table, for the players' appreciation, a shiny nine-millimeter. Everyone duly appreciated it, and then he wrapped it up and stuck it back in his sports jacket. Apparently Stan stocked a great variety of merchandise in his jewelry store. Jimmy took out a piece of folded-up paper with the extra coke Stan had given him. "Take it," Stan had said. "This stuff makes me buggy." Jimmy hadn't done coke in years. He hunched over and licked his pinky and put a little more up each nostril.

Chumley was digging a hole with one hand, scooping out sand into a pile by his right leg. Jimmy wrapped his arms around himself, concentrating on Chumley's movements. His head felt scraped out, clear. He wished there were stars to look at. Finally, he quit watching Chumley and focused on the surf, crystals gathering on the water and splintering into diamonds on the smooth, packed sand at the water's edge and spreading out like glittery confetti. It was amazing, beautiful. The pale sand stretching north and south of them was beautiful. Chumley and Stan were beautiful. Drake was an annoying cocksucker.

"I need to get laid," Chumley said. "In the worst way, man. You know what I'm saying?"

"No," Jimmy said, turning back to him.

"My dick's gonna fall off from lack of use. You know, like we used to have tails. We had tails just like monkeys. Use it or lose it. You know what I'm saying?"

"No."

"Whatever happened to your old lady?" Chumley said. "You ever see her?"

Rita was beautiful. She smelled like the vanilla oil she bought on Castro Street that came in a little glass vial like a coke vial. She had a slight catch in her laugh, like a hiccup. She had long, slim hands that seemed to move independently of her wrists when she was talking excitedly, waving them around. At night, under the covers, she rubbed her feet together restlessly. Sometimes he had held them and massaged them. She had a little birthmark on her face, which she hated, that he found adorable.

Two days after he started washing dishes at the restaurant, he was on a bus headed for work and he thought he saw her on the street, walking quickly, arms crossed across her chest, her head down and her hair half in her face. He should have jumped off the bus. He wanted to, but he was afraid to be late to his new job. Maybe it wasn't her, anyway, but he was pretty sure it was. He should have gone back later and looked for her. He didn't know why he hadn't.

"Rita," Jimmy said. "I don't know, man."

He knew why he hadn't looked for her. Things might not work out. Things might get all screwed up between them, like they had before.

He imagined where he would be now if he had gotten off the bus. Not all coked up with Chumley, that's for sure. He'd be at home in bed with Rita, with her curled up small against his back, one light arm thrown over him. He couldn't think about it. Every time he did, he felt how he had failed her. When they were together she had said, over and over, *Don't leave me*, and he had promised her, *I won't*. He had held her and lied to her, even though he didn't know he was lying at the time.

Work was the important thing. So he told himself. Stay focused on doing a good job and on not getting into any shit. Shit was everywhere, and you had to step carefully. It was there waiting for you, and if you didn't watch where you were going you'd find yourself up to your neck in it, wondering how you got there and how to wash it off. As for the loneliness, the only thing that really helped—besides just holding steady to some sort of discipline, getting to work each day—was music. Playing the riffs he'd learned off cassettes, listening over and over to Little Walter and Sonny Boy Williamson I and II, to songs like "Lost Boy Blues" and "Off the Wall," "Help Me," "Eyesight to the Blind." Big Walter

Horton and James Cotton, Charlie Musselwhite, Sonny Terry with his whoops and Jimmy Reed up in the high register. Anybody he could find no matter the style—country blues or Chicago, acoustic or electric. He tried to catch local guys like Mark Hummel and Michael Peloquin whenever they played. Once, sitting at the bar after playing a set at the Boom Boom Room, Peloquin had given Jimmy a nod of recognition over his club soda.

"Lovely Rita, meter maid." Chumley was singing the Beatles song. "Rita, Rita, pumpkin eatah," he said. He switched to Springsteen. "Rosarita, jump a little higher. Señorita, come sit by my fire—"

Chumley's hole in the sand was as deep as his elbow now. He took out a last fistful of sand and flung it into the wind. Glittery bits of it clung to his forearm. He stood up, swaying a little.

"Hit me," he said, tapping himself on the stomach.

"Aw, no, man," Jimmy said

Jimmy stood up. He and Chumley circled each other, feinting, and then Jimmy hit him in the solar plexus with a left.

"That was a pussy shot," Chumley said. "You pussy."

"That's what my old man used to say," Jimmy said.

"Your old man was right."

"I'm not gonna hit you," Jimmy said.

His father was long dead. His mother was dead, too, of cancer, nearly three years ago. Jimmy had gone back to Trenton to take care of her at the end, and that had been bad. Missing Rita every day, but he hadn't wanted to bring her there, into that sickness. He drove a delivery truck for DHL and at night listened to his mother moan. Then the hospital where her stomach was swollen like she was pregnant, while the rest of her—arms, legs, breasts, even, it seemed, the bones of her face—wasted away. The volunteers in the hospital, old ladies in matching tan pantsuits with teddy bear pins, kept acting like she was going to get better, when it was clear she was totally fucked. He had watched her die.

"I'm not gonna hit you," Jimmy said again.

"Here, kitty kitty kitty."

He had visited his father's grave to give him the news, had stood there in the rain and talked to him like he was listening, which Jimmy knew he wasn't. You die and that's it. No one waiting in a halo of light to welcome you, no angels to carry you to heaven or demons to drag you down to hell. His mother had been cremated; Jimmy's uncle had kept her ashes and for mysterious reasons had recently mailed some of them to Jimmy. He had them in a box in his closet. Somehow he couldn't get rid of them, scatter them further. Whatever the proper thing was.

Jimmy swung, and Chumley twisted away. "Okay, never mind," Chumley said. "It's too cold. Let's go back."

Jimmy followed him up the concrete steps that led from the beach, along the asphalt path through the dunes and across the street. The cars along the street all had a thin sheen of moisture from the fog. Jimmy stopped and drew a heart on someone's back windshield with his finger. *J & R*. An arrow through it, aimed upward. Then he wiped it off with the side of his hand.

"Come in for a little nightcap?" Chumley said. "Beer? Line?"

"I'll get the streetcar," Jimmy said. "It's work tomorrow."

The café at the Judah Street turnaround was long closed. A couple of dark empty streetcars sat there, looking abandoned. The street was oily between the rails. Jimmy started up Judah; he was too restless to stand and wait. Besides, he wasn't sure if anything ran this late.

It seemed to have gotten even colder than it was on the

beach. He jogged with his hands in his pockets, pressing his arms close to his sides, holding himself together, apart from the night, a contained world moving through a larger, indifferent one. After a couple of blocks, his teeth finally stopped chattering. The clear-headedness he'd felt sitting in the sand with Chumley, the exultant sense of the rightness of everything, had leaked away. His thoughts were confused, little sparks zipping around in his brain, fizzing and dying. This was why he'd never liked coke; it took you up for a few minutes, like a wave, and then it sent you straight to the bottom of the ocean.

*

Rita was now a resident of the Barker Hotel on Eddy Street, just off Polk. At four A.M. Wednesday morning, she lay curled in bed, her head on a flat, moldy-smelling pillow, studying a series of spidery cracks in the wall. She listened to the drip of the sink and the hacking cough of the man next door.

Her room was next to the bathroom. You had to bring your own toilet paper when you went. Sometimes, after people flushed, the water kept running; that was a sound that was kind of soothing. Earlier, she had listened to people clomping or stumbling down the runner of faded brown carpet in the hall, arguing or laughing or screaming. From the room above her, just after two A.M., had come the sounds of someone rearranging the furniture, dragging what must have been the dresser across the room, and then the bed.

Now there was a bad smell, too, keeping her awake. It was different from the other hotel smells of unwashed bodies and stale urine and disinfectant and alcohol that seemed to have been absorbed into the yellowed plaster walls, different from the smell of burned chili coming from a hot plate in somebody's room, or curry and onions in the lobby. She'd first smelled it earlier tonight, coming in from an afternoon of panhandling around Union Square, a sign propped next to her that read KIDS AT HOME, PLEASE HELP US. This had seemed to strike a sympathetic chord for a number of people, especially women. But then a woman who actually had a kid, a baby wrapped up in a sweater instead of a baby blanket, stopped and tried to give Rita a quarter. Her left arm, cradling the baby, was bandaged in dirty gauze. Blood seeped through the gauze and made a rusty stain. Rita gave her three of the twelve dollars she'd collected. "Bless you, sister," the woman said before moving on. "Bless you and your little ones."

Rita tried to keep her breath shallow. Maybe a rat had died in the walls. Maybe somebody's cat had kicked off. You weren't allowed to have pets, but people snuck them in anyway. The man next door had a bird named Penny. "Pretty Penny," he'd been saying all evening. "Pretty bird, pretty bird," he had crooned, then paused to hack up phlegm. The bird sometimes responded with little raspy chirps. There was a bell on the cage that rang with a pleasant tinkling sound. Rita knew the bird wasn't dead because she could hear it right now, gently ringing its bell.

"Oh, hell," she said, and got out of bed in her T-shirt and underwear. She pulled on her jeans. She had to pee, anyway. Maybe she could figure out where the smell was coming from. In the morning she'd tell the Indian man who sat behind the counter in the lobby, and maybe the man would do something about it. "Yes, yes, all right," he'd say in his funny accent. Rita wasn't sure he actually understood English.

She took her roll of toilet paper from the table beside the

bed and stepped barefoot into the hall, locking the door behind her with her key. It was late and nobody seemed to be up or hanging around, but she didn't want to take the chance that somebody might show up to casually stroll down the hall, trying doors to see if any were unlocked.

The smell was stronger in the hall but not as bad in the bathroom. The bathroom light socket was empty. A little illumination came in from a streetlight in the alley behind the hotel. She struggled with the hook on the door, which wasn't quite lined up with the eye screwed into the door-frame. She got it latched, put down the toilet seat and squatted above it.

As she was about to stand she heard people in the hallway. They sounded like they were at the door to her room. She heard whispering as they passed the bathroom, then stopped at the end of the hall. They must be at the door of the supply closet—empty of supplies except for a box of roach powder, some dusty plastic cups, and a naked Ken doll with one arm missing. Rita had opened the door by accident when she first arrived, thinking it was the bathroom. A little later, she had thought about getting the cups, but by then the door was locked.

She got up quietly, wiping herself and pulling up her underwear and jeans. She put her ear to the bathroom door. There was a loud click and a whispered, "Fuck!" followed by the other person's, "Shh."

"Locked," a man's voice said.

"Wait. It's easy."

"Wish I wasn't here," the first man said.

"Wish you'd quit saying that. You been saying that all night."

"I've been meaning it all night."

"Get over it."

Rita's feet were cold from the bathroom floor and her neck ached. She rolled her head toward her right shoulder, then her left. She heard the closet door open, the bottom of the frame sliding over the carpet runner. Then more fumbling noises.

Her hand was on the doorknob, turning it so slowly she almost wasn't doing it. She turned it all the way.

Don't, she thought.

She opened the door the little bit it would go, held by the hook and eye. She could see the back of one man—a broad back in a tan corduroy jacket and matching pants that were too long, crumpled over his shoes. He wore a tan hat that didn't quite match his suit; it was a shade lighter, made of some soft material like felt, with a brown leather braid on it that held in place a colorful trio of tiny feathers. It seemed like a costume of some sort, not something a normal person would wear. The man backed up, dragging something out of the closet—a nylon sleeping bag. A mummy bag, that actually looked like it had a mummy in it. She had seen a show on TV once about the pharoahs, and she imagined one of them inside the bag, arms folded across his chest, a gold mask on his face.

The smell was stronger now.

"Oh, man," one of the men said. She thought it was the one she couldn't see.

"I said get over it," the other one said. "The sooner we do this, the sooner it's done."

"Won't be too soon for me."

"Be quiet."

"You know what the kids say? Take a chill pill and be still."

"You know what I say? Shut your piehole."

The man in the corduroy suit moved out of her line of

vision. She watched the sleeping bag slide past the door. Where the strings were pulled together at the top, a few long strands of bright red hair fell out. They looked fake, like doll hair.

She caught a glimpse of his profile as he shut the closet. Then he turned and looked right at the bathroom door. He had the kind of glasses that magnify your eyes to anyone looking; his big pale gray eyes were on her, eyes that seemed to have a yellow film over them, but could see right through that and the scratch on the right lens of the glasses, down into where her soul was crouching and trying to hide deep inside her body.

He raised one hand, as if in greeting, and let it fall limply to his side. There was something wrong with the hand; it was curled up and stiff looking and scarred all over the knuckles. Burned, maybe. She followed the motion of the hand as it fell, and then she looked at the man again, at his eyes that were on her, watching.

For a minute she couldn't move. She knew she'd been stupid to look in the first place. The way to survive was to know what was going on around you but not to look at it directly. Don't meet people's eyes, don't give them a reason to notice you. Now she was looking into this man's eyes, and he was looking back, probing her, knowing her, claiming her somehow; it was like he owned some part of her and could collect it whenever he wanted.

She backed slowly into the bathroom, to the wall across from the toilet, where he couldn't see in. She couldn't feel her body at all; it had dissolved. She was part of the wall, the pipe running alongside it, the toilet, the particles of air that smelled of human sweat and waste. She heard his breath at the door, his hand on the knob, testing, but he didn't pull very hard; the hook and eye held.

Down the hall a woman started screaming, "Pay me, pay me, pay me." She sounded like a police siren, her voice sliding back and forth between two shrill notes.

"Ssst!" the other man hissed. "Let's go, man."

One more pull. Rita waited, her eyes on the door. Now she felt her body again, sweating, dampness starting at the roots of her hair, between her breasts and thighs, under her armpits, breaking out all over her.

"I'm leaving," the other man said. "I don't want any part of this."

"Wait." The first man's voice was calm where the other's was frantic.

"No, I'm going. You deal with it."

"It's all right," the voice at the door said. Then it whispered. "You're dead," it said to Rita.

"I'm outta here," the other man said.

Rita waited, sweating and shivering, clenching her teeth together to keep them from chattering. She felt something light—a cockroach, the tail of a vole or rat—skitter over her foot. She flinched, but stayed where she was. In slow motion, she moved her hand to the pocket of her jeans and wrapped her palm around the solidity of her room key.

I'm dead.

The woman kept screaming. "Pay me, motherfucker."

"See you later, sweetheart," the man whispered.

She stayed there, clutching her key. She heard them go but waited a couple of minutes more, then went to the door and listened. The prostitute had stopped badgering her client. Now there was music coming from down the hall. Thumping bass, and a rapper's voice: "She got the bomb-ass pussy." *Duh-dah-DOOM, duh-dah-DOOM.*

She listened, trying to decide whether she should go back to her room or stay put. Maybe they were coming back. Or weren't gone yet. Maybe the man in corduroy was standing quietly in the hall, waiting for her to step out, waiting to put his damaged hand over her mouth and his other arm across her body and drag her into a dark place in himself and in her.

There was a noise in the alley outside. She climbed up on the wooden shelf on top of the radiator and looked down through the rusty wire mesh of the window. Directly below was a large Dumpster filled with plastic bags of garbage and stray stuff people had tossed in, or had uncovered tearing open the bags, looking for something they could use or sell. Parked on the other side of the Dumpster was a dark-colored van. The man in corduroy had slid open the side door—that was the noise she'd heard. He went around to the driver's side while the other man pushed the sleeping bag in, closed the door, and climbed in the passenger side. They drove off without lights.

Rita went back to her room and locked all three locks. Doorknob. Bolt lock above that. Chain at the top. Turn off the light. The dark was like thick, black water. She was having a hard time breathing, and the sweat on her body had dried but she was cold all over. She ran into the bedside table and the sharp edge jabbed into her thigh and she fell into the bed gasping from the pain. She lay down and pulled the blanket over her head, taking a few deep breaths under the blanket, the water weighing her down. She crossed her arms over her chest and pressed her legs together. I'm dead. I'm dead and I don't have to be afraid, no one's going to hurt me, I'm all right, I'm all right, I'm dead. I'm dead.

2. Gary Shepard stood outside the Barker Hotel, thinking, Krishna Roach Palace. The Krishna family owned a number of hotels in San Francisco, all of them falling apart, all inhabited by people down on their luck or people who'd never had any to begin with. Two of them were leaving the Barker right now. A brown woman in a tight dress, her features slurry from heroin or crack or alcohol, clung to the arm of a skinny black man in plaid pants and a Panama hat who was trying to shake her off, saying, "I gots to go, woman! I gots to *go!*" Gary watched them stagger off toward Polk Street, pushing and pulling, locked together until the moment they'd separate and lurch off in different directions, looking for someone else to hold to or be dragged down by. So long, lovers, he thought, and went in through the double glass doors.

He'd never been to the Barker, but he knew this part of town. Miz Brown's on the corner: two people stabbed outside. The bar two doors down: good beer selection, generous shots, transvestite raped in the bathroom. Around the corner, an adult bookstore a murder suspect had ducked into while running from the cops. Someday, Gary thought, he should write a crime guide to San Francisco. Instead of going to John's Grill, where Sam Spade had eaten in *The Maltese Falcon*, people could tour attractions like the Eagle Diner, where the waitress had been shot to death by the cook. History was everywhere.

An Indian man stood behind a barred window at the front desk. The lobby smelled of cumin and curry and, under that, moldy plaster and urine. There was a yellow plastic radio on the counter, tuned low to a pop station. "Light rock, less talk," the announcer said, and then Linda Ronstadt came on singing "Blue Bayou." The man looked at Gary impassively. No greeting, no acknowledgment that a person was walking into his place of business. This wasn't that kind of business. He wasn't going to smile and say, "Good morning, sir. What can I do for you?" He didn't look like he wanted to do a thing for Gary.

"Good morning," Gary said. "I'm a private investigator." He slid his card forward. "I'm working on a court-appointed case and I need to talk to you." He said the same words almost every day, to crack whores and drug dealers and car thieves, to fourteen-year-old girls whose boyfriends were in gangs, to grandmothers raising their grandchildren in tiny apartments. He said it to murderers and landlords, to people who were insolent or terrified, as he looked for ways to help his clients, trying to mitigate the consequences of whatever crime they had been accused of. Whether or not they were guilty was beside the point. Or was supposed to be anyway.

He worked for another investigator, who kept offices on the first floor of a spacious Victorian in the Mission district. Before this, he'd been an investigator with the California State Bar, busting lawyers who stole their clients' money and put it up their nose or into their arm, or who beat up their ex-wives or were in on insurance scams. He'd been good at it, so good he was taken mostly out of the field and given a substantial raise. When he met Annie three years ago, it seemed things were falling into place. They got married within a year, and for the first year of their marriage everything was fine. He was making good money, and they started driving around the city on the weekends looking at open houses. But he found he was happiest when he was out roaming around or sitting in his car at three A.M. in a bad neighborhood waiting for someone he would stroll toward with a smile and a subpoena. He had quit the State Bar when he could no longer come and go as he pleased; his boss was fired and replaced by a supervisor who expected him to account for every minute and spend at least three days a week in the office. Now his finances were more uncertain, but he felt like he was in his element. He only wished Annie could see it that way. What Annie saw was her secure, upwardly mobile life with the rising star of the State Bar going up in flames. They hadn't bought a house; they ended up renting a small one in the Parkside District. And now, ever since her sister died last year, she was on this baby kick and bugging him to get a better job. They'd had another fight that morning. He was trying not to think about it.

The hotel clerk showed him a mask that said, *I know nothing, I can tell you nothing. There is no information for you here. Go away and leave me in peace, I can't help you.* Gary was used to it.

Behind the man, a woman in a gold and purple sari sat in front of a TV. She glanced up and turned back to her program. *The Jerry Springer Show.* Two women were pulling at each other's hair onstage. The TV was down to a murmur, faint screams and boos underneath the music on the radio.

"I'm looking for Carol Miller," Gary said. "Cher, Sherry, Cherry. She's staying here. Or was. I need to find her. I have a client who's in trouble, and she may be able to help him." He paused. "You know how it is," he said, "with these people."

He'd counted on striking a chord with that; for a minute the man held his expression, and then it changed, became animated. "These people!" he said. "They live like animals, some of them. They steal the toilet paper from the bath-rooms, then there is none. They come to the desk and I give them a few sheets. If I give them the roll, it disappears. What can you do with such people?"

Gary shook his head in sympathy.

"Drunks," the man said. "And liars. And on drugs, so many of them."

"What about Carol Miller?"

"She stays here, but she has to take her dirty business to the street. We are respectable people," the man said. He reached for a pack of Marlboros and shook one out. "I have not seen her for a couple of days."

"How long has she been here?"

"Two weeks. She paid to the end of the month. Then—" he shrugged. "They come, they go."

"So sad," Gary said. Carol Miller was a prostitute. Gary's client was a man named Freddie, who claimed to be Carol's boyfriend. Freddie had a coke habit, a chest covered with tat-toos of naked women and snarling tigers, and a felony assault charge pending. Under the three strikes law, Freddie was going to do time; he had two priors. Freddie wasn't a bad guy, as far as Gary could tell. He'd gotten in a bar fight, was all. But the other guy, who also claimed to be Carol's boyfriend, wanted to narrow the playing field and get Freddie sent up. It was a bullshit case. Gary wanted to take Carol's temperature, to see if maybe she'd talk to boyfriend number two. They could call the DA, refuse to participate, and get a Cessation of Investigation. Then, as far as Gary was concerned, Carol and her boyfriends could go back to their chaotic, unexamined lives without clogging the courts and prisons.

The doorway at the back of the office had a curtain of col-ored plastic beads. A little girl came through them and climbed onto the woman's lap. She was about five years old.

Black hair, big dark eyes, with tiny gems of some kind sparkling in her ears and an orange dot in the center of her forehead. She studied Gary, curious and shy. Little sweetheart, Gary thought. What a place to raise a kid.

"Do you know if Carol Miller's here right now?"

"No," the man said. He had smoked a few drags of his cigarette and put it out. Gary resisted the urge to have one himself. When the man took out another Marlboro, Gary reached for his Camel Lights and lit up, too.

"No, she's not here? Or no you don't know?"

"I don't know."

Gary was trying to quit smoking, for Annie. She cut out newspaper articles and left them faceup on the kitchen table—"Definitive Link Established Between Smoking and Lung Cancer." "Tobacco Companies Accused of Covering Up." Ads for Nicotrol and Nicoderm. She didn't seem to worry that he might get killed on the street one day, walking up to the wrong person, or being in a place he shouldn't. But then, she didn't really know how dangerous his job was. He never talked much about it because he knew it would upset her and make her more anxious to see him behind a desk. He was careful on the streets but he knew how unpredictable things were. You could spend your whole life being safe, and in one instant someone could take it all away from you, knife you to death for some reason only discernible to the voices in his miswired brain, then take five dollars from your wallet and head for Church's Fried Chicken.

A girl came down the stairs, but she wasn't Carol Miller. Carol Miller was a tall redhead. Freddie had described her to Gary. He'd also described her method of giving blow jobs. Freddie said he didn't know what he loved more, Carol's tits or her blow jobs. Freddie said the guy he'd fought with didn't know what true love was, but he, Freddie, knew all about it.

Great tits, red hair, and that mouth around your dick. That's love, Freddie said.

Gary watched the girl. She was about five-four, thin, with dirty blond hair. She wore a tight jeans skirt and a white tank top that showed her navel. She kept her head down, but he could see she was pretty. She looked like a junkie—pale, afraid of the light, curled up in some corner of herself. She cut her eyes at the front desk as she passed, and he saw they were an unusual shade of blue, the shade you usually only got from colored contact lenses. He wondered if they were real.

"Listen," Gary said to the man, "I need to see her room. I know you're not supposed to let me up there. But I really need to see it."

He was met with silence. The man smoked. The camaraderie was over.

"Thanks anyway," Gary said. "Thank you for your trouble."

Outside, the girl was standing on the corner of Polk and Eddy, looking lost. The light turned from red to green, but she just stood there like she was waiting for somebody to help her across. Gary had once followed a schizophrenic for three days, a guy whose parents were trying to get him committed, and the guy had stood on a corner in Berkeley watching the light change for half an hour. The light had changed, but the little red electronic hand beneath the light had stayed there instead of turning to the white figure of a walking man. Finally, the schizophrenic had thrown his arms out and his head back, like he was Christ on the cross, and—miraculously, it must have seemed to him—at that moment the electronic sign started working again, and he strolled across. Gary wondered if the girl was mentally ill or what. She had a story, he knew. Everyone did, and it was always a story you'd rather not hear and already had heard before anyway, at least some version of it.

Two boys armored in black leather jackets walked by. There were zippers all over the jackets, and chains hanging down from the belt loops of their jeans. Their ears and noses and eyebrows were pierced, and they wore studded bracelets on their thin wrists, all of it glittering in the sunlight as they tromped past in heavy black boots. Gary fell into step behind them and approached the girl, stopping at the corner beside her.

The light changed. The girl looked up at him through a wispy fringe of bangs. Her lower lip was swollen and the lower side of her face bruised, a purple-black bloom under a layer of makeup. She stepped into the street. Gary crossed with her, hands in his pockets. He could feel her trying to pretend he wasn't there. She'd see only a big man, older than she was by ten years, heavyset, muscled. Gary's face bore a few pockmarks from a long-ago acne condition. He used to think he'd be handsome without the scars, when he was younger and worried about his looks. Criminals usually thought he was a cop, and cops sometimes took him for a criminal. His looks were an asset on the street. Most people, even criminals, took the path of least resistance, and Gary made it easy for them to look for someone else's day to ruin.

They had reached the other side of the street. The girl turned blindly and was walking, fast, Gary keeping pace.

"Hey," he said. "I'm a private investigator. I'm working on a court-appointed case. I need to talk to you."

She slowed but didn't answer.

He had a card in his hand, extended toward her. "I'm not a cop," Gary said. "I was just in the Barker, remember?"

She stopped then and gave him another quick look. She crossed her arms over her chest, glancing over her shoulder at the Vietnamese restaurant they'd stopped in front of. She turned back and put one hand up to her face in a gesture that made it look like she was considering him or his offer, but was probably meant to hide the marks of whatever had happened to her. He didn't step toward her, just waited, and that seemed to reassure her.

Gary held his card out again. "Hey," he said. "I only want to talk to you. My name is Gary Shepard. I'm a private investigator, working on a court-appointed case."

"You said that."

"But I didn't tell you my name before."

"No, you didn't," she said, reluctantly agreeing.

"I just need some information," he said.

"I haven't got any information." She brushed her hair back with her hand—a narrow hand, with long fingers, the nails bitten short, a little dark polish on them. She caught him looking and quickly pulled some strands back across her face, over the bruises.

"Listen," Gary said. "Let me buy you a cup of coffee."

"I'm busy," she said. "I got things to do."

"I'm sure you do." He could imagine what they were. Get high. Climb into some guy's car and put her head in his lap or kneel down in front of someone in an alley. Get knocked against a wall in a crummy hotel room.

"Important things," she said, defensive. She looked down the street at whatever important things she was inventing for herself.

"I'm sure you're busy," Gary said, sounding as sincere as he could manage. "I don't want to keep you. Just take my card. You can call me anytime." He handed her the card and she studied it.

"Gary Shepard," she read. "You need a license to do your job?"

His California PI license number was on his card. "Yeah," he said.

"Like beauty school."

"I guess so." He could see she was impressed. A licensed professional. She was looking at him doubtfully, taking in his unprofessional appearance—jeans and sneakers, a sports coat over a T-shirt.

"I heard it's supposed to rain later," he said, squinting up at the sky. Weather: the most innocuous of conversational gambits. Unless, of course, you were on the streets. Weather was a whole different topic then.

At least she's got a roof over her head, he thought. For the moment.

"It rains too much here," she said.

"Well then, you take care." He stepped back. "Stay dry. And really, call anytime."

"There's a Miz Brown's on the corner," she said.

"That would be fine."

"Let's go, then," she said, and started off ahead of him.

*

He watched her eye the plates of waffles and eggs the waitress carried past them to the next booth. She was dragging a Lipton's tea bag through the hot water in her mug. She lifted the bag, wrapped the string tightly around to squeeze out the liquid, and set it carefully on a napkin.

"Let me buy you some breakfast," Gary said. "What's your name?"

"What's it to you? I haven't done anything."

So much for the pleasantries. "I just want to know who I'm talking to," he said. "You already know my name."

"It's Rita," the girl said. "And, no, I don't have any ID if you're going to ask for it."

He wanted to ask her why not, but left it alone. It might

make her close down further. "Well, Rita," he said, "I was actually thinking about ordering some eggs."

"I guess I could have some waffles then," she said. "And maybe some bacon." She scratched at her shoulder, looked around the room, then settled on staring fixedly at the napkin dispenser.

Gary signaled the waitress, a gaunt woman who looked to be in her sixties, wearing heavy makeup and a wig of tight black curls. "Morning, Fran," he said, reading the pin on her brown uniform. "I'd like the number two, sunny side up, and my friend will take waffles with a side of bacon."

"And two eggs scrambled," Rita added, hunching forward so her voice came from behind a curtain of blond hair.

"Sure, hon," Fran said, not looking at either of them; she jotted on her pad, as she'd probably been doing for the past forty years. Gary found himself trying to calculate how many times she must have written *coffee* and *#2 scram* in that time.

"Orange juice?" Rita said, moving her hair aside and looking at Gary like he might not allow it.

"Large or small?" Fran asked.

"Small," she said. "Large," she said, looking at Gary again.

"And, Fran," Gary said. "I bet you're beautiful when you smile."

Fran focused on him for an instant and smiled, showing her gums and a missing upper tooth. "Be still, my beating heart," Gary said, and clapped his hands theatrically over his chest.

Fran went off, still smiling. It took so little. Gary had been raised in Eau Claire, Wisconsin, where people greeted other people on the street—even strangers—and joked with the waitresses, and if somebody's car or truck was broken down at the side of the road, someone pulled over to offer help.

After thirteen years in San Francisco, the kind of people he'd grown up with had come to seem unreal. And naive. He hadn't been back home in ages. But sometimes the Midwest boy in him surfaced.

"So, Rita," Gary said. "How long have you been at the Barker?"

"Too long, already."

"Do you have any place else you could go?" He wondered again what her story was. "Any place at all?"

"You said you wanted some information." She studied her tea bag.

"I'm just doing my job," Gary said. "It's my job to ask questions. I swear I'm not like this normally," he said. "If we were just sitting here and I wasn't working, I wouldn't ask you a thing. I'd just sit here drinking this crappy coffee, not saying a word."

"Yeah, right," she said.

"Okay, I lied."

"I don't even know you and already you're lying to me."

"Better not listen to a word I say. I'm full of shit."

"Just like everybody else."

"No, Rita," Gary said. "I'm one of the good guys. I won't bullshit you," he said earnestly. Or hit you, he thought, wondering who had done that to her face. It hurt to see her prettiness marred. She was very pretty. Small shoulders, thin arms, long shapely legs. He'd once seen some dancers from the San Francisco Ballet after a performance, sitting in Max's Opera Café, eating big slabs of cake (afterward they had walked outside and lit cigarettes); he could picture Rita among them, her hair up to reveal her long neck. She had to be tougher than she looked to be staying at the Barker.

When their meals came, he watched her press the pats of butter into her waffles with the tines of her fork, then

drench them in syrup. He thought of Annie, always count-
ing calories, watching her weight. Doing those stupid aero-
bics videotapes, jumping up and down in their living room.
Feel the burn. There was one with Jane Fonda that was espe-
cially idiotic, where Jane Fonda said things like, *Howdy, part-
ner,* while pretending to ride a pony, and bad Western music
played. He waited until Rita had taken a few bites and then
asked about Carol.

"I don't think I know her," she said, reaching for the bacon.
She took a napkin and carefully blotted the grease off a strip.
"I only seen a couple people going in and out. Most people
keep to themselves."

"You'd know her if you saw her. She's tall, with long red
hair. Hard to miss."

Rita kept eating, digging the side of her fork into her pan-
cakes and shoveling in big bites, her eyes on her plate. "No,"
she said. "I didn't see nobody like that ever."

She was gripping her fork a little too tightly. Gary knew she
wanted to distance herself from any trouble Carol might be in.
People lied to him every day, their eyes wide with feigned
innocence, their voices trembling with righteous indignation.
They sat in an interview room, making up one fantastic story
after another, trying to hit on the one that would get them out
on the streets again. "Listen, Rita," he said. "I just want to talk
to her."

"I'm sorry, I can't help you. I appreciate this breakfast
you're buying for me and all. But that's as far as it goes."

"Look," Gary said. "Maybe we could help each other out
here."

"I already told you, I don't know her."

"But you might see her," Gary said. "You might run into
her."

She surprised him by laughing. "I doubt it," she said.

He took a twenty out of his wallet and slid it across the table between her plate and the sugar dispenser. "Here's the thing," he said. "I'm not supposed to do this. But maybe you could use a few bucks."

"Maybe," she allowed. They both looked at the money. "I'll think about it," she said.

"You've got my card. You can call anytime."

"This is my card," she said, tapping the center of the bill, where Andrew Jackson's face appeared. "It's got my name on it. Right there. Jackson. I'm Rita Jackson."

"Pleased to meet you, Rita Jackson," Gary said. "The picture doesn't do you justice, though. You're much prettier."

"Don't give me any of that shit," she said. She folded the bill, tucked it into her jeans, and returned to demolishing her breakfast.

*

After Gary Shepard left, Rita lingered over the last bites of waffle, cutting out the remaining four squares and moving them around in the lake of syrup she'd poured on her plate. She looked out the window, watching the daily lives of the poor, the destitute, and the insane. She could feel that she was in trouble. The man in the Barker last night had seen her, and now there was this investigator coming around. She was right in the middle of a situation here. *Don't go looking for trouble, trouble will find you.* One of Jimmy's tapes he used to play. I don't want any more of that. *Bad luck and trouble, been my only friend.* That was another one he liked.

Well, I'm not going back to the shelter or to Terrance's craziness. I can't go backward no matter what. I have to change my direction here.

A man in a black suit walked by with a sandwich board—

GOD LOVES YOU in big letters, under it a list in smaller letters
that looked like Bible verses. As he passed the window, Rita
saw the other side of the board; it was covered with tiny
writing, the words all crowded together, unreadable.

If God loves me, where the hell is he? I could use some
help right now. You'd think God could do more than show
up for a couple of minutes in a cloud. That was a long time
ago. What have you done for me lately? I know you've got a
lot of people to show yourself to and all, but maybe you
could spare me another minute. Give me some kind of sign.
Or send one of your angels down to help me out here. I've
been lost and I know it. Take me back into the fold, let me lie
down in green pastures, leadeth me beside the quiet waters,
for I shall fear no evil. She had seen a poster once that fin-
ished that thought: For I Am the Meanest Son of a Bitch in
the Valley.

Polk Street was a far cry from any green pastures. It was
more like the valley of the shadow of death.

You're dead, the man had said. He had said it like a thing
that was going to happen, like a prophecy. *See you later, sweet-
heart.* He was an evil prophet, and he had looked straight
down into her and seen her guilty, tarnished soul, and she
was afraid.

*

Jimmy had slept late, right up to ten thirty, and as he rushed
to get ready for work he felt the coke still crackling inside
him, his nerves like fraying wires. He finished a cigarette,
put on the pants he'd stayed up to iron last night—he'd had
to walk about two miles before he found a cab with a
depressed driver who talked nonstop about his ex-girlfriend
and her new husband all the way to the Mission. He tucked

in his white shirt and felt, as he always did, a little better and purer just from putting it on. He shaved and brushed his teeth and gargled with Cool Mint Listerine and slapped on some Tuscany cologne, then cracked a smile at his image in the mirror. He'd seen a movie on TV once about a guy who did a lot of drugs every day and night, then got up in the morning, did a little ritual with a shower, Visine, Dexedrine, and Alka-Seltzer, opened his hands, and said to the mirror, "Showtime, folks."

"Hi, I'm James and I'll be waiting on you today," he said to the mirror. "Why don't you give me a big tip, you rich son of a bitch?"

He put a little gel on his hair and scrunched it up on top where it always got flat. He'd have to get it cut soon. His boss, Walter, had long graying hair he kept in a ponytail, but he wanted the waiters to keep theirs short. Walter didn't mind an earring, as long as it was a stud. Jimmy had a tiny ruby in the hole in his left ear. He'd stolen it a few weeks ago from the jewelry box of some girl who had taken him home from a bar. He couldn't remember now what she'd looked like, only that she'd had a white dresser trimmed with gold paint and that the jewelry box had also been in the shape of a dresser with little drawers in it lined with blue felt. He'd taken some money from her, too, a couple of twenties from the wallet in her purse.

"Can I get you something from the bar?" Jimmy asked the mirror. "You think you're something, don't you," he told it. He passed his hand down over his face, over his forehead and eyes and nose and mouth, and by the time his hand got to his chin the smile had been replaced by a frown. Then he brought his hand up again. Now he was smiling. A kid's game he remembered playing.

"Showtime, folks," he said.

★

"Hey, Rita," Marco said. "How you been, girl? You looking for anything?"

Marco was an old connection. He was standing in front of the Bagel Shop on Polk Street—one of the places she and Jimmy had gone, where Jimmy had not appeared again—smoking a joint. He looked like some seventies rock star, only scuzzier. His dyed orange hair fell around his shoulders. He wore a jacket that looked like it was made from snakes, and alligator cowboy boots.

"I don't do that stuff anymore," Rita said. Maybe this was God's sign. He was testing her again, putting temptation in her way. He hadn't wasted any time; she'd left Miz Brown's this morning, gone and sat in a church for a while, and wandered back to Polk Street, not wanting to return to the Barker in case the man in the corduroy suit had come looking for her.

"Listen, I'm flush," Marco said. "I'll turn you on for free." Marco had some relatives who were rich, Rita had heard. Once, one of them died and left Marco some money, a few thousand it had taken him about a week to spend.

"You're looking good, Rita," Marco said ironically, but didn't inquire as to why her face was banged-up and swollen. "How've you been? Hey, how's your old man? How's Jimmy?"

"Don't even ask," Rita said. Then she wished she'd said something different. Like, *Oh, Jimmy, he's doing good.* Then Marco would have thought they were still together. Obviously, Marco hadn't seen Jimmy, either.

"Come on, let me turn you on," Marco said. "For old time's sake."

Rita remembered the old times. Sitting around in hotel

rooms on Sixth Street, watching guys look for a vein in their arm that wasn't collapsed. Or shooting up between their toes. Then their eyes rolling back in their head. Waiting in a parked car or a stranger's apartment while someone went around the corner, and three hours later you were still sitting there, bored and crawling out of your skin, wondering whether you'd been burned or if you'd soon be feeling your salvation, entering and soothing you like a lover you wanted. Or having enough to just stay in for a few days with Jimmy, and the TV. With all the bright, talking people moving around in their nice houses and driving places in their cars, and the curtains closed so you hardly knew if it was day or night out there in the world where all the shit was, and it was far away, it had forgotten all about you.

She thought of how sick she'd been when she'd quit.

"No, thanks," she said. There. She'd passed the test. No, thanks. Simple as that.

"You sure about that?" Marco said. He looked over her head, his eyes scanning the street.

She wasn't sure. She seemed to be having a stretch of bad days. In church she had prayed for the soul of her mother, like always, and for some way out of her life. She wanted to know how to do it, how to feel normal and have a normal job and just live like other people seemed to. She wanted to know where Jimmy was. Jimmy, the one she had promised to love and honor until death, the only man who had ever made her feel like he really saw her and knew her and loved her no matter what. He had seen her at her worst, unwashed and junk-sick and depressed; he'd made her tea and wiped her down with a damp towel and held her on nights she shook and cried out and talked like a crazy person, lost in dreams of wolves and blood and Karl Hauptmann's violations. In the nearly empty church, she sat in the front pew and cried and she didn't know how anything was going to change for her or how she was going to find Jimmy, ever. Jesus, hanging on his cross behind the altar, had his own troubles and had offered no advice.

"Just come over and chill, then," Marco said. His purple silk scarf had fallen down and he flipped one end over his shoulder, effeminate as a drag queen. "I've got some vodka," he said, "and I think some rum. I've got Mountain Dew and Oreos and some other stuff."

She followed him back to his studio apartment, a block away. It had green wall-to-wall, the kind she always thought must be made by the mile in some big factory somewhere because she'd seen probably a hundred apartments with the same carpet. Heavy brown drapes covered the single window. The walls were adorned with black-light posters of Jimi Hendrix and Janis Joplin and the Grateful Dead and of nude women intertwined with garish, unlikely flowers. Marco handed her a can of Mountain Dew and she settled into a deep armchair that was covered with a pink blanket and watched him fix. He sat on the coffee table and ripped open the paper wrapping on a Plastipak cylinder. He lit a zebra-striped candle and held over it a blackened spoon with a bent handle that looked like something dug up from about a million years ago, boiled up some brown granules, and dropped in a Marlboro filter to soak up the liquid. She watched him hit up, his face relaxing into the rush of the high.

When God tested Job, he killed his cattle and sheep and camels. God sent a wind and killed Job's ten children. Later, God gave Job more animals and let him have more children, like the new babies would be just as good as the old ones. That part of the story had always bothered Rita. Job had still lost his children no matter what God did afterward.

Marco smiled at her. He didn't have a care in the world right now.

She was too weak. She couldn't do it. Just a taste, to help the anxiety. Then she would go back to the Barker and make sure no one was lurking around, and she would lie in bed and deny any bad thing that tried to gain access to her thoughts.

"I guess I'll have some after all," she said.

"Wise decision," Marco said. "Just give me a sec." He sank back into the couch, eyes closed, his head fallen to one side, mouth hanging open. She felt the old impatience. After what felt like about a year, he stirred himself and came over to her with the necktie he'd used to tie off and prepared her a shot.

"Just—about—ready," he said, flicking at the needle with his finger.

"It's been a long time," Rita said.

"Let me do you." He leaned close, slapped at the crook of her left elbow, raising the vein she used to use. The needle slid in, then the plunger. Then, immediately, there was the sensation of pure relief, her blood turning to thick, slow, blue light in her body. With a feeling of wonder, she watched a little blood wash back into the cylinder. Like a nature show she'd seen. *Secrets of the Deep* or something. An octopus squirted its ink into the ocean. A beautiful suspended swirling thread of blood. Marco booted the shot a couple of times and then pulled out the needle. Rita sank back into the chair. She could sink forever. Marco was standing over her and she felt a wrenching sensation in her gut and doubled over and threw up on the floor.

"Hey!" Marco said. "Hey, whoa. Here."

He thrust a plastic bowl at her and she gagged a little more into that. All those waffles. She tasted the bacon and syrup.

"Come on," Marco said, "let's clean you up." He led her to the bathroom, half-dragging her. Water in her face and mouth. Marco was laughing. Rita laughed, too. She was so happy, happier than she'd been in a long time. She was on a ride of some kind. You sat in a log and went whizzing down a chute of running water and hit the big pool with a whumping sound and the water splashed all over you. She held on to the sink, watching the hole at the bottom where the water kept disappearing. The ride was going to take her down there, through the pipes and into the sewers, until she flew out and landed in the ocean. She slid to the floor, still laughing. Marco was calling her from somewhere. He was high up above her, like God in the clouds. He was the Man in the Moon.

"Oh, Rita," Marco said, in a high, false trill. "You don't want to stay in the bathroom, do you?"

She laid her head on the toilet lid.

"Marco in the moon," she said.

"Get up," Marco said. "Come on, sweetheart." She felt him lifting her again and she slid down his body like it was a wall. She leaned against his knees. There were little snarls of hair along the wall. There was a tiny roach, a baby one, lying unmoving on its back.

He moved away and she crawled out after him. She crawled over to a bed in the corner, a mattress on box springs with a pale blue electric blanket on it, and Marco helped her onto it. "Man, I feel so good," she said. "I feel so goddamned good."

"Once a junkie, always a junkie," Marco said. He was above her again.

"You look like the moon," she said. The bed was hot; the blanket was turned on. Marco disappeared and music started up—something without words, only a beat that pulsed relentlessly inside her head. The lights went off, and she was in outer space, and the stars were green and purple and orange flowers, whizzing around. Janis Joplin smiled at her. Jimi's bandanna and vest blazed, brighter and then dimmer, his heart was in the shape of a guitar. Then she was falling away from everything. Even Marco, undoing her jeans, was a million miles away. She was traveling, faster than the speed of light, getting farther and smaller at once.

*

In Union Square, the shoppers hurried by close to the storefronts, holding their coats around them or angling their umbrellas through the crowds on the sidewalks. It was the middle of November, and the rainy season was just beginning. The thought of all the bad weather to come, while the days got shorter and darker, gave Rita a hopeless feeling. She sat dully in the shelter of an awning, under a window full of gold jewelry, still nodding on the junk Marco had given her, with a sign that said simply, PLEASE. She'd found a round cookie tin, and that was set in front of her, and only a handful of change was in it. Down the block, a girl in a silver plastic helmet with wings on it was playing an electric keyboard and getting the lion's share of any handouts.

The rain smelled good at least. Fresh. It would wash away the dirt on the sidewalks and streets and make them glitter. Rita closed her eyes and thought about the rain seeping into the ground, into the roots of trees in Golden Gate Park. For an instant, she thought about leaning against the tree a few days before and getting kicked. Forget that. Move on. Redwoods had shallow roots, she knew; they needed dampness and fog, couldn't survive in a dry climate the way other trees could, trees that could sink their roots deep into the earth to find water. A redwood could topple over in high winds. She thought about all the roots that were under the ground, even, probably, under the sidewalk she was sitting on. Sometimes spreading tree roots would come right up through cement and buckle it.

She opened her eyes and watched a woman walk past, a bulky Macy's bag swinging in one hand. A little girl held the woman's other hand and hop-skipped beside her with her face turned up to catch the drops. That was the thing to do. Just go into the park and stand there with her head back and her arms out, letting herself get drenched with the delicious chill of the rain. Then she'd go someplace warm and quiet, and Jimmy would be there to hold her and undress her, and they'd crawl into a big bed with very white sheets and make love.

She blocked out the image of Marco that appeared. She couldn't think about that. If she thought about it, she would hate him. The message of God was supposed to be love. She saw the point in loving your neighbor, but having to love the people that were your enemies, the people that wanted to use and destroy you, seemed not only impossible but stupid. The most she could attempt was not to hate them, because she knew hate would eat you up from the inside out and do worse things to you than your enemies had. But she felt it anyway—hate and shame and anger—and as usual there was no way to dig that feeling out of her and get rid of it. She hated Marco, and herself, because of what she had let him do, and that was that. It settled inside her, making her feel hopeless again.

The woman and child had stopped a couple of stores down, and the woman was looking at whatever was in the window. The little girl gazed up at her mother, then turned and saw Rita.

"Mommy," she said. "Why is that lady sitting there?"

The woman glanced over. Rita closed her eyes again.

"Never mind," the woman said. "Come on, honey."

"But why?" the girl asked, and if her mother had an answer, she didn't say.

A siren started up somewhere. Voices passing, the keyboard's high notes drifting from the corner. Tires on the wet street, hiss and hiss. Why am I here? Why am I sitting here when I should be in a house somewhere, raising kids. Putting down my roots. I should have my own kitchen and a little garden, like my daddy did, and a living room with some TV trays so me and Jimmy could eat there sometimes, and a dog to sit and behave and not beg, that's a good boy, here's the leftovers. Now she was sitting on the concrete stoop in the front of the house and rain was coming down in her yard and she would have to bring in the tricycle and the bike with the banana seat so they wouldn't rust. She would have to get back inside and cook dinner because the kids (two girls, she wanted to have girls) were getting hungry and she was, too, and Jimmy was coming home any minute to lift her hair and give her a kiss on the back of her neck and say, *Man, that smells good, baby,* and he would open the refrigerator for a beer. She loved him so much she thought she'd die just looking at him sometimes, he was so handsome with his longish dark hair and dark eyes and long muscled arms, the slim waist and his hips that moved against hers at night and claimed her for his very own. She was so happy to be close to him like that and they were a family and their girls crawled into bed with them on weekend mornings and watched cartoons on TV and she could feel their warm little bodies against her side.

When she opened her eyes again she tried to pretend it was all a TV show, that she could make everyone and everything disappear if she wanted to, just by turning off the set. She closed her eyes again and drifted, seeing Jimmy and then Marco, trying to keep one close and push the other one far away, trying to reverse what the world really was.

*

Annie was on the phone giving a Tarot reading when Gary got home. She looked up from the kitchen table, where a row of cards faced her, and gave Gary a distracted look before turning back to the cards. She hadn't paged him all day; she was still mad about this morning, then. Or else, as sometimes happened, she'd just decided to bury her dissatisfaction until it was ready to erupt again. He went to the refrigerator and took out a Beck's, popped it open, and went to the living room couch.

"We all struggle with attachment," Annie said. "There's a Spanish proverb that says, 'Where one door shuts, another opens.' But we often can't see that other door until we've closed the first one. And that's a hard and scary thing to do." Her voice was soothing, nurturing. Annie worked five mornings a week as a receptionist for a brokerage firm in the Financial District and spent the afternoons taking pictures around the city or holed up in her darkroom in the basement. Lately, because money had been tight, she'd been doing this Tarot thing. She'd sit in the kitchen for hours some nights, drinking white wine and turning over cards, murmuring solace and encouragement and bullshit to whoever was desperate enough to call a stranger for some mumbo-jumbo advice.

"The World, reversed," Annie was saying. "There's something holding you back—fear of change. It's hard to let go of the known, I know."

Gary clicked on the TV, hoping to catch the last of *NYPD Blue*, but it was already over. He flipped through the channels with the sound muted and found some black-and-white footage of the Nuremberg trials. Hermann Göering's face appeared in close-up. Gary thought for the thousandth time about the fact that evil didn't have a face you could recognize—there was no mark anywhere, nothing that might let people know you were capable of torturing and killing, of ordering executions and then sitting down to dinner. He thought of how ordinary most serial killers looked, how you'd never even notice them if you saw them in the grocery store. Göering sat straight in his chair in his gray suit, looking like any businessman in a meeting. Occasionally he turned to talk to the man next to him, but mostly he sat impassively, like someone politely listening to a boring speech.

"Four of Swords," Annie said in the kitchen. "I think this is going to be a good change in your life."

He wanted to call out, *What about our life?* Annie was reading cards because he was downwardly mobile. Annie's phrase. He was bad with money. She took care of all the bills, the credit cards, the taxes. How had things changed so radically in less than two years of marriage? When they met three years ago, he was flush and she thought he was fascinating.

They had met at the Art Institute, where she was a grad student. Gary was living in North Beach, and he usually hit the café there after his morning run along the Marina for a cappuccino and a look at the *Chronicle* before heading to the State Bar or the Hall of Justice or Superior Court in Sacramento. They had shared a table one morning when the café was crowded. Gary liked the serious way she talked about her photography, how she would stop in mid-sentence to think of the exact word or phrase she wanted next, growing still and staring out the window, then suddenly starting up again with intense animation. He liked her dark eyes, the tiny row of diamond studs up her left ear, her uncertainty about whether she had enough talent. Her parents had wanted her to do something more practical, but they were footing the bill for the Art Institute. She referred to herself, without any apparent irony, as a rebel. She was twenty-three, and he had just turned thirty-one. She seemed a little lost. He'd liked that about her, too.

He heard her get up and go to the fridge, and knew she was pouring another glass of wine. Annie liked Chardonnay, and if it cost less than ten or twelve dollars a bottle she would turn up her nose at it, like you were offering her Boone's Farm or Thunderbird instead of a perfectly decent Glen Ellen or Mondavi. She could go through a bottle a night, sitting there with her cards. He should have thought to bring home some Kendall Jackson as a peace offering.

"I know," Annie said in the kitchen. "Not to worry." She laughed, and Gary felt jealous that she could be so light-hearted with a stranger.

She hung up the phone, and he clicked to another channel. Annie didn't want to see black-and-white images of Nazis and death camps. Usually, late at night, there was bound to be some old footage being shown, of rallies in Berlin or German soldiers freezing in a snowstorm on the outskirts of Stalingrad or concentration camp victims with emaciated bodies and haunted eyes staring at the camera.

He watched a nature show on the Discovery channel for a couple of minutes. There was always some life-and-death drama going on in the natural world. Right now, some dwarf mongooses were coping with a snake entering the termite mound where they'd made their home. He switched channels again. MTV was showing *Singled Out*, a nineties version of *The Dating Game*. A group of teenaged girls jumped up and down, madly waving their arms. One of them stepped forward and knelt down in front of the blond cohost, looking like she was going to be either knighted or beheaded.

Annie came in and sat down next to Gary, holding her wine.

"Weird," she said, looking at the silent TV.

The cohost, a woman Gary remembered seeing on a magazine cover at the grocery checkout, her mouth wide open in a feral snarl, was slipping a paper bag over the head of the girl on her knees.

"Annie, I'm sorry," Gary said.

"You always say that," Annie said.

What was it she had said on the phone a few minutes ago? Something about fear of change. Annie wanted him to change, to become somebody he wasn't. What could he say? "I'm sorry we fought," Gary said. Then he felt stuck. It would be the same discussion again, the same brick wall. Annie wanted a child. She wanted him to get a better job. More money, more security. As if security were possible.

Annie took a sip of her wine and put her bare feet on the coffee table, atop a pile of *New Yorker*s. His wife had beautiful feet. High arches, elegant toes. She thought her thighs were fat, but there was nothing wrong with them. It had taken about six months of marriage before he realized how truly insecure she felt about everything—not just money, but her body, her intellect, her talent.

"Mom called today," she said. "She wants to know if we'll host Thanksgiving dinner here. She doesn't want to cook this year. She says without Laura—"

"I'd love to cook," Gary said, relieved that she was ready to make up. Annie's sister Laura had died last year of ovarian

cancer. Maybe that was why Annie had become so focused
on having a child. Maybe she'd gradually change her mind.
Besides, she had her photography. She was always talking
about updating her portfolio from grad school and trying to
get a show. Gary doubted it would happen, but Annie
seemed to need something, and a wall of photographs was
infinitely preferable to a child. As soon as he thought it he
felt guilty. There was nothing wrong with wanting a child, it
was what a lot of women wanted.

"You know what a terrible cook she is, anyway."

"No kidding," Gary said.

"God, the way I ate as a kid," Annie said. "I can't believe I
didn't get rickets. Or scurvy. All we ever ate was processed
food. Frozen pot pies. Kraft American Cheese Singles. Hot
dogs. Scooter Pies—did you ever have Scooter Pies? They
were big, round chocolate-covered cookies, with marshmal-
low or something in the middle. Did you ever have those?"

"We had Mallomars. They had marshmallow in them."

On TV, there were now three girls with bags on their
heads, kneeling in a semicircle behind a boy in a chair. It def-
initely looked like some weird execution ritual. He put his
arm around Annie, and she leaned against him.

"You cook," Annie said. "It'll be a great dinner. She won't
appreciate it, but I will. You could make that pine-nut stuff-
ing."

"No problem," Gary said. He inhaled the fruity scent of
her hair—her creme rinse. He put his mouth to the back of
her neck and thought of rubbing his face against her soft nip-
ples and freckled breasts. He remembered that Rita's nipples
had been hard under her white shirt, outside Miz Brown's
that morning, two little points his eyes were drawn to.

"I do love you, you know," Annie said.

"You just love me for my stuffing," Gary said.

"Yep," she said.

"And my osso bucco."

"Your osso bucco is excellent." She tucked her feet under her and put her head against his shoulder.

"Like everything I cook."

"When you cook. You don't cook like you used to."

He wanted to say, *You don't love me like you used to.* "I've got a big caseload right now," he said. "Soon as it lightens up, I'll make a great osso bucco."

"You know," Annie said. "You could *be* a lawyer, instead of working for them. You could do corporate investigations. You could open your own firm and hire people to do the shit work."

"I like the shit work." He stroked her hair. He loved her. He'd tried to stay with the cubicle job, for her. The spirit was willing, but the flesh said, To hell with this, I want to be where things are happening. Where I feel like I'm making a difference to someone, and can look into their eyes and know that I did what I could to help them.

"I just don't understand why you want to be out there, dealing with the crime and ugliness of the world."

Gary thought of Annie's photographs. Black-and-white studies of poppies and lilies. Kids splashing in fountain spray or running across wide lawns. It's not that they were bad photographs. It was just her idea of beauty; it contained no difficulty, no darkness. He couldn't explain to her the kind of beauty he saw in people who were being pushed down, not allowed to bloom. Just that they survived was astonishing to him.

She finished her wine, kissed his shoulder, and got up and went to the kitchen to refill. "Let's go to bed," she called.

Gary went into their bedroom and stretched out on top of the comforter. He waited for his wife to have another glass of wine, to come and lean against the doorjamb to steady her-self, and then weave toward the bed, fall on it, and let him make love to her.

*

Chumley was losing at foosball and having a great time, banging on the sides of the machine and flipping the players in their striped uniforms around in circles on their metal rods. Jimmy tuned him out and listened instead to two girls on his left at the bar, waiting for one of them to make a remark that left an opening he might casually fill with his own comment. But they were deep into some discussion about the place they worked, an office somewhere in which a man named Dexter made their lives miserable.

"And do you know what he said when I gave him the files?" the one right next to Jimmy said. "He said, '*Finally.*' Like I'd had all day to do it or something."

The other girl murmured her assent and took a Merit Ultra Light from the pack on the bar in front of her. You weren't supposed to smoke anymore in bars in San Fran-cisco, but in most of the neighborhood places the bartender would look the other way and slip you a coffee mug for the ashes. Jimmy wished the other girl was sitting right next to him, so he could offer her a light. She was the pretty one. He took out a cigarette for himself and lit it, then turned to Stan, who was nursing a third martini and also lighting up.

"Hey, you know what I read somewhere?" Stan said. "I read that if you want to get a chick to notice you, you do what she does. Like, the way that chick just lit a cigarette and we did, too. It's like body language or something. If she crosses her legs, you cross your legs. Pretty soon you're on the same wavelength." Stan leaned in close to Jimmy, his gin and cigarette breath washing over him. "Man, that pot got me *high*," he said confidentially.

"Thanks for turning me on," Jimmy said. He was glad that Chumley and Stan had invited him out tonight. It had been a bad day. The floor manager at the restaurant hadn't shown up, and things were tense and disorganized, and Walter kept going into the kitchen to yell at everybody. Jimmy had wanted to just crawl into his harp all night, to get lost in the predictable repetitions of the blues, eleven bars and the V–IV turnaround rounding out the twelfth, back to the I chord, the third note of the scale sounded, then flatted as the reed bent, the soulful mournful flatted third. But now it felt good to be sitting here, drinking a beer. The place was bathed in dim red light. Bar light. Timeless, gentler and softer than twilight, transforming tired faces into restful ones, anxiety into ease, anticipation into gaiety. Blues into swing. The girls next to them were laughing now, Dexter and his demands receding, their office lives disappearing into the far distance. Jimmy loved bars, the intimacy with strangers encouraged by too many drinks, the stools where you sat shoulder to shoulder, the reflections of glasses on a polished bar. Piles of neat square napkins and plastic compartments for lime slices and curls of lemon rind and olives. Behind the bar were four long rows of bottles with yellow pour spouts, each bottle with a tiny Exit sign on it. Off Ramp. Rest Stop. This Way Out.

There was a sign behind the bar: If You Lived Here You'd Be Drunk By Now.

Stan put his arm around Jimmy. "Hey, Jimmy," he said. "You're all right, man. You know that?"

"Fucking A," Jimmy said, and raised his beer.

"You should come by my shop sometime," Stan said. "Come by anytime. Hey." He leaned across Jimmy. "How's it going, ladies? How are you all doing tonight?"

The one nearest Jimmy—an overweight blonde with dark roots about an inch wide—looked at Stan, then turned away. Her friend looked at Jimmy and held his eyes for a second.

"Hey," Stan persisted. "Let me buy you a drink."

"No, thanks, we're fine," the blonde said.

"Hey, Sam," Stan called to the bartender, a skinny kid with corks stoppering the huge holes in his earlobes. The kid was sitting on a stool in a corner of the bar, reading an *X-Men* comic, and didn't look up.

"Sampson," Stan said. "Samsonite. SamTrans."

The bartender sauntered over, still holding the comic.

"Give these ladies another round." He turned to the blonde. "Hi, I'm Stan. This is my buddy, Jimmy."

"I said we were fine." The blonde's voice was hostile.

"You want to get high?" Stan said. "I've got some dynamite weed."

"Stan," Jimmy said. "I don't think they want to talk to us." He could feel the other girl watching him. She had short, curly dark hair, dark eyes. Spanish, Italian, Puerto Rican. A tight black T-shirt with *New York* in different-colored letters slanting across the front. The bartender brought the women their drinks. They were both having Cuba Libres.

"And one for me and Jimmy," Stan said.

The dark-haired girl jiggled her skinny red straw in her drink, took it out and chewed on it, set it on her napkin, picked it up, and started folding it. "I'm Robin," she said, looking at Jimmy. "And this is Patricia."

Patricia shot her friend a look. "Don't," she said. "*Robin.*"

"I'd love to get high," Robin said. She picked up her drink suddenly and took a long, giddying slug, tipping her head back, her eyes closed. It was a gesture Jimmy understood.

"You always do this," Patricia said helplessly. She twisted her bleached hair around her finger.

"I just want to smoke a little pot," Robin said.

"Well, I don't," Patricia said. "I'm staying right here." She put both hands around her drink, as though it was attached to the bar and she could cling to it if something or someone tried to pull her away.

"My car's right around the corner," Stan said. "Come on, go for a ride with us. Christ, we're not gonna do nothing to you. We're not rapists or anything."

Jimmy wondered again about Stan's prison term. It had to have been drugs. He wanted to tell Stan that bringing up rape wasn't the smoothest way to get a skeptical woman into your car, but Stan was pressing on.

"Look, here's my card," Stan said. He took his wallet from the inside pocket of his sports jacket—the wallet was black-and-white cowhide, Jimmy noted, which probably further diminished their prospects—and pulled out a card that read Stanley Thompson Jewelers. Patricia held it dubiously between long, peach-colored nails.

"I'll tell you what," Stan said. "Let's all finish our drinks. Then I'm going to go get in my Cadillac and drive out to the beach and smoke some pot, and whoever wants to come with me is welcome."

The bartender brought their Cuba Libres and took Stan's martini glass away. Jimmy thought about the other side of bars: men telling their life story to the ice in their glass or throwing curses at some stranger or sliding carefully off a barstool, managing a controlled stagger toward the door with car keys in hand. Women running to the bathroom to puke, or making out with somebody they wouldn't have looked at three drinks ago.

"Cheers, dude," Chumley said, picking up his new drink. He drank it in an imitation of Robin's chugalug. Doing what she had done, getting on her wavelength.

Robin and Patricia were huddled together, earnestly negotiating the evening's next activity in low voices.

Jimmy heard Chumley scream, "Score! Score! Score!", pounding the side of the machine in rhythm to his voice. He caught Robin's eye, and she gave him a slight smile. He raised his glass, titled his head back, and drank. One Fuck-idol pill, going down.

"Ready," he said to Stan.

*

"Bad to the Bone" was playing on Stan's car stereo—George Thorogood and the Destroyers. Jimmy had seen an MTV special once, about the influence of blues on rock and roll, and George Thorogood had been a big part of it. The special had been narrated by a girl who obviously didn't know dick about the blues. At one point she had said, "About Robert Johnson virtually nothing is known. He lived, he played. That's it." That was the lamest thing he had ever heard. There was a lot that was known about Robert Johnson. Jimmy could have told them plenty about him if anyone had asked. Robert Johnson had started out playing the harmonica. He was a terrible harp player before he became a great guitarist. Jimmy wasn't terrible, so he figured he was already ahead of Robert Johnson, in a way. Of course that was bullshit, but there was value in bullshitting yourself. It kept you playing instead of giving up, figuring you'd never be any good.

Stan had the music cranked up, so Jimmy could only wonder what further negotiations were going on in the backseat between Patricia and Robin. They sat close together, quietly arguing.

Stan passed Jimmy his pipe. Jimmy turned the music down and offered Patricia a toke.

"No, thanks," she said.

"Robin?" Jimmy said, holding it out to her. She took it from him.

"Nice bracelet you have," Jimmy told Patricia, pretending to admire a big hammered-silver band on her left wrist.

Patricia stared out the window, her face set. She wasn't having any. The pipe went from Robin to Jimmy to Stan, back to Jimmy. He was taking two hits for each one of theirs.

"Hey," Jimmy said. "Stop here." He went into a corner store and bought a six-pack of Budweiser, a pint of vodka, some grapefruit juice, and Fritos. He got back in Stan's car, which was filled with fragrant smoke. "Refreshments," he said.

Patricia, as it turned out, would like a cocktail. There weren't any cups, but Stan had a small thermos. Jimmy poured in vodka, topped it with a little juice, and passed it back. He and Stan opened beers.

"I'm fine," Robin said.

"I'll say," Stan said, leering at her in the rearview. "You sure are, babe."

"Don't mind Stan," Jimmy said. "He's an animal."

"Yeah!" Stan roared, throwing back his head. "A god-damned party animal!"

"He's harmless," Jimmy assured the girls, not knowing if it was true.

They were on the Great Highway now, heading south. Jimmy looked out at the blackness that was the ocean. He tried to imagine living things under its surface—fish, sharks, strange sea creatures floating around in the cold and dark. It seemed impossible that there was anything out there. He rolled his window down a little and inhaled the salt breeze. He suddenly wished he were alone, so he could walk on the beach and maybe sit somewhere and play the A harp in his back pocket, play something low and sorrowful like the ocean. The sand stretched out, lunar and empty.

Stan pulled the Cadillac into a big parking lot and up to the sloping concrete wall that separated it from the beach. There were a few other cars and a black van, all of them spaced far apart. Music thumped from the van.

"How's everybody doing?" Stan said. "How are you two fine ladies feeling?"

The fine ladies giggled. Patricia thrust the thermos into the front seat. "How about some more of that," she said.

"Coming right up," Jimmy said.

Stan was snorting coke from a vial with a tiny spoon attached to it by a thin silver chain. "Here, man," he said, giving it to Jimmy.

"Is that coke?" Patricia squealed. "You didn't tell us you had coke."

Patricia was turning out to be something of a party animal. She was clearly drunk now. Robin sat quietly in a corner of the backseat, but Jimmy wasn't worried about her. They had an understanding. He didn't really want the coke, but here it was, and Just Say No was about the stupidest advice he'd ever heard. It was complicated, turning down drugs, even those you didn't particularly want. There was a promise in them you knew they would eventually betray, but in the moment, it was easy to overlook that. It wasn't peer pressure that got people. It was the pressure of the instant, the single split-second Yes that called to you. The No was in there somewhere, but it was harder to locate. He took a generous scoop of powder and put it up one nostril, then the other, and passed the vial to the backseat.

"You want to hear my speech about drugs?" Stan said.

"What, are you reading my mind?" Jimmy said. Wavelength. "What am I thinking now, Stan?" Jimmy closed his eyes and conjured a great white shark with black BBs for eyes, willing it into Stan's brain, but Stan ignored him.

"I'm taking a speech class and we all have to make a speech," Stan said.

"Oh, you're a student?" Patricia said. "You look kind of old to be a student."

Stan didn't take offense. "I like learning things," he said. "I'm gonna get my degree one day."

"In what?" Patricia said.

"I don't know yet. So far I've taken Creative Writing, Speech, and Sociology. I dropped Sociology, though. It was too hard."

"Tell us your speech," Robin said.

"It's called, 'Why Should Drugs Be Legalized,'" Stan said.

"Good title," Jimmy said.

"Okay." Stan paused to collect himself, then turned to them all and started talking in a voice that attempted formal discourse.

"Why should drugs be legalized?" Stan began. "Drugs should be legalized—uh—for one reason, to take all the crime associated with drugs . . . And it would do a striking blow to organized crime and the Mafia. Drive-by shootings would be history and, let's face it. Studies have proved that only ten percent of our population are the addictive kind of people. And they're gonna be high on any kind of drugs no matter what anybody says. So if we give it to 'em, we can *tax* 'em, and when they get high enough, they can find their *own* ways to the hospitals because there'll be a lot more *money* for hospitals. There ain't gonna be this war on drugs that has never, uh, netted anything. In the thirty years since the nineteen-sixties, it has only managed to stop about ten percent of the illegal drugs. And what does that do?" He paused dramatically. "All that does is drive the prices of the drugs *up*"—he raised his finger in the air, jabbing it toward the roof of the car—"so that the *dealers* make more *money!*"

There was silence in the car after Stan's speech, as everyone contemplated the sorry state of affairs that led to expensive and illegal drugs. He passed the coke around again. "Hey," he said finally. "I didn't mean to bum everybody out. It's a party. Who wants to take a walk?"

They stumbled from the car, entered through an opening in the wall and descended the steps to the beach. The wind was gusting. No one was around, though farther up, toward the Cliff House, a bonfire was lit. Patricia went ahead, with Stan close on her trail. Jimmy and Robin walked side by side. After a few minutes he put his arm around her.

"Cold?" he said.

"I guess so. I mean, I'm shivering, but I don't *feel* cold."

Patricia was already down by the water, wading along the white edge of the surf. "Whoo!" she screamed.

"I used to come here sometimes," Robin said. "Now I hardly ever do."

"You know what I like?" Jimmy said. "I like being able to look out there and not see any buildings or telephone poles."

"In Santa Barbara, where I went to college," Robin said, "there were oil platforms."

"I'm from Jersey," Jimmy said. "I kind of miss the boardwalk at Seaside sometimes."

"Yeah, there's one in Santa Cruz," Robin said. "I like the roller coaster there."

Jimmy thought about Little Walter's "Roller Coaster," which he was trying to learn, by ear. It was slow going. He was also working on tongue-blocking, which he wasn't very good at yet. "I've never been to Santa Cruz," he said, bored with the conversation, wishing he had someone to tell about the tongue-blocking, knowing Robin wouldn't be interested. Rita had listened to the tapes he played her, though when he started talking about chords and sevenths and harp positions she got that blank interested look that said, *Yes, yes, honey, that's great, I have no idea what you're talking about.*

Jimmy turned Robin toward the dunes at the south end of the wall. They walked for a while until they found a wide depression in the sand, surrounded by tall grasses, the wind passing over them. Jimmy took off his jacket and laid it on the sand, so Robin could sit on it, and squatted down next to her. This was the part he hated, having to find something to say while waiting for the sex to happen. Everything surrounding the sex, the before, the after, the being where he didn't want to be—it was just like drugs. He didn't really want her.

He leaned in and kissed her. Soon they were rolling together on the sand. He heard Stan laughing on a snatch of wind, then nothing. Robin was warm beneath him. He pushed her T-shirt up and then her bra, black lace, stiff underwire. There was a small iris tattooed just above her left breast. She smelled like mangoes and chocolate and smoke. He felt her hands fumbling at his belt and unzipping his jeans. Her hands were icy, though, like the hands of a corpse. The mangoes were too soft, rotting from the inside, their skins blackening; he was suddenly afraid to look at the flower on her breast, afraid it had shriveled. She was holding him, trying to get him hard. There were bells in his head, a steel ball hitting them and making them ring, like a pinball game, *ba-bing, ba-bing.* It was just a game.

He was sick of girls, he realized. He moved up over her to put himself in her mouth, felt the wetness of her tongue.

Nothing. He fell off her, into the cold sand, and lay on his back. She followed him, her mouth working on him.

Ba-bing. Nothing.

"Forget it," he said.

"What's the matter?" Robin said, stopping.

"Just forget it," he repeated. He didn't want her to touch him. There were the stars, all bursting inside his head. What was she doing? He'd told her to stop. She had started again. He felt like he was being devoured by some animal. He pushed at her head, her shoulders. "Get off me," he said.

"It's okay," Robin said. "Just let me."

No.

Let me, let me.

No.

Her mouth working.

He grabbed her by the hair to raise her off him and instinctively gave her a quick right with his fist. He saw her head snap back.

Then he was up and running. Tucking himself in, protecting himself. The sand tried to pull at him; his boots sank in. He couldn't tell which way the ocean was, though he could hear it rushing in his ears. The dunes were full of little pathways, little hollows to hide in. But he had to run. There was a hole, waiting for him to fall through it, and he had to catch the ball on the flippers and not let it shoot straight down between them.

He kept running, and now there were streetlights and silent cars with wet fog on their windshields and squat houses facing the ocean, so he knew he was going in the right direction, away from the water. And there was a streetcar sitting with its lights blazing at the turnaround. He got to it, his breath ragged, and stepped inside. The driver, a weary black man in a brown suit and cap, flicked a cigarette past him and pulled the doors closed with a lever as Jimmy fumbled for his Fast Pass and fell into one of the long seats in front with a sign above it that read Please Reserve These Seats for Seniors and Disabled Passengers and with a little jerk the streetcar started up.

Ba-bing.

3. At five in the morning a week before Thanksgiving, two of the five tables in the San Francisco Medical Examiner's Office were occupied. Section 27491 of the Government Code of the City and County of San Francisco had a long list of reasons a person might end up here, among them hanging, gunshot, stabbing, drug addiction, and "death in whole or in part occasioned by criminal means." In the aftermath of whatever bizarre dramas had occasioned their deaths, the victims lay quietly inert on white porcelain, their fingerprints taken, their fluids drained out, red tags fastened to their big toes.

Gary wasn't supposed to come here, as an investigator. But he and Sanchez, the tech on duty, had a history. They'd dated the same woman at the University of Minnesota, and had decided they would rather drink with each other than with her. Gary had moved to San Francisco first, to the Inner Sunset District, and Sanchez roomed with him when he hit town and started medical school at the University of California on Parnassus Street. In those days, Sanchez was always up for heading to the Mitchell Brothers on O'Farrell or to one of the strip places that lined Broadway or just roaming around the city. Now Sanchez and Gary were both married. Jim Mitchell had shot his brother Artie, and Carol Doda and her blinking red neon nipples no longer presided over the intersection of Columbus and Broadway; a sports bar was there now. But Gary and Sanchez were still tight. If it was late enough at night and Gary called first, Sanchez would let him sneak in for a few minutes.

"Mr. Shepard," Sanchez said.

"Doctor Sanchez," Gary said. Sanchez had started out to be a doctor, but changed his mind, skipping his first year exams in favor of a trip to Vegas.

"You want some Niners tickets?" Sanchez asked. "I can't use 'em. Maureen claims it's our anniversary."

"Tonight?" Gary said. "Tonight. I can't." He had promised Annie earlier he'd be available for dinner; she'd made reservations at some trendy restaurant she wanted to try. It was supposed to be good, and he loved eating out, but he hated trendy. Once, he and Annie had gone to someplace in Marin called Fork. They gave you so little food, he thought, they should have named it Tine. "Got any Jane Does on ice?" he said. "Red hair?"

"You want to look in the freezer? They brought one in earlier. Make it quick, though. It's my ass if you get caught in here."

"Yeah, yeah." Sanchez was fond of reminding him what a risk he was taking to let Gary come here. But Sanchez loved anything illicit. He sold Ecstasy to a few lawyers and at least one cop Gary knew of. Sanchez liked the edge. You'd never know it from looking at him. He was pudgy, almost bald, and wore glasses that made his eyes look unnaturally small. In spite of this, he had managed to find a wife and was currently juggling liasons with a court stenographer and a nursing student.

Sanchez never seemed to need much sleep. Right now he was merrily wide-awake, while Gary felt like lying down on one of the examining tables.

The freezer was kept at thirty-four degrees. Three black

body bags were in it. Sanchez led Gary to one of them. "They found her in an oil drum down in Hunters Point, at the ship-yards."

He pulled the zipper down. There was something about the sound of a body bag zipper. It was a long sound. It went on and on.

She had probably been pretty; it was hard to see it now. The eyes might have once been hazel, or green, or brown; now the eyeballs had a white film over them, and bulged out. Her mouth was a smear of red. Gary thought of what his client, Freddie, had said about Carol's blow jobs.

"Is there a cause of death yet?"

"From the looks of her, they strangled her," Sanchez said.

Gary had Annie's Polaroid with him. He took a picture. He had come here because it was a place he might find Carol Miller, a possible place if not a likely one. He had hoped she was still out there somewhere, walking the streets, going in and out of bars, climbing the stained carpeted stairs of the Barker Hotel. He watched the Polaroid develop, the woman's ruined face floating toward him. Whoever she'd been, Carol or somebody else, she was no one now. He turned away. He'd grown more or less inured to seeing photos of bodies on which violence had been enacted, but it was still difficult to be in the actual, eerie presence of the dead. There was so clearly nobody home—they were so blank, not human. But they still looked human. That disconnect was hard to absorb. And the knowledge that he, too, would one day be one of them—

"I dated a redhead once," Sanchez said. "Bonnie Some-body. Irish Catholic. Used to drink me under the table, can you believe that?"

"Impressive," Gary said. He followed Sanchez out of the cold air. The smells in the room hit him harder than they had when he'd come in from outside. He gagged, and forced down a wave of nausea. "Listen, I'm out of here," he said.

"Take care, man," Sanchez said. "*Vaya con Dios.* Give my best to the Missus."

"Happy anniversary," Gary said.

"We're taking off for a few days," Sanchez said. "Mexico, baby. Margaritas on the beach."

"Have fun," Gary said, and walked fast through the door and the outer office, down the hall, and into the blessed dawn air of a new day.

*

Thursday and rain again. Rita sat in bed in her room at the Barker, smoking, watching a large brown stain in a corner of the ceiling bleed drops of water into a yellow plastic bowl on the floor. The moisture would slowly condense and form a bead that hung on, trembling, until it finally fell and hit the other water that had collected in the bowl with a gentle pocking sound.

I should leave here. At least change rooms. I shouldn't even have come back. *You're dead. See you later, sweetheart.* The word *sweetheart* had given her a sickening feeling. It was just what people said, what men said. Karl Hauptmann had said it: *Rita, be a sweetheart.* And Marco, yesterday. She didn't want to think about what she had done with Marco. It was over. She had to move on, and not go backward. She'd had to move on from a lot. Most of it, when she thought about it, was stuff that had happened with men. Why she couldn't move on from Jimmy was that there had been a lot of good things, and you had to figure out a way to hang on to those, because without them the world would just not be worth living in.

Yesterday, after Marco's junk had worn off, she'd been too upset to think about going someplace new. The Barker had only been her home for two nights, but she clung to the bare familiarity and sense of autonomy it afforded her. Besides, she had paid through the weekend, and there were no refunds. She had bought some vodka with the money from spare-changing and come back after dark, moving quickly from doorway to doorway before ducking into the hotel.

Now she wished she had a hot plate, so she could at least make tea. Maybe heat some soup. Campbell's chicken soup, with white and wild rice. That, and some steaming tea. It's freezing in this room. And why just a hot plate? Why not a whole damn kitchen? Every day on the streets she walked among people who had kitchens, who could go home to their flats or apartments or big houses and put a kettle on the stove to boil up some water. They could microwave a cup of soup and have it hot in three minutes. They could open a refrigerator and take out some cheese singles and go to a cupboard and get a box of Wheat Thins and put them together on a plate and have a snack, and they didn't think twice about it. Right now she despised them.

In the room above her, furniture scraped across the floor. She watched the ceiling carefully to see if the leak would worsen, but it stayed the same. Whoever was up there redecorating their goddamned room kept moving things until she reluctantly got out of bed and dressed to go out, just to get some peace. She didn't have a coat, so she put on a man's shirt over the long-sleeved thermal shirt she was wearing. Clothes were easy to find. A buck an item at the Goodwill on Twelfth Street, all mixed together in gray plastic bins in a warehouse with high dirty windows where the sun filtered down and made everything look kind of holy. Toys were four for a dollar, black-and-white TVs and stereos were ten apiece, household items two bucks. Most of it was broken—busted-up suitcases, old computer monitors, record albums lying a few feet away from their sleeves along with stray articles of clothing that fell out while people were digging through the piles. But it was hard to find coats there; they usually got snatched up right away. Whenever a new bin was rolled out from the back of the shop, from behind the metal fence, everybody converged on it, pushing and shoving to be the first to find something warm. She could probably get one at a thrift store in the Mission that sold clothes by the pound, but she needed to conserve the little she had. Either way, she had to do something soon, if she wasn't going to get caught back on the streets. No way she was going back to Terrance's, even for a free place and free drinks. Nothing was free. You paid for every damned thing. Sometimes, you overpaid.

I'll just go down to Miz Brown's. It will be warm there, and I can sit at the counter and have my tea. And if that man is around he won't mess with me in broad daylight, in public. I hope.

The investigator, Gary Shepard, had given her his card. Maybe it would be a good idea to tell him what she had seen after all. She might need some protection. She dug his card out from the back pocket of a pair of jeans tossed on the floor. She put some makeup over her bruise—it was yellowing now, easier to cover, and her lip was no longer swollen—and tried smiling in the mirror. Not bad. But her eyes—she had that spooked look no matter what. It was what men saw, what the man in corduroy had seen.

Don't think about it.

In the lobby, she passed the little girl who belonged to the Indian couple, playing with her Barbies. Six or seven of them were lying on the carpet, fanned out around her like a bomb had just exploded. All the Barbies were white. Rita knew there was a Black Barbie and an Eskimo Barbie. She wondered if there was an Indian Barbie.

The little girl held a naked doll in her lap, brushing its long blond hair with a tiny pink comb. Rita stopped and said hello.

"Hi," the little girl said shyly.

"That your favorite one?" Rita asked.

"I don't know," the girl said. "Her name is Shakti," she volunteered.

"Pretty name," Rita said. The girl was pretty herself, like a doll. Rita had had a Barbie. She took her to the beauty parlor, which was located on the kitchen table, and then out to the park, which was in front of the couch in the living room. Ken would pick her up in a pink convertible. Barbie would be dressed in something shiny, carrying a pink pocketbook that hooked over her wrist, and wearing tiny plastic heels that fit her arched feet. Though sometimes Barbie would just lie in a corner of the couch and say, *I'm too tired to do anything today. You fix yourself something. Take some money from my purse and go to the store. Make yourself useful for once. I just can't,* Barbie would say.

"Do you want to play with me?" the little girl said. She straightened Barbie's legs, which squeaked, and then held her by her legs and gazed into her painted eyes.

"Oh, honey, I can't," Rita said, wanting more than anything to do just that.

"Yesha!" The girl's mother emerged from the back room behind the counter and came swiftly toward them, swathed in an electric green sari, brandishing a plastic spatula. Rita backed away.

"We were just talking," Rita said, but the woman didn't look at her again. She picked up the girl and began scolding her in their strange language. The girl put her thumb in her mouth, still clutching her Barbie, and looked down at the others on the floor as though they might disappear. Her mother carried her off. Rita wanted to follow the mother and try to explain. Maybe the Indian mother would slap her daughter, for talking to one of the scum that had the nerve to stay at her dirty hotel and try to have a little normal conversation like a normal human being.

Outside she looked around nervously, then walked fast to the pay phone on the corner. Amazingly, it was working. She dialed the number on Gary Shepard's card. A male voice answered, "Investigations."

"Mr. Shepard, please," Rita said.

"He's in the field right now," the man said. "Can I take a message?"

"Tell him—" Rita said. She wasn't sure Gary Shepard would know who she was if she left just her name, but she didn't know how to describe things to this voice on the other end. She contemplated a small sticker someone had stuck on the phone that read Jesus Sucks.

"Do you want to leave your name and phone number?" the man said.

"Well, I'm at a pay phone here," Rita said. "Just tell him Rita called him. From the Barker Hotel. Concerning that matter we spoke about." She was pleased with her formulation, with how official it sounded.

"Right," the man said.

"Will he get the message soon?"

"He'll get it," the man said. He hung up.

She was disappointed. She had hoped to speak with Gary Shepard, to hear his voice saying he'd meet her, that he needed the valuable information Rita could give him.

She felt exposed, standing there at the phone. She put the

receiver back on the cradle and hurried into Miz Brown's and took a booth in the back, where she could watch everyone who came through the door.

*

"Oh, fuck," Freddie said. "Fuck, fuck, fuck."

They were in a bar a couple of blocks from the Hall. How Freddie had gotten out on bail was a mystery. Gary began to revise his previous good opinion of Freddie, who must have some major connections to be walking the streets again after a third-strike charge.

"It's her," Freddie said and started crying.

"Are you sure?" Gary said.

"Fuck, fuck, fuck," was the only opinion Freddie could offer. His shoulders were jerking in little spasmodic movements. He made a high sound back in his throat that sounded like a baby kitten being strangled. Gary handed him a bar napkin and he balled it in one hand, not using it.

Gary bought him a beer, and left him there. No more great head for Freddie. On the bright side, Freddie probably wouldn't have to worry about the assault charge. Now Freddie might be a suspect in a murder.

He headed for a Vietnamese restaurant he knew and sat by the window with a big bowl of noodle soup. The soup was fragrant with spices, full of beef and vegetables, and absurdly cheap. Outside, the rain was driving the hookers and crack dealers into doorways. He wondered whether Carol Miller had any family who would come to claim her body or whether she'd be marked "Indigent" on a form and shipped off to medical students for practice. Whether she had loved Freddie and would have been gratified that he had cried over her, that as Gary left the bar her boyfriend was getting drunk and repeating her name to a bald bartender and a black transvestite named Sugar.

The rain was coming down in sheets now, a real downpour. This place needs a good scouring, Gary thought. He looked around the restaurant at his fellow diners, all of them Asian—people who had come from Vietnam and Cambodia and Laos looking for a better life, who had landed in the Tenderloin among drunks and addicts and prostitutes and elderly people scraping by on social security. It didn't seem they had a lot to be happy about. But they looked happy, or happy enough—the young waitress bustling around, the two old men in animated discussion over plates of rice and fish, the family with the two toddlers in black plastic seats to raise them high enough to see over the table, waving their chopsticks around and frequently dropping them. All most people wanted, Gary thought, was to be left alone to live their lives. Not to be fucked with. Too bad there was always someone, somewhere, intent on doing just that.

It baffled him why anyone would want to bring a child into a world like this. He tried to imagine Annie with a baby—their baby. He saw her standing in a terry cloth robe, holding the child on one hip, an angry expression on her face as he headed out of the house to the local bar. He saw his own mother and father, heard his mother saying, *Can't I get some help around here?* His little sister, Sandy, would be squirming in his mother's arms; Gary would be sitting on the floor of the living room, his hands over his ears. When his parents argued, he seemed to split into two boys, one who didn't want to hear and the other who was desperate to listen. So instead of flattening his palms to his ears, which would cut off all sound, he cupped them just enough to hear everything. *Don't you dare leave me here alone with these two children. They're your children, too. I know what you're up to, Mis-*

ter. Don't think I don't know. His father's side of the argument was a muttered, *Yeah, yeah, yeah* and a slam of the front door.

His father had been a math professor at the University of Wisconsin. Now he taught at a private college in upstate New York. Gary's memories of him before the divorce were few—an office at the university that smelled of Glade air freshener with books of numbers and diagrams instead of pictures; a tan overcoat with snow crystals clinging to it; a dim booth where Gary sat with a basket of fried cheese curds and a 7Up and watched a silent TV bolted above the bar, while his dad joked with the bartender, probably one of his students, probably one he was sleeping with. Though at the time, Gary wouldn't have known that. His mother had only told him about his father's infidelities later. He remembered always being mad at his father, tensing up and withdrawing on the rare occasions his father suggested throwing a football around the yard or going ice skating. After his father got remarried—to one of his graduate students—he'd had another son and done all the things with him that he'd never done with Gary. Gary had met his half-brother once, years ago, a pale kid clutching a plastic action figure to his chest and holding onto his father's hand with a fiercely proprietary intensity.

The waitress stopped at his table and picked up his empty bottle of 33. The rumor during the Vietnam War, a vet had told him, was that 33 contained opium. This vet lived on the streets. He had been a decorated Marine staff sergeant; now he was a guy in a filthy thermal shirt and overalls who slept on a piece of cardboard. "You like another?" the waitress said.

"Thanks," Gary said, "I'm thirsty." He considered his options for the afternoon and thought getting drunk might be one of them. Or he could head home early, surprise Annie in her darkroom, and maybe they would make love. Or he could continue working—he had a new case, one involving a thirteen-year-old boy, a knife, and a dead eleven-year-old boy who had apparently given the wrong nonverbal signals one night at a playground in the Sunset. There was a girl there, too, who might have seen what happened, but so far she wouldn't talk to anyone. He could head over to her junior high when school got out.

Or he could fall by the Barker Hotel and see if he could learn any more about Carol Miller. Of course, Carol Miller wasn't his problem anymore; the cops would step in now. Unless they came up with a suspect and Gary was assigned to the case, he was done. But he was curious about what had happened between the time she was at the Barker Hotel and the night she ended up folded into an oilcan. Freddie had seemed full of grief for her, but maybe the grief had been for himself, for the thought of going down for murder one. Freddie had seemed like a good guy, until he got out on bail so fast.

A man knocked on the rain-runneled window by Gary's table, and he looked up. The man had on glasses over one brown eye and one gauze-and-tape one, and no coat or shirt. He held an umbrella turned completely inside-out. As Gary looked through the glass, the man did a couple of dance moves, like he was Fred Astaire—a mock soft-shoe, holding the umbrella horizontally in both hands and swinging it from side to side. Then he tipped an invisible hat and went off into the rain.

In the land of the blind, the man with one eye is king. A line from a Tom Waits song. There went the one-eyed king of the Tenderloin, bare-chested, with his ridiculous umbrella. King of pain and suffering, king of loss and bad decisions and impoverishment, of voices in your head and toxic substances in your blood. Wherever you looked, he ruled, and nobody was ever going to depose him.

*

Jimmy usually worked Thursdays, but a waitress had begged him to trade shifts with her. He was going to have to pull a double next week. He stood at his apartment window looking down on the rain-shiny street and sidewalk. The green awning over the fruit and vegetable market on the corner darkened with the water that slid down in a steady waterfall onto the sidewalk. People ducked quickly under the awning, toward the wooden bins of apples and avocados and plantains, filling net bags or plastic shopping baskets. Inside, there were bins of dried chiles, pasillas and anchos and guajillos, along with waxy-looking jalapeños and serranos and the hottest ones of all, habaneros. There were tortillas and sopes and octagonal boxes of Mexican chocolate with sugary crystals, cans of lard, packages of frozen banana leaves, piles of green tomatillos. Mexican food was one reason Jimmy had decided to live in the Mission. Also, things were still cheap here, compared to most of the city. He liked the life on the street, too. Dark-haired girls in threes and fours, giggling and jostling each other along. Women pushing strollers (some of the girls, too, who looked like they were still in high school, were already mothers). Grizzled old men, benignly drunk, staggering out of the bars in the middle of the day, blinking like they'd just come up from underground.

Of course, plenty of shit happened here, too. If you looked for it, you'd find some wasted girl in short cutoffs and heels, standing in a doorway with her back to the street, hunched over a crack pipe, or another one throwing up between two parked cars, or some guy in a long black coat and no shoes muttering intricate obscenities to invisible spirits who seemed to hover in the air in front of his upraised face. But around them, during the day at least, people went about the business of normal life. There were kids everywhere, and bridal shops and toy stores and thrift stores, and a photography studio with silver-framed pictures of smiling babies and smoky-eyed women in feather boas. Taquerias and little restaurants and bars and a twenty-four hour donut shop where in the middle of the night people inside sat in an eerie greenish light that made them look even more drunk and hopeless than they were. At night in the Mission, all the families were tucked into their railroad flats and crackerbox apartments, and the buildings had iron gates or roll-down steel doors, and all the messed-up humanity seeped up like raw sewage.

Jimmy called Chumley to see if he could work out in Chumley's mother's basement and maybe spar a little. Chumley had recently set up the basement like a regular gym: weights, mirrors, heavy bag, speed bag, a stationary bike. He had installed a stereo system and hung speakers in the corners of the room. The walls were covered with pictures of women from muscle magazines with long hair and tiny string bikinis and bulging thighs, flexing their massive oiled biceps. The couch Jimmy had slept on in July was still there, since it weighed about a ton. Nobody was ever going to move that couch, unless they took an ax to it and hauled it out piece by piece. Chumley had showed off the weight room the night they'd gone to the bar with Stan. Seeing the couch had reminded Jimmy of how he'd felt the night he spent there, unable to sleep, figuring Rita was probably out getting high. He had chain-smoked the rest of his cigarettes, thinking about how to make things right. Get her off the junk. He'd shot up with her a couple of times, to see what it was she found in it. He understood why she did it. But it was funny about drugs—some you could take or leave, and others took you. Heroin was something he liked, but it hadn't taken him. It was genetic maybe, or chemical.

On the couch, there was a tiny burn hole he remembered making on one cushion.

"Hey, what happened to you the other night?" Chumley said.

"Nothing," Jimmy said.

"That's not what Stan said. He said you tried to rape one of those chicks you went off with."

"Stan's full of shit."

"I'm just telling you what he said."

"Well, Stan doesn't know anything."

Robin. Her mouth on him, her voice. *Let me, let me.*

"He said she went to Taraval Station to file a police report. Or maybe he said she *said* she was going to. I don't know. Talk to Stan. Anyway I can't work out today. I have to go to my *j-o-b.*"

"I didn't do anything," Jimmy said.

"You left me at the bar without a ride."

"You said you didn't want to come."

"I did? I don't remember that. I hate it when I can't remember things."

"You said, and I quote, 'Go fuck yourself.'"

"Okay," Chumley said, evidently convinced by this. "Whatever. Talk to Stan."

"Later," Jimmy said and hung up.

He sat on his couch with a cigarette. He lit a match and looked at the flame, watching it burn down and expire. The matchbook said Rick's Restaurant & Bar. The cover showed the front of a ship, the prow pointed up, like it was either cresting a wave, or about to break apart and sink like the

Titanic. He lit another match. It burned a little longer, but still went out before it reached his fingertips. He struck one more and lit his cigarette and sat smoking, trying to empty his head. She was just some girl he'd never see again. Only now he might see her in a courtroom. He shouldn't have hit her. He shouldn't have talked to her in the bar in the first place. He backed up to the moment he'd first noticed Robin, then backed up further. If only he hadn't gone out that night. If he hadn't run into Chumley and his tow truck before that on the street. If he'd stayed in Trenton after his mother died and brought Rita back there, instead of returning to San Francisco. Or gone back to the hotel the next day, instead of going out with Chumley and his friend Rudy that night and getting arrested.

It all seemed inevitable, like there was nothing he could have done about it.

He pictured the cops showing up at the restaurant, dragging him away in front of customers. Chelsea standing behind the bar with her mouth open, Walter frowning, coming up to ask what was the matter. The diners putting down their forks, their glasses stopped in midair on the way to their lips, the whole place frozen like in some science fiction movie. Everybody would see who he really was: not James, a decent hardworking waiter, but Jimmy—violent offender, good-for-nothing shit.

He ground the cigarette into a glass ashtray he'd taken from Little Joe's in West Portal. Once he and Rita had gone there for breakfast and ordered glasses of champagne, and the waitress had brought the whole bottle over and set it on the table. He'd taken the ashtray as a memento of that day, a day with bottomless glasses of champagne and Rita looking in his eyes and jiggling back and forth in her seat with happiness; later they'd gotten their fortunes from

Laffing Sal at the Musée Mécanique at the beach, and put quarters in to watch the miniature Ferris wheel made of toothpicks go around. They paid to watch the figures in a little diorama called "Opium Den"—the man lying on the couch rose up and then sank back down—and tried to capture gumballs inside a glass box with a small crane, but they only got three. In the photo booth they took one picture looking very serious, straight at the camera, and the next one silly. In the third Rita was kissing him, and in the fourth you could only see part of his face and the back of her head. They went into the Camera Obscura and for a dollar they watched the ocean, reflected somehow and projected onto a surface like a shallow bowl that people gathered around in the dark room. Afterward they went upstairs into the Cliff House and had drinks and watched the sun go down.

That was a perfect day. It was hard to understand how he had gone from making Rita so happy, like on that day, and making her cry the way she did later. He had loved her, but not so she could feel it. That day he'd seen her on the street—it had to have been her—his heart had lurched forward with the bus. He should have gotten off. He was a coward. Afraid for his job, afraid to confront the hurt in her eyes.

On the coffee table sat a gray plastic Hohner Special 20 case with a C harp in it. Harmonica cases looked like little coffins, he thought for the hundredth time. Somewhere on the street a car backfired. It sounded like a gunshot. The man who lived downstairs from Jimmy had been shot, but he didn't die. Now he got around in a wheelchair. There was somebody with real troubles. But it didn't change the sour feeling in the pit of his stomach.

He went for the Pepcid in the bathroom cabinet. That usually helped when his stomach was bad. Maybe he had an ulcer, but he wasn't going to pay a bunch of money to a doctor to find out. He brushed his teeth, ran a comb under the faucet, and then through his hair without looking in the mirror. Back in the main room, which was both living room and bedroom, he pulled a cassette from a stack on the floor and put it in the deck. Sonny Boy Williamson II started singing, "Somebody help me, please help me." But he was talking about something other than a possible rape charge. "Help me get my baby back tonight." Jimmy lit up another cigarette, discouraged to see it was the last in the pack.

At the window again, he smoked and watched rain drip off the fire escape. There was a dying plant he'd bought sitting on an upside down Berkeley Farms milk crate. The plant was a mess of shriveling brown stems and yellowed leaves in rock-hard soil. Rita used to have a lot of plants when they were together. She was always finding ones people had thrown out, and bringing them home and taking care of them. Maybe the rain would revive this one. He listened to the harp solo, one he had learned by heart. Sonny Boy's first album, made for Chess in the 'fifties, was titled "Bummer Road." That's what he was looking at, not Mission Street. Bummer Road Apartments. Bummer Market. Bummer Donuts, Open 24 Hours, We Never Close. He decided to go down the street to the bar for a drink and to buy some more cigarettes, and let that be the last decision he'd worry about making until tomorrow.

*

All the counter stools at Miz Brown's were taken. It was past lunchtime, but outside the rain was heavy, so several patrons were lingering over brown mugs of coffee and picking at slices of homemade lemon meringue or Dutch apple pie. Rita slid into a booth that had a sign above it reading,

Booths Reserved for Two or More People. Fran, the waitress
who had served her and Gary Shepard, came over.

"Hi, hon," she said. "Isn't this rain something? Looks like it
won't ever let up."

"At least it's not freezing out," Rita said. She was glad Fran
didn't tell her she couldn't sit there. And that she called her
hon, even though she probably said that to everybody. The
day started to look better.

"Is the pie really homemade?" Rita said.

"It comes in plastic containers we throw in the trash. But it
tastes all right. Go for the apple."

"I'll have some of that, then. And hot tea." She watched
Fran bustle over behind the counter, stopping to refill a few
coffees before getting the tea and pie, chatting amiably with
the men hunched on the stools in their sweaters and coats.
The other waitress, a stocky, pale girl with a bright orange
crewcut, looked about Rita's age. She was made up with a
thick layer of heavy foundation, her eyes were circled in
black, and a silver ring pierced her left eyebrow. She plodded
back and forth behind the counter. Rita watched her take a
plate of eggs from the window where orders from the
kitchen came up and slam it down in front of a customer.

She had about finished the pie when Gary Shepard came
through the door. The rain had finally quit, and when it did,
Miz Brown's quickly emptied. One booth was taken by a
couple of nuns, and a man still sat at the far end of the
counter. Gary Shepard had on jeans and sneakers and a
striped button-down shirt, untucked, and a beat-up brown
leather bomber jacket. He was big and solid and confident,
walking in and bringing the rain smell with him and smiling
like Rita was his long-lost sister.

"Hi, Rita," he said, and slid in across from her. "I went by
the Barker, but they said you'd gone out. Glad I found you."

"You found me," Rita said. "Good job, Mister Detective." She meant to say it lightly, like a joke, but it came out slightly sarcastic. "I tried to call you. Did you get my message?"

"That's why I'm here."

"You said"—Rita looked around, then lowered her voice— "you said maybe you could pay me for some information." She watched him reach into his inside jacket pocket and take out a wallet. The little plastic windows for pictures flipped open as he removed some bills. She saw a silver Visa card, a picture of a dark-haired woman, and another of a little baby. He flipped the wallet closed.

"Here's sixty dollars," he said.

"That isn't much, for the information I got." Actually, she'd expected only twenty. But, fine. Sixty. Great. She put it in her pocket before he could change his mind.

"I can probably get you some more."

"I could use more," Rita said. "But what I could really use is some kind of job. I don't want to do what I've been doing." She didn't want to tell Gary Shepard what that was. He seemed to like her. He would look at her differently if she told him.

"Actually I've been thinking about that," he said.

"You have? You've been thinking about me needing a job?"

"Among other things."

Fran was suddenly at his elbow. "I remember you," she said.

Rita wondered why Fran hadn't said that to her.

"Fran, darling," he said. "How about a cup of black coffee."

"I'll make you a fresh pot." Fran's nose was covered with tiny broken blood vessels, and so were her cheeks. She looked flushed from excitement, or drunkenness.

Rita wanted more hot water for her tea, but the waitress had turned away. Meanwhile, for Gary Shepard, an entire fresh pot of coffee was being made, just like that.

"Ever thought of being a waitress?" he said.

"I don't know. Maybe." She was disappointed in him now. He saw her and Fran the same way. He thought she couldn't do any better than this, a waitress in a shithole diner who'd gotten old bringing people their eggs and gluey hash browns. He probably acted interested in everyone, pretended they were special when he didn't even care. She licked her finger and pressed it into the last crumbs of pie on her plate, then stuck it in her mouth. She felt him watching her and was embarrassed. She wiped her mouth with a napkin, not look- ing at him.

"You seem like a smart girl," he said. "And you're pretty. There are a lot of places that would hire you."

"Yeah, for you know what," Rita said. "I didn't even grad- uate high school." When she was with Jimmy she had worked as an erotic dancer at the Lusty Lady in North Beach for a few months. It wasn't too bad—women ran it, and most of the other girls were nice to her, and everything was behind glass so you never had to actually deal with the cus- tomers. But finally it had been too hard to go into that little mirrored room and go through the moves, wiggling and touching herself and dancing up close to the low windows they watched through, thrusting her hips at them, pretend- ing like she was happy they were there, putting their eyes all over her. Some of the other girls seemed to actually like it, they were proud of their bodies and their dancing and to them it was a kind of game, being looked at by all the men and sometimes even couples and some pairs of women, too, who came in. But Rita had felt uncomfortable, and that's when she had started getting high again; it made it so she could face going in there. Then the night manager saw a needle mark and that was the end of that. Heroin had messed up her job, and messed up her and Jimmy, too. She wasn't going to do it anymore. So she'd slipped with Marco. You pick yourself back up is all. But still, any job I could get, I'd be a piece of meat. Same old same old. Never been any different, never will be.

"No, I mean places you wouldn't be exploited," Gary Shepard said.

"People like me," Rita said, "are always, uh, exploited."

"It doesn't have to be that way."

"But it *is* that way," she said. "Some girls, they can walk down the street minding their own business, and hardly anybody bothers them. But there's something wrong with me. I had a guy last week pull over through three lanes of traffic to offer me a ride." She was agitated, trying to make him see. "I attract bad people," she ended helplessly. She thought of the man in the Barker. She had drawn him to her somehow, just as she had drawn Karl Hauptmann, without even being aware of it. The wrongness was something certain people could feel.

"You can change that."

"Easy for you to say. You don't live around here."

"No," he said. "I don't."

"I'm nobody," Rita said. She didn't feel she had any particular skills or talents except for the illegal kind. She didn't even have her ID thanks to the guy in the park who had kicked her face in. "It's like there's a wall." She couldn't explain it to him. You either got it or you didn't. "It's just how it is," she said.

"It doesn't have to be."

"Says you."

Fran came back with the coffee, and they fell silent. Rita stared at her used tea bag lying on the napkin.

"Tell me about Carol."

"Carol's troubles in this world are over, if I saw what I think I saw." She told him about the two men dragging the sleeping bag out of the closet, about waiting scared in the bathroom, about the van in the alley. The man in corduroy with his weird hat and damaged hand and the long red hair falling out of the bag and the bad smell. Gary Shepard was looking at her steadily with his kind eyes. She wasn't used to being looked at like that, someone making eye contact and not looking away at the walls or the air or her breasts. She wanted to keep on talking, giving him what she knew, giving him all the evil and poison and believing for a minute he would know what to do and how to make it better.

"Did you get a look at their faces, either one of them?"

"One of 'em. I saw one."

"That's good. That's really good, Rita," he said. "It's great. You're great."

"No, I'm not," she said, pleased. She looked intently into her empty brown cup. She could feel Gary Shepard's eyes still on her, like physical warmth.

"Did they see you?"

"I just had the door cracked, I backed away. Not really." Of course he had seen her. There was no hiding from the truth of what she was. Whore, harlot, sinner. She thought about his hand, how he had raised it in greeting. He knew her. *If she profanes herself by playing the harlot, she shall be burned with fire.*

"Maybe you'd better stay away from the Barker, just in case."

"Yeah." She decided not to mention the Barker's no refund policy. She'd find someplace else after the weekend.

In the meantime, she was glad she was with Gary Shepard. He looked like he could kick the shit out of anyone. He had money. He thought she was a smart girl.

"Listen, I have an idea," he said. His idea was to forget all this for a while, to go somewhere and play pool. Did she play pool?

"Pool," she said. "I guess that'd be okay."

He called for the check.

*

Stan's jewelry shop was in Noe Valley. He had a signboard with a drawing of a gigantic diamond ring set out on the sidewalk on Twenty-fourth Street. The street was lined with clothing stores and restaurants, with gift stores that sold Guatemalan dolls and Balinese masks and educational toys. There were delis, pizzerias, bookstores, cafés, and a supermarket where an employee policed the lot to make sure everyone who parked there was actually a customer; parking was at a premium. This afternoon all of these places were doing a brisk business, but Stan's shop, which you reached by walking down a small alley near his signboard and through a courtyard filled with rain-wet restaurant tables, was empty of customers. In the laundry next door, a desiccated Chinese man stood at a steam presser. The store on the other side of Stan's had gone out of business.

When Jimmy walked in, an annoying electronic bleep announced his presence to Stan, sitting at his workbench behind the counter at the far end of the shop. Stan was soldering a necklace with a small torch. He looked up and set the torch in its stand.

"Hey, dude." He flipped up his visor. "You found my shop."

"Yeah," Jimmy said. "Kind of out of the way, isn't it?"

"No shit, Sherlock. When it rains like this, it's deserted. At least on nice days, people are sitting outside at the restaurant, and I've got some company. You ever eaten there? The food's great. Much better than the previous joint."

"Never been," Jimmy said. He never came to Noe Valley. "Nice place you got here." There was a display of different-colored wax molds for rings on one wall. Several wooden clocks with brass pendulums hung around the store. A long jewelry case held rings, gold and silver chains, and watches. Above Stan's workbench was a framed photograph that looked like it was taken about twenty years ago—Stan on a beach with a woman and a couple of little kids, only the woman's face had been cut from the picture so the cardboard backing showed. Several silver flasks sat on a shelf next to some pocketknives.

"Business isn't so hot," Stan said. "I had a guy come in yesterday who might want me to make a ring, though. He wants a big diamond for his girlfriend, if she says she'll marry him. Man, I hope she says yes." Stan laughed. "Speaking of chicks. What's the deal with this Robin babe? She's pissed off at you big time."

"What did she say?"

"She said you tried to rape her. She came walking up the beach after you took off on her. She was freaked out, crying and shit."

"I didn't try to rape her," Jimmy said.

"Well, I hope the cops believe you and not her," Stan said. "She split. Said she was going down to Taraval Station to file a police report."

"Did she go? Or did she just say she was going?"

Stan thought a minute. "I dunno," he said.

"Great," Jimmy said. He thought about how he'd felt the instant before he hit her. It was like a reflex, an automatic response. Like he was back in the ring, when he used to fight, years ago in New Jersey. He hadn't done it professionally—just a few bouts with the New Jersey Police Athletic League on Saturday mornings. It was like his opponent had just thrown a jab that Jimmy jerked his head away from, and in the opening, before the guy had his gloves back up, Jimmy was ready and let loose on him. That was the deal; every punch the other guy threw left him vulnerable. Wait for an opening. Keep your hands up. Counterpunch. Stick and move.

"Why'd you hit her?" Stan said.

"I don't know," Jimmy said. "I just lost it."

"Men and women," Stan said. "I think I'm gonna do my next speech for school on that. Everybody I know is having trouble with women. Including me," he said, and threw his head back and laughed. "'The War Between the Sexes,'" he said. "That's gonna be my title."

"Leave me out of it," Jimmy said.

They both took out cigarettes. Stan lit his off the small blue flame on his torch. He sat back in his chair, looking up at Jimmy.

"Well, hey," he said. "It ain't the end of the world. Let's go get some lunch."

Jimmy wasn't really hungry. But he didn't want to go home, either. He wanted to go backward. Back in time. No bar, no Robin. Maybe he could talk to her. Maybe she'd calmed down, after she came down off the coke, and hadn't reported anything. Maybe he should go see her and tell her he was sorry. He was, in fact, sorry, so it wouldn't be like he was lying. Maybe a cop was at his door right now, looking at the decal Jimmy had pasted on it, a Beware of Owner sign with a black-and-white drawing of a gun, the barrel pointed at the viewer. Not that he had a gun, but what if the cops thought he did? He was still on probation. Now he might be looking at a felony conviction. A felony was a strike. Three strikes and you're out, done, finished as far as the state of California was concerned. A voice in his head said, *That's never gonna happen.* But he heard another voice, a surer one, whispering, *Yes, it will.*

They went out to Stan's Cadillac, parked a couple of blocks away. Stan lit up a joint as he cruised them down Dolores Street. Jimmy took a few drags and laid his head back against the crushed velvet seat, looking up at the palm trees sliding by. They were whispering, too. Long fronds in the wind. They said warm weather, breezes weighted by the smell of flowers, white sand beaches. Southern California or someplace in Mexico. Lying back in a deck chair or swinging in a hammock, drinks with paper umbrellas, glass stirrers that curved into the tails of monkeys on one end. The smell of suntan lotion—cocoa butter, a smell you could almost eat, deep and chocolaty. A girl rubbing it into his skin, her hands moving in slow circles. Rita used to massage rubbing alcohol into his neck and shoulders. Her voice was another whisper. The times she was afraid, shutting him out. *Don't touch me. Leave me alone.* Curled up small in a corner of the bed, her back to him, after another bad dream woke her. The palm trees swung across the windshield. Stan sang along with the radio, a song by Counting Crows that was popular a couple of years ago. "Round here we stay up very, very, ve-ry VE-ry late . . ." The car was filled with pot smoke and sunshine, and Jimmy's thoughts were shreds of clouds, some dark and some nearly invisibly white, and there were a few stray clouds left in the sky from the last rain. He'd go find Robin and talk to her. It would be okay. Everything will be okay, baby. Let me hold you. You can trust me. You're safe. *Jimmy. Hold me. Please don't leave me all alone.*

*

Rita was a better pool player than Gary Shepard. He could usually get the ball into the pocket hitting it straight on, but she saw he was lost when it came to banking shots off the bumpers, aiming at just the right spot so the cue ball would ricochet back and hit the ball you wanted at the perfect angle. She was beating him easily, leaning over and lining up her shots, a cigarette in her mouth. She had won two games already, and now she only had to sink the 8-ball. It was lying along the railing between the right side pocket and the corner. She drew on her cigarette and set it on the edge of the pool table before aiming. Magic eight ball. It clunked into its intended pocket and she let out a yell.

"Gotcha!" she said. "Pay me."

He handed her a twenty. She went to the bar and ordered another Beck's and a vodka cranberry. Two men were playing bar dice, slamming the cup down. The theme of their conversation was *Feck you* and sometimes *Feck you and yer fecken ma, too.* A haggard old woman in a Yankees cap sat in the corner, blearily eyeing Rita. The bartender, a fortyish pink-haired woman with pornographically large breasts and long glittery earrings, put the drinks and a dollar down before Rita and asked her to play the jukebox.

"D4," the bartender said. "I'm feeling sentimental today."

Gary Shepard put his pool cue back in the rack on the wall. Four striped balls were still scattered on the red felt of the table. Rita's cigarette had burned itself out.

"I guess pool isn't my game," he said.

"Guess not," Rita said, setting their drinks on a round table nearby, next to their empty bottles and glasses. She went back to the pool table and took a shot, aiming at a blue-striped ten ball, narrowly missing sinking it in a corner.

"Great," he said. "*Now* you start missing." He followed her to the jukebox.

She pressed D4, then looked at the selections through the glass, dirty with fingerprints. "As Tears Go By" by the Rolling Stones floated from the speakers behind the bar.

"They've got some Billie Holiday on here," Gary Shepard said.

He was standing close to her. She didn't mind. She was having a fine time, winning at pool and getting slightly drunk. "This is a sad song," she said. The bartender was singing along, sounding much better than Mick Jagger. *And yer fecken ma.*

Rita scanned the titles of songs and put in "Lover Man." Then Bessie Smith doing "St. Louis Blues." Jimmy used to play a Bessie Smith tape. There was another song she remembered that went, *Gimme a pigfoot and a bottle of beer.* She had always wondered what a pigfoot was—whether it really meant the foot of a pig or if it was slang for something. She had heard of people eating monkeys' brains, so why not pigs' feet? But the way Bessie Smith sang it made her think it meant something else, like *cold in hand* meant not having any money and *another mule kicking in my stall* meant somebody stealing your lover. She played Stevie Ray Vaughan and T-Bone Walker and Robert Johnson's "Hellhound On My Trail." "Wow, this is a cool jukebox," she said.

"Good picks," Gary Shepard said. "Where did you learn about the blues?"

Rita just looked at him.

"Hey, I love the blues." He touched her shoulder. She moved away, crossing her arms. "I love everything that begins with *b,*" he said. "Blues. Beck's. What else. I love the Bay. And boxing. And booze."

"Booze," she said. "Well, who doesn't." She already had Jimmy on her mind, and now he'd brought up the blues, and boxing. Jimmy had owned a pair of red six-ounce gloves. Sometimes he'd put them on and just throw combinations at the air, his movements fluid, a kind of dance. He was a good dancer, too. He didn't flop or jerk around like a lot of guys. He stayed focused, contained somehow. She went to put her pool cue away, then took her drink to the bar while Gary Shepard punched in a few more selections. Rain and tears going by and children playing at the evening of the day turned into Billie Holiday feeling sad and cold and alone, no one to love me, where can you be. Karl Hauptmann had first shown Rita the thrill of romance, and it sure as hell wasn't any heavenly dream.

Don't get all depressed again, which is what you'll do if you keep on like this. She gazed at a Budweiser clock behind the bar, that showed a snowy scene with a couple of elk walking around. Bud. Bar. Babes, bimbos, bitches. There's a lot of words for women beginning with *b*. She tried to think of more of them. Next Bessie Smith came on and the bartender started singing along again. Go find a karaoke bar, babe, Rita wanted to say to her.

Gary Shepard sat down next to her. It felt like too much of an effort to be nice to him. She chewed on the straw from her drink, feeling his eyes on her.

"You know what?" he said. "I love my job."

"Good for you," she said.

"No, really. I love being down at the Hall. All the deals being cut. Cops and criminals and attorneys. All the shit that goes down."

"I guess." In her opinion, shit going down did not seem like something to be glad about.

"Even at night," he said. "The Hall's peaceful at night, everyone put to bed in their cells. Nobody around but bail bondsmen, and cops bringing people in."

"Uh-huh," she said.

"You know where I'd kill somebody, if I was going to do it in the Hall?" he said. "Third floor, end of the hall, there's a little balcony that overlooks the freeway. You stuff something in the door so you don't lock yourself out. That would be the place to shoot someone. The noise of the freeway, two sets of doors—probably no one would hear it. You could leave the body there and saunter back in."

"Thanks for the information," Rita said, "but I haven't got any plans in that direction."

He signaled the bartender. The bartender danced around, pulling out another bottle of Beck's from the low fridge, raising the vodka bottle high to pour a huge shot into Rita's glass before adding the cranberry juice, doing everything with an exaggerated flourish. Like she was fucking Tom Cruise in *Cocktail*. The juice in the glass dissolved quickly, registering as the palest pink effusion. Blood in a syringe. Octopus ink.

"That's going to get me drunk," Rita said as it was placed before her.

"Then I guess I'll have to get drunk with you," Gary Shepard said. "I'll have a shot of Cuervo Gold," he told the bartender.

"All right!" the bartender said gaily. "Party time!"

"Don't let him have any more," one of the men at the bar said. For a few minutes now he had been slumped forward over his glass while his friend played dice alone, but now his head snapped up suddenly. "Are you driving?" he asked Gary Shepard. "Are you seriously fecking going to drink and fecking drive?"

They ignored him. Rita took a long swallow and felt the liquor burn down her throat and into her stomach. She felt better and, also, as though she had to pee immediately. She took another swallow and got off the barstool, on the side away from the men.

"Don't go," Gary Shepard said.

"I'm just going to the Ladies. Women's. Room." She looked around to see where it was. "Bathroom," she said. Another *b* word.

"Promise me you'll come back."

"Jesus Christ." She walked away from him. When she returned, he'd drunk the first shot of Cuervo and the bartender was pouring him another. Well, he was paying. He was buying the drinks and he had chosen the music that was playing now, Prince singing about the purple rain, and that's how it is, she thought, that's just how it *is*. She held up her glass and looked at him through it. Gary Shepard under pink water, a red-faced fish in her glass. "Babes, bimboes, bitches," she said. "Barbie. Any I missed?"

"Broads," he said. "Dance with me."

The jukebox had started the next song. "A Whiter Shade of Pale," sung by Annie Lennox. That was a good choice. Rita loved the way she sang it.

"What, here?" she said, looking around.

He took her hand and pulled her off the stool.

Her head came up only to his chest. She let him put his arms around her. He pressed his palm against the small of her back and maneuvered her backward, and they shuffled around between the pool table and the bar. It was strange, how every man had a distinct smell that was his, under the cologne and deodorant and aftershave. She could always smell it, no matter how much stuff they put on, and she didn't like it. Except for Jimmy. She had liked to lick the sweat from his armpits; even that had seemed sweet and clean. Gary Shepard was slowly and subtly grinding himself into her. It was easier to go with it. Her sadness was dissolving in the vodka, like the cranberry juice. A little flame, drowning. Maybe if she could drink enough she could extinguish it. The song ended and he was still moving her around, pressing against her.

"Hey," the bartender said. "Do I need to get a hose?"

The old woman at the end of the bar laughed at that. Rita looked into her filmy brown eyes.

"Get it while you can," the woman said, and made a circle of her left thumb and forefinger and rapidly poked her right index finger into it several times.

"Can we go now?" Rita said.

Outside it was late afternoon, the sky overcast again. The street was full of trash and sadness. A man bent toward a parking meter, earnestly talking to it, discussing something of immense and private importance. A prostitute in red shorts and matching spiked heels was on the pay phone at the corner, her thick legs covered with a mess of varicose veins like tangled blue threads. "You know what I'm saying," she said. "Don't you tell me you don't know. You know exactly what I'm talking about."

Gary Shepard had started walking, fast. Rita almost had to run to keep up. They passed a store with ADULT XXX on its marquee.

"Where are we going?" she said.

"Out of this neighborhood." He slowed and looked at her. "We should have gone someplace else."

She had put on sunglasses. He was looking at her, trying to look into her eyes she knew. But he had no business doing that. No business at all.

"Whatever," she said. "Where are we going now?"

"I was thinking about a motel," he said. "That okay with you?"

"Fine by me. Just so long as it's not the Barker." Another *b* word. "I'm bombed," she said.

"Blitzkrieg," he said.

"Well I have no particular feeling on that, whatever it is."
She let him take her arm.

*

"My disease used to be sadness," Stan yelled. "But now it's
not madness, or badness. It's gladness!" he roared. He went
on about happiness, not sappiness or crappiness, joyness not
coyness. Amity, not calamity. A group of Japanese kids at a
table listened raptly. A thin pale man with a cauliflower
nose, reddened from broken capillaries, turned to Jimmy at
the bar and said, "My disease is drinking and thinking. I usu-
ally drink alone at home. My wife left me, and my left leg
was amputated. Diabetes."

"Yeah, Stan!" Chumley yelled. "Hey, Jimbo," he said.
"You ought to get up there and play your harp."

Stan's act followed a couple of guys who had played Irish
songs on guitar and pennywhistle. Before them, a girl with a
unicorn tattooed up one leg had wailed her way through No
Doubt's "I'm Just a Girl." It was open mic night at the Four
Deuces, and anybody could get up on the tiny red-carpeted
stage and display their talents, mostly imaginary, for the
patrons.

Jimmy ordered another shot of Jägermeister. He had his A
harp in his shirt pocket. He always carried a harp with him,
and he'd often play waiting for a bus or streetcar, hunched
over and turned toward the wall of a building or in a door-
way. Sometimes, someone who was also waiting or just
passing by would call out, *Hey, you sound good* or *Thanks for the
music.* In jail, he had jammed with a guy named T.J. who
played guitar, and they talked about doing a few gigs
together when they got out—Petaluma, Santa Rosa, San
Jose. T.J., according to himself, was acquainted with a few

influential people and had been in a fairly decent band called The Doors of Deception before he was—again according to himself—*set up and sent up.* But one day, T.J. felt compelled to stab somebody in the cafeteria with a homemade shiv and was sent over to Ad Seg, Administrative Segregation, and that was the end of the proposed tour.

"C'mon," Chumley said. "Get up there, dude."

"I don't think so," Jimmy said.

"You okay?" Chumley asked. "Because you look a little down, my man."

"I'm good." He had planned to try and find Robin earlier, but instead he'd gotten drunk with Stan at lunch and then gone back to Stan's shop and taken a nap in the upstairs loft. There was a futon on the floor, next to a jumble of boxes and a large dusty machine, probably once used for some mysterious jewelry-related purpose.

"Lock the doors, piss and weep," Stan was yelling. "Nothing can stop a fucking creep." This had the Japanese table, and several others, in stitches. "I love America!" one of the Japanese yelled, and another said, "Bukowski rules!" and pumped his fist in the air.

Jimmy drank his shot and ordered another. He was already too drunk and he had to go to work tomorrow and he hadn't gone to find Robin to straighten things out. He took his harp from his breast pocket and blew a few tentative riffs, hunched toward the bar. Around him, people were yelling and laughing and talking. Stan stepped off the stage to wild applause and a few offers of drinks. The jukebox came on, Bruce Springsteen singing "I'm on Fire." Jimmy closed his eyes and lost himself in his own barely audible music.

★

The TV in the Holiday Inn south of Market Street was set inside a cabinet, so you could close the doors if you wanted to, and not see it. With the remote control, you could push a button and watch ads for any of several movies—New Releases or Hollywood Hits—and with another push of the button you could see the movie. But that cost $7.95, so Rita just left the TV on and got out of bed to wander around the room. She picked up the wet towels she and Gary Shepard had left on the bathroom floor, mopped up the water from their shower, and wrung out the towel over the tub, then hung them both neatly on a rack. She looked at herself in the mirror and smiled. She took the small plastic bottle of pale peach shampoo, still half full, from the edge of the tub and brought it back into the room and set it on the dresser next to her bag, a big patent leather purse she'd plucked from the dumpster behind the Barker.

She lifted one corner of the heavy gold curtains and peered out the window at the lights of cars blearing by, the bright signs of bars and restaurants shimmying up and down the street. The rain had started up again, and everything had a shiny surface. The cars seemed to be swimming by silently, the sound of their motors muted by the window glass, the whooshing of warm air from the heater beneath the window, the murmuring of the TV. There was a pad of notepaper on a table, and she put that next to her bag, too. Then she got back into the bed, under a quilted spread with a pattern of green and pink and blue leaves, and plumped up the soft white pillows and relaxed.

Gary Shepard had left half an hour ago. He had been a gentle lover, and had held her afterward while she laid her head in the crook of his shoulder. He'd asked her, *Are you all right*, and she had said, *Yes*, even though she was sad and still thinking of Jimmy, but there was no reason to mention that to Gary

Shepard. Before he left, he hugged her tight against him and she breathed in the smells of his leather jacket and cologne and cigarettes. He said the room was hers until eleven A.M. tomorrow and he would talk to her soon and she should take care of herself, and he had given her forty more dollars.

According to a plastic card on the dresser, this was a non-smoking room. Not anymore it wasn't. She lit a cigarette and flipped through channels on the TV, not really seeing them. Gary Shepard had told her, as soon as they got in the room, that he was married.

"So am I," Rita had said.

"You are?" he seemed surprised.

"Yes, I am. Very much so." She regretted telling him.

"So where is he?" They sat on edge of the bed, side by side. He seemed too nervous, now that they were alone, to touch her. Their thighs brushed, and he moved away slightly.

"I don't know where he is," she said. "And I really don't want to be having this conversation, so can we have a change of topic now?"

"We can talk about anything you want."

"Those pictures in your wallet I saw at Miz Brown's. That your wife and baby?"

"That's my little brother, about a dozen years ago. I don't know why I still carry that. Actually he's my half-brother. Annie and I don't have any kids."

Annie. Rita didn't like knowing her name; it made her more real. Gary Shepard should know better than to talk about his wife, by name, to someone he wanted to get with. "Do you feel bad?" she said. "Being here with me?"

He had moved closer then and put his arm around her. "I guess I should," he said. "But I don't."

"That's good. I guess." It wasn't good. He should feel bad about committing adultery. Rita felt sorry for his wife. She looked at his muscled thighs in his jeans. He was much bigger than she was, much stronger. But she didn't think he would try to hurt her. Of course, she hadn't thought that about Terrance, either, and look how that ended up.

He pulled her into him, and then they were kissing, and he was lifting off her shirt and saying *Sweet girl, sweet girl,* and it made her feel sweet, even though she knew she wasn't, she was doing wrong and so was he, and they were naked on top of the bedspread and kissing some more. He put on a condom before guiding himself inside her, asking, *How does it feel, does it feel good, tell me how to make you feel good.* But she didn't say anything. He felt like the others who had moved in and out of her, breathing into her ear, saying, *Come on, let it go, come for me,* even though of course she couldn't; Jimmy was the only one she'd ever felt that with. Gary Shepard didn't take all that long. Soon he groaned and came, burying his face in her neck.

On the TV, Sheryl Crow was in a music video singing, "Every day is a winding road." Isn't that the truth. You never know what's next, good or bad. You wake up and shit happens. This morning I woke up in the Barker, feeling like I might as well die as do anything else. Now look at me, in a nice hotel with soft sheets and pillows and a couple dozen channels to watch and forty dollars in my pocket. I'm doing all right. "Thank you, Jesus!" She imitated a TV minister. "Thank you, *Je-sus.*" She was lying to herself but sometimes it was necessary. You lied to yourself and you knew you were lying because how could you fool yourself? I'm doing all right. Thank you, Jesus, I am just fine with all this cheating on husbands and wives and some maniac out there somewhere looking for me. And Jimmy might be dead for all I know. Maybe he really is dead and maybe there's no point to walking down the damned winding road all alone.

She tapped her cigarette into an empty Dr Pepper can and made a mental note to remember to take the packets of tea and sugar from the tray with the in-room coffeemaker along with her in the morning. And a towel from the bathroom, too; they'd probably never miss it.

4. Gary pulled into his driveway, turned off the engine of his Honda Accord, and lit a cigarette. He sat smoking, looking at the house. Annie's cat, an overweight gray tabby, streaked across the grass through the light from the living room window and disappeared into the bushes separating their yard from their neighbor's. The privacy of the house's location—last on a cul-de-sac—had been part of its appeal when they moved here. It was on top of a hill, so that from any window you had a sense of exactly where you were in the city. You could see the Pacific Ocean from the deck. Too bad they couldn't afford to buy it.

He finished his cigarette, jammed the filter into the car ashtray, and lit another. Annie would be in the kitchen with her Tarot cards and wine; or already in bed, reading a book; or up watching TV. Waiting for him to get home, not knowing when he'd be there. He was always canceling plans, getting hung up with one assignment or another, calling to say he'd be late. Don't count on me for dinner. Call a friend and give her my ticket. That afternoon, after leaving the bar with Rita, he'd stopped at a Shell station and called Annie, while Rita went inside for cigarettes. He'd lied easily, and Annie had accepted it, had believed he was doing a surveillance instead of heading for a Holiday Inn with another woman, who was at that moment coming out of the Shell mini mart with a pack of Marlboro Lights for her and Camel Lights for him, holding a can of Dr Pepper. A tentative smile flickered across her face, disappeared and flickered on again.

He had said good-bye to Annie without telling her he loved her.

He had leaned across the seat and opened the car door for Rita, who looked surprised, then pleased, and got in.

That was the moment he might have changed his mind: sitting in the car in the Shell station after talking with Annie. There was an attorney at the Hall who he'd been flirting with for months, but it was just a flirtation. Rita was a prostitute, maybe a junkie, a scared girl he wanted to help somehow. He felt protective of her. He shouldn't sleep with her. He should drop her back at the Barker, and go home to Annie. But then a vision of Rita's small white body, naked on a bedspread somewhere, floated over his deliberations.

He had driven them to the Holiday Inn, received a slim plastic card that would open the door to their room, and then, on an anonymous bed, he had cheated on Annie for the first time.

As he sat there smoking, it started raining again, the wind carrying handfuls of water and flinging them against the car. He had heard on the radio, driving home, that there was a whole series of storms lined up out in the Pacific. Winters in San Francisco were always rainy, but this one looked to be especially bad. He got out and stood in his front yard in the downpour. He liked the sound the rain made hitting the leaves of the bushes. The cold seeped into his skin. His hair quickly got wet, and his jeans, and the rain splashed on his face and into his mouth as he closed his eyes and raised his face toward the thick dark clouds letting go of their burden, bringing it in from the empty middle of the ocean to drench the dense population of the city, the poor and wasted citizens living on a peninsula on the western edge of the continent, the cruel and stupid and hopeless, the generous and kind and confused and deluded—the wealthy were all inside, he imagined, not paying much attention. He wondered where Rita was. Hopefully, she'd stayed put at the Holiday Inn and wasn't out in this somewhere.

Annie came to the door and pushed it open, a little too hard. It hit the big ceramic pot of bamboo on the stoop. She stood on the square of cement, swaying a little.

"Gary?" she called. "What's up?"

He felt like a dog being called in, or a little kid. She took a step forward, out from under the shelter of the overhang, and backed up abruptly.

"Wet!" she said. "Too wet for me. Come on, honey. Don't stand there in the rain. Didn't your mother ever tell you that? Not a good idea to stand in the rain. You get wet."

He realized she was drunk. He waved at her, crossed the grass and climbed the two steps toward her, and followed her into the warmth of the house.

*

Jimmy followed Stan out of the Four Deuces into the rain. They got into the Cadillac and headed for Stan's. Stan hadn't wanted to drive back across the city to his own place, and Jimmy felt too drunk to deal with it, so he was going to crash on Stan's couch. He was only vaguely aware that the car was moving, then stopping, and then he felt the rain on his face and heard the ocean as they walked across the street and up an outdoor staircase with a wrought-iron railing, down a row of apartments and into a room with paintings of misshapen nude women on the walls: Stan's living room. Two blue-and-white-striped couches sat at right angles, a square corner table between them holding a squat lamp and a pile of books. Jimmy sat on a couch and picked up a few of them. They all had little prize announcements on them—finalists or winners for the Pulitzer or National Book Award. Stan and his self-improvement bullshit. Jimmy opened one and flipped through the pages, looking at the lines of type, not seeing the words.

Stan went into the tiny kitchen. Cupboards opened, a pan banged down onto the stove. The faucet running. Rain poured heavily from a drainpipe somewhere outside. Jimmy thought maybe he could still hear the ocean, the waves that kept washing in and wearing down the jagged oily rocks, taking bites out of the crumbling cliffs, erasing the footprints of whoever had walked there that day and making the sand smooth again, the edge of the surf littered with broken sand dollars and bits of seashells and crab claws. In his mind's eye, he saw a dead seagull, its eyes gone, tiny black mites swarming its feathers.

"We need some *food*!" Stan yelled. "Otherwise we're really gonna feel like crap tomorrow."

"I have to work," Jimmy said.

"So do I, dude. Hey, check this out." Stan came out of the kitchen and unwrapped a piece of gray flannel and showed Jimmy a coin. "Twenty dollar gold coin. Worth about five hundred. Gold's down. People are buying platinum rings now. I swear, platinum has magical qualities." He wrapped up the coin again. "You know what I did today? I melted down an eighteen-karat bracelet to make two wedding rings because I didn't want to lay out the money to buy new gold. That's like a farmer eating his seeds." He put the coin in his pocket and looked toward the window. All I need's a few big sales," he said. "I'm dying, man. My debts are killing me."

Jimmy sank back on the couch and closed his eyes. Stan put on a Nirvana CD. Jimmy wanted to ask if he had any blues. He'd just seen Buddy Guy on a TV show a few nights ago, playing and singing his heart out, sweat pouring off his face and his shining black hair. That guy was so humble. "I couldn't be in the same room with Muddy and Howlin' Wolf," he had said. On the stereo, Kurt Cobain was singing something about "I'll kill you, I'm not gonna crack," but Jimmy was hearing Junior Wells doing "Good Mornin' Little School-girl." Then his mind jumped back to Sonny Boy II singing "So sad to be lonesome, so *unconvinient*"—Jimmy always got a kick out of how he said that word—"to be alone." Then he thought of having a cigarette, but instead he passed out.

*

Gary shucked his wet clothes, took a long hot shower, and put on a robe. He walked into the living room, toweling his hair dry. Annie was on the couch watching a black-and-white movie on TV—*Lost Weekend*, the part where Ray Milland sat in his brother's apartment with the shakes, having torn apart the place looking for liquor, trying to remember where he had stashed a full bottle. In a minute, he would look up and see it in the light fixture. Annie had a glass of wine in her hand.

"Did you have to stand out in the rain?" Annie said.

"It felt good," Gary said, sitting down next to her.

"I hate getting wet. Wet wet wet. Yuck. Sometimes I even hate taking a shower in the morning."

"You're like a cat."

"Mreo*ow*," she said, imitating her cat's annoying voice. Her cat was old and cranky. She'd had it since she was a girl. "Where's Pru?"

"I saw her outside."

"Forgot I let her out. I'll go get her."

She took a drink, tried to set her wineglass on the coffee table but knocked it over onto a book the woman attorney at the Hall had given Gary. *Who's Who in Nazi Germany.* Gary handed over his towel and Annie mopped at the spill.

"Oops," she said. "Wait." She went to the door and opened it. "Kitty kitty kitty!" she said in a high voice. "Come on, sweetheart! Kitty kitty kitty kitty kitty!" The cat streaked in, ran past Gary and into their bedroom. Probably it would lie on his pillow with its damp muddy fur. Gary hated that cat. Annie went to the kitchen for a refill. When she came back, she set down the glass with extreme care, as though it was made of something infinitely more breakable.

"You didn't have to wait up," Gary said.

"I felt like it." Annie was wearing an old torn T-shirt of Gary's, from The Joint, a place in Eau Claire where he'd tended bar one summer during college. The illustration showed a man and woman with martini glasses set in front of them. The woman was about to feed the man a large banana. The T-shirt had a couple of holes in it and Annie's skin showed through in a way he'd once found provocative. She tucked her legs under her on the couch and leaned her head drowsily against his shoulder. "Tell me about your day," she said.

"I didn't know you were interested." She rarely asked him about his day anymore. Usually, he just told her. Or didn't.

"I'm interested in why you promised to take me to dinner tonight and couldn't. I'm interested in what's so damn compelling at work that you can't spend any time at home, with me."

"My day started at the morgue around five A.M.," he said. "You sure you want to hear about it?"

"Oh, no," Annie said. "No, no, no. Never mind." She closed her eyes.

Gary waited for some further elucidation of her feelings, not wanting to antagonize her more.

"Look at that," she said, apparently referring to something on the table. "Unbelievable," she said.

"What?"

"I went to school with her."

Gary looked at the mess of magazines that were always there—*Harper's*, the *New Yorker*, the *Atlantic*, the *Nation*. He subscribed to all those. There was an issue of *Doubletake* that Annie had bought. She had submitted her photographs there recently and been rejected. She picked it up and gloomily regarded the cover, a color photograph of several black women in sacklike dresses and vivid head scarves, smiling in front of a pockmarked wall.

"She slept with our professor," Annie said. "Now her stuff is everywhere."

"I'm sorry," Gary said.

"I don't know what it is," Annie said. "Everything just keeps changing. Today's the anniversary."

"The anniversary?"

"Laura. Remember Laura? My sister?" She sat up, agitated, looking like she wanted to hit him.

"Of course I do. I didn't realize. You didn't say anything earlier."

"I just wanted to have a nice dinner. I knew it would be a bad day. I just wanted to go someplace nice afterward. Someplace fun. That's all I wanted." She sat rigid on the couch, looking sorrowfully at her glass of wine, telling it about her feelings.

"Babe, I'm truly sorry. I should have remembered. I'm an asshole." He felt a surge of self-loathing.

"Mom and I went to the cemetery. She goes all the time, but you know, I haven't been there since the funeral. She was talking to her, that's what she does, she goes and talks to her like she's still alive, and tells her everything, like how her yappy little Pekinese threw up on the wall-to-wall, and how she bought Daddy a new set of golf clubs for his birthday, and—God."

Annie stopped talking and they both looked at the TV. Ray Milland was plastered now, wasted, pathetic. A commercial for Huggies came on, and Gary wondered why whoever bought TV time for commercials would think that young mothers were likely to be up late at night, watching a years-old movie about an alcoholic hitting bottom. But here was Annie, who wanted a baby, so it seemed they'd nailed their demographic after all.

"I just looked at the ground and the flowers getting ruined in the rain, and I thought about Laura being down there and wondered if the earth was wet as far down as her coffin was. And I tried to imagine what her body would look like after a year. My mother babbled away, acting like we were all sitting at lunch together. She was almost *happy*. Like a crazy woman. I cried the whole time and she actually asked me what was wrong. So the morgue sounds about right."

"I didn't realize," he said again.

"Sometimes I can't believe it."

"What, that she's gone?"

"Any of it. That Laura's dead. That she'll be thirty-three forever and will never be here on Thanksgiving. That everything has to change. I mean, I know change is a law of life and crisis is supposed to be some kind of opportunity."

"You sound like you're giving one of your readings."

"I believe it," Annie said. "I just can't feel it sometimes. I guess that's what I mean." She started hiccuping. "I've been crying all fucking day," she explained.

Gary held her, let her curl up against him. She sobbed and

hiccuped in short, tight bursts, as though she had to let it out slowly, a little at a time; then the sobs came faster, and he waited for the deluge of tears, but it didn't arrive. She would subside a little, wipe the dampness from her eyes, start up again. He wished she would just wail. He thought she would—if she knew where he'd been that afternoon, knew that her husband had been with another woman while she had stood at the grave of her dead sister.

At the Holiday Inn, Rita had gone to the bed and bounced on the mattress like a kid. She was wearing a man's shirt, and jeans with a small rip at the knee; he'd wanted to put his mouth there; later he had. She had long, slim legs. Like a deer. He'd thought of the one time his father had taken him hunting, in the woods of northern Minnesota; he couldn't shoot it, it was too pretty; they'd never talked about it or gone again. It was surprising that Rita looked so good, considering what she'd probably been through. But she was still well under thirty. Pretty soon her life would catch up to her. He'd seen it over and over, beautiful girls whose skin was once dewy as camellia petals, who after a few years on the streets grew coarsened, their features losing their fineness. Bruises and scabs all over them, their teeth rotting, their once-flat bellies slopping over the waistbands of their tight skirts. Women with dull eyes and heavy makeup, whose lost loveliness might still flash out at you. But Rita was still a flower, with her strange eyes and her navel pierced with a tiny bright bit of pink glass, and her sweet nipples that he had longed to suck on and finally did. Her white cunt was a flower, her cunt's scent and taste different from Annie's, not as sharp, deliciously thick, liquid; he could still taste it.

Annie grew quiet in his arms. He had gotten hard, thinking of Rita.

"Look at you," she said, and reached to touch him, opening

the robe. "Death turns you on, doesn't it." She moved to straddle him, bracing her hands on his shoulders. "I knew you were sick when I married you," she said. One hand moving down his chest. Her familiar light touch. She stopped suddenly, stood up and took off her panties, and was there again, lowering herself.

Again he saw Rita on the bed at the Holiday Inn. Annie was moving against him. He cupped her ass, raising and lowering her, his eyes closed. One minute she was Annie, his wife; he loved her, he loved this desire in her. And then he was with Rita again, delighting in all the myriad small ways she was different, was herself, mysterious, unfamiliar, vulnerable. He wondered about other men living secret lives, having whole separate families sometimes, shuttling back and forth between them. The Nazi commandants torturing Jews by day and coming home to tuck in their children at night. He felt like he should keep Rita and Annie separate, in different rooms inside of him, but he couldn't. They were there together.

Annie moaned. He knew how close she was to coming, knew how she would sound when she did come—those strangled sounds again, like her sobbing. Carol Miller had been strangled, marks around her throat. He pictured Carol with her long red hair down her naked back, kneeling in front of her boyfriend Freddie, saw her lying down, alive, on the morgue's steel table, opening her legs.

That was the image that made him come. He held his wife tightly, felt her trying to arch away—she hadn't gotten there yet, she wanted him to wait—but he held her, grabbing her hair, forcing her head back, still with his eyes closed, for that moment not caring that she was Annie, not caring about anything except that he was inside of a woman and was going to take the release he needed.

When he was done he let go of her and lay back on the couch, exhausted. Annie was rubbing herself, moving against his flagging erection until she had her own orgasm.

He felt sickened by himself.

Annie was climbing off him. She went to the bathroom. The toilet flushed. She came back wearing a red silk kimono he'd bought her last Christmas. "That was kind of rough," she said. "You've never been like that."

Gary closed his eyes. He thought, She must be able to see it—how I am, what I did this afternoon.

"I liked it," she said. "It felt—passionate. Real." She settled herself next to him again. "I know we've hardly made love in months."

"It's all right." He desperately wanted a cigarette. He wanted to get away from her, to stand on the deck and smoke and think. He forced himself to open his eyes and smile at her.

"My parents have been married almost thirty-five years," Annie said. "I wonder if they still make love?"

"Why don't you ask your mother?" Stop, he told her mentally. Just stop talking now. You're drunk. Go pass out and let me do the same.

"Right," Annie said, and chattered on. "Like she'd ever tell me. You know my mom. She'd be shocked. She's so conservative. Remember how freaked out she was when we moved in together? And Daddy, too. Did I ever tell you he rewrote his will? He showed it to me and everything. Then he changed it back, but still. That was pretty extreme, don't you think? Did I tell you that?"

"Yes. You did." He knew about Annie's father, an internist who still hoped his daughter would stop fooling with photography and go to medical school. He knew about Annie's childhood, her arguments with her mother, and her jealousy of

Laura, whose husband had made a fortune with an Internet startup—she felt guilty abut the jealousy now that her sister was dead. He knew about Annie's abortion at nineteen, her terror of getting cancer because an aunt and now Laura had died of it. He knew she disliked parties and was addicted to white wine and television and sometimes believed in reincarnation. He knew, he thought, far too much about her.

"I'm going to the deck for a smoke," he said, getting up. He kissed her; she clung to his neck for a moment, then let him go.

"It's still raining," she said. "You'd better wear something."

"Yes, Mom."

"Oh, shut up," she said. "Gary—"

"What." He tensed. For a moment he was sure she was going to say, *I know where you were this afternoon. I know what you've been up to, Mister.*

"I do love you," she said. "I do."

"Me, too," Gary said, and headed for the back door.

★

Jimmy called in sick to the restaurant on Friday. Stan had gone to work, leaving him alone in the apartment. He sat on Stan's couch with coffee and a cigarette, wishing his head would clear. He read a few articles in the morning's *Chronicle*, got up for more coffee, peered out the window at the tan apartment building next door, went back to the couch, and lit another cigarette. He studied the nude paintings Stan had done in some art class he'd taken. They weren't very good. Finally he pulled on his jacket and went outside. It was a cloudy day, windy and fresh, and he decided to take a walk on the beach.

He crossed the Great Highway and took off his boots and socks when he got to the sand, then walked down to the water carrying them. There weren't many people around; occasionally a jogger passed, or somebody with a dog. He walked south along the edge of the ocean, watching the waves coming in, the gulls diving, the sanderlings standing still and then running all together in the same direction, like a wave themselves. His anxiety was a wave, pulling him under.

He didn't know how the hell to find Robin. And it might be too late, anyway. Again he went back to the moment he'd hit her, to the panicked feeling he'd had. Why had he been so freaked out by a girl? And why hadn't he just turned away or just pushed her down into the sand, gotten up, walked off . . . Because you're stupid, he answered himself. *You stupid little shit.* He thought of the apartment in Trenton where they'd lived before his father died, his father on the couch having a sausage sandwich and a beer, saying, *C'mere, you stupid little shit.* Saying it affectionately that time, inviting Jimmy to sit in his lap and watch TV with him, giving him sips of beer. His mother cleaning up in the kitchen, the smell of the sausages and beer, and his father's sweat, and his mother's cigarette smoke; she was always smoking. Cancer sticks. Some comedy on the TV with a tinny laugh track, his father laughing along with it.

He wanted to crawl back into that memory and stay there, in that apartment that had long since been torn down; a three-story parking structure was there now. When he'd gone back to take care of his mother before she died, he had walked around the old neighborhood and hardly recognized it. The only thing that was the same was the New Jersey State Prison across the street, whose south wall he'd played under as a kid with Chumley on the strip of grass that ran alongside.

Now, walking along the packed wet sand at Ocean Beach, he found himself thinking, prison, prison, prison, with each step. He turned and walked away from the ocean, cutting diagonally across the beach. He couldn't go to jail again. He couldn't let it all fall apart. But he felt it had already happened, somehow, and he was helpless to do anything about it.

*

Rita watched a small mouse cross from under the bed to a hole in the baseboard on the other side of her room. Maybe she could get a cat. I want a TV like the one at the Holiday Inn and a big fluffy cat. Or maybe a Siamese, they're so pretty. But maybe those don't catch mice, or maybe some kinds of cats are better than others at it. Anyway, I'm only staying here because I paid in advance and have two more days. Time to figure out the next move.

It was Friday afternoon, and for the moment the sun was shining. She'd left exactly at eleven A.M. that morning, with a few small items from the Holiday Inn in her bag, and picked up a pint of vodka and a pack of cigarettes as she walked back, enjoying the way the rain had laid a freshness over the streets.

Now she fumbled for a cigarette and lit it, forgetting she had one going in the ashtray on the bed. It had been a good day until she saw the man in the corduroy suit. Only he wasn't wearing the suit anymore or the funny hat from before—he had on a long tan raincoat and a green John Deere cap and he was inside the adult bookstore she passed on her way back to the Barker; he didn't see her, he was pulling a magazine from the rack near the door, his back mostly to her, reaching with his ugly hand. She ran the block back to the Barker and locked all the locks to her room and took out the vodka. She'd meant to pick up some cranberry juice at the nearby market but, fuck it, she would drink it straight. Now because she was drunk she was not as afraid, though she kept an ear on the door. The Indian man at the desk wouldn't let anybody come up. That was how it was supposed to work, anyway. But sometimes he left the desk to go back through the bead curtains to the bathroom, or to run around the corner for cigarettes. Hopefully, he had a full pack and an empty bladder right now.

The mouse poked its head out of the hole, came halfway across the room, stopped, and looked at her. Actually it was kind of cute. She didn't mind it, as long as it didn't try to get up on the bed with her. It was the roaches she hated and feared more than anything, but they usually came out only at night. What she needed was a gecko. She'd heard that if you kept one of those around, they ate up every roach in sight. She took a drag off her cigarette and leaned against the wall, wanting some big pillows to sink into.

"Add them to the list," she said. "TV, kitty cat, gecko, and some feather pillows. And while you're at it," she directed an imaginary servant, "how about a big pot of tea with lots of sugar." And some of those butter cookies with the dark chocolate on top with the picture of the castle. Now she was doubly sorry she hadn't been able to stop at the store on Polk Street. She waved her cigarette around, watching the curls of smoke spiral up in the air. She took another drag and let her hand drift to the bed.

Her head fell forward. Her eyes closed; then she jerked awake, looked around the room. The mouse was nowhere in sight. The vodka bottle lay beside her on the bed and she tucked it in next to her. The sunlight coming through the window was molten, a rectangle of light burning on the bed.

She brought her hand to her mouth for another drag but the cigarette had disappeared. She stared at her fingernails, painted a metallic blue. Pretty. She'd painted them for Gary Shepard. Gary Shepard was all right. He'd given her money. She still had some, she could go out and buy cookies, or she could go into Miz Brown's and order a big pile of pancakes drenched in maple syrup. But watch out for the Bogeyman. Something her mother used to say. *Who's the Bogeyman?* Rita would ask, but her mother wouldn't tell her; Rita imagined him as a shadow animal-man with a long tail, claws for his hands and feet, waiting outside the door or under her bed for her to fall asleep. *B* word. She would tell Gary Shepard that one. The bed was burning hot by her hip. She smelled smoke and realized it was burning for real; she rolled away from it, to the edge.

Once, Rita and her friend Shandi had started a fire in the empty lot behind the apartment building in San Jose where Rita and her mother had moved after Reno. They were playing with matches in the weeds, starting little fires and stomping them out, but then there were too many fires, and they got scared and ran toward the building to find her mother, screaming that someone had set the lot on fire. Rita's mother called through her locked bedroom door, *Don't bother me. I'm trying to rest.* Rita remembered how to dial 911, and then the firemen arrived, giants in big black slickers and boots with yellow stripes. Her mother finally came out of her room, wearing a stained bathrobe, her hair hanging in her face, and Rita was more ashamed of her than of starting the fire. The firemen sat the girls down, after the fire was put out, and lectured them about never, ever playing with matches again. But after that they still did it. They tried to set the woods by the Catholic church on fire, and the bushes behind the shopping center, and they succeeded in starting a big one in somebody's trash can a few blocks away. Rita thought about all the fires she and Shandi used to start while she watched the thin blue blanket smoldering on the bed. It wasn't much of a fire. Finally she took the pillow and smothered it.

After the fireman came, she had to sneak around to see Shandi. Her mother said it was because of the fire, but Rita knew it was because Shandi was black; *I never liked that girl,* her mother said, *she's not our people.* It was news to Rita that she had a people.

Black. Another *b* word. She should make a list.

It was getting kind of smoky in the room, so she went to the window and tried to open it, but it had been painted shut. After a minute she gave up and went back to bed. Someone was pounding on the door a long way off. Then they stopped.

She woke to find the Indian desk clerk standing over her.

"Get out," the man said. "Get out. You take your things and leave and don't come back."

"Hey," Rita said. "Hey. Okay." She sat up. Her cigarettes were somewhere in the bed; she felt around for them, trying not to listen to the man, who was going on about decent people. Apparently they weren't her people. She found her cigarettes on the floor, finally, and threw them with her few clothes into a white plastic trash bag. She slid her Baggie of money out of her pillowcase and tossed it into the trash bag, not wanting to put it down her pants in front of the man. She quickly began to take down the postcards she had tacked to the wall to try and brighten up the room. A pouty Marilyn Monroe in a striped bathing suit. A picture from *Gone With the Wind,* only it said *Via Con Vento,* Rhett Butler carrying a passed-out Scarlett O'Hara from the flames of Atlanta. In her favorite one, a man with angel wings strapped to his back knelt and kissed a woman on a bed. Soft light came in through the windows of the room, and the angel had his hand under the woman's chin, raising her face up for the kiss. On another postcard the Virgin Mary smiled sadly with her eyes downcast and her palms out as if to say how very sorry she was about everything that was happening to Rita.

She pulled the cards away from their thumbtacks and dropped them into the bag, the man hovering near her with his strange smells and harsh rapid words.

She grabbed her purse and looked around to see if she'd forgotten anything. The clerk was taking the blanket and sheets and pillow off the bed. A little spot on the mattress was blackened, but it didn't look too bad. He took her arm and led her to the door, hissing, "Out, out, out!" as he hustled her down the hall to the stairs. The transvestite who lived across the hall stood at his door in a halter top and jean shorts and bare feet, watching. His toenails were the same blue as her fingernails.

"Let go of me," Rita said at the top of the stairs. "I'm going, I'm going." She hurried down, holding onto the railing, the man still chattering from the hall. She passed the little girl in the lobby, who was playing with her Barbies.

"Out, out, out!" the little girl said, in perfect imitation of her father.

*

On the street, she felt afraid. She started walking fast, then running. Miz Brown's was too close to the Barker. She ran a couple of blocks, walked a few more, and went into the Copper Penny. She called Gary Shepard from the pay phone in the back. He had given her his pager number. She punched in the number and the pound sign and sat at the end of the counter and ordered some tea. A woman with a rip in the underarm of her uniform took her order.

Hopefully, the man had bought his dirty magazine and taken it home to relieve whatever craziness or violence was in him. She regretted not telling Gary Shepard the man had seen her that night, had said he would come back for her. She would tell him now. Maybe he could take her someplace safe. Ha, ha. No place safe from the Bogeyman.

"And an English muffin," she told the waitress, whose tag read SUNNY. The waitress stalked down to the end of the counter, took one from the package, and crammed the two halves into the toaster like she was mad at Rita for having the nerve to order anything at all. Then she disappeared into the kitchen, ignoring an older tattooed man at the counter who was holding up his coffee cup and staring hard in her direction.

If I *was* a waitress, Rita thought, I'd try to be like Fran. I'd be nice to people, and make them feel welcome. The voice of the clerk played in her head, wearing a groove into her brain. *Get out. Out, out, out.* Every *t* of the word *out* was sharp and precise.

You are nothing, the voice in her head said.

I've never been anything. I can't play the harmonica like Jimmy or have an important job like Gary Shepard. I'd probably be a bad waitress, I'd get the orders all mixed up. I can't be anything but a whore, which is nothing, nobody.

Whore was what Karl Hauptmann had called her. Not at first. At first he had been nice, bringing her M&M's or 3 Musketeers bars or magazines like *Seventeen* and *Cosmopolitan* when he came to see her mother, and she had liked him. He had built her a platform bed—a four-poster, something she'd always wanted—and helped her hang lavender sheets around it as curtains; she liked feeling enclosed, making a room of her bed inside the larger room. A few months after she turned thirteen, her breasts got to the point where she needed a bra, and then Karl was always looking at them, making her uncomfortable and embarrassed, and she started avoiding him as much as possible. But that day, her mother was at the doctor's, and Rita came home from Shandi's, and there was Karl sitting at the kitchen table with a bottle of Crown Royal. He explained to her that he was celebrating getting fired from his construction job.

"Come have a drink with me," he said.

"No thanks." She had gotten drunk and sick a few months before from some of her mother's vodka mixed with orange juice and she didn't want anything to do with alcohol. Or Karl.

"Suit yourself," Karl said, and she went to her bedroom and turned on her radio and got out her diary that had a plaid cover and a key to lock it. *Today me and Shandi set another fire a small one I know its a sin I will pray to be better. I got a C on the math quiz I HATE MATH!!! I think Brian Martin likes me he followed me to my locker. He is so gross.* Karl came in through the hanging sheets, carrying his glass and another one, both of them full. "No fun to drink alone," he said, and sat on the bed and handed her the glass.

"I don't want any," Rita said.

"Drink it," Karl said, and the way he said it made her take a small sip. She made a face.

"That's better," Karl said. "You get used to the taste. Take another sip."

She did. It was warm and slightly less unpleasant.

He started stroking her hair. "You're such a pretty girl."

She wanted to say, *Stop it.* She wanted him to stop. But she was afraid of him. He was a mean drunk, unlike her father. Her father, when he drank, had just stumbled around and then gone to bed. But Karl yelled, and cursed, and was mad at the world. Once, he had slammed her mother's door so hard the full-length mirror on it fell off and broke into pieces and he got so mad about that he kicked the door off its hinges with his heavy boots, and then he stood in the midst of the wreckage and punched the wall and broke two bones in his hand and they all had to go to the Emergency Room.

When he tried to kiss her, she turned her face away. "Don't," she said.

He pulled back and took a swallow of his drink, and she thought he might go away then. But instead he set the glass on the floor and then took hers and put it on the floor, too, and then he took hold of her hair and proceeded to rape her.

Now you know what it is to have a man. I did you a favor, sweetheart.

Afterward, the bed was bloodstained all the way through the sheet and mattress pad and down to the mattress.

You're both whores. You and your mother both. He walked back into the kitchen ranting while she lay there curled up with her hand between her legs, pressing it hard on the place he'd been, on the pain he had seared into her.

But her mother wasn't a whore. And Rita shouldn't have told her what Karl did. She should have been strong and kept it in. If she had pushed it all the way down inside her and not let it get out, her mother would still be alive.

She sat nursing her tea for over an hour, waiting for Gary Shepard to call, but after she'd eaten a second English muffin and had a refill of hot water and paid with the four dollars in her purse, the pay phone still hadn't rung. The waitress kept looking over at her and Rita could hear her thinking, *Haven't you left yet, you piece of trash?*

But Gary Shepard had said she was smart. She tried to hold on to that word, to the image of herself as a smart young woman, who could do things because she was so smart, who still was going to make something of her life. With Sheryl, at the shelter, she had talked about what she might do, and Sheryl had been excited to hear that Rita liked taking care of plants, that she used to garden with her father. "You could do that for a living," Sheryl had said, and Rita hadn't believed her. Sheryl had promised they would go to some of the city's community gardens together. But of course they hadn't. People were full of shit. They never followed through.

She wasn't safe here. A thin needle of pain and anxiety started somewhere back in her brain, a tiny circle that became dime sized, then quarter sized, until she had a headache blooming in her left temple.

Her second cup of tea had grown cold. She didn't want to ask the girl to dump it out and give her more hot water, especially since people were starting to come in for lunch. Reluctantly, she slid off the stool. She went into the bathroom, brushed her hair and put on makeup, peed, washed her hands, and gave her underarms a quick bath, all the time listening for the phone's shrill ring. Maybe Gary Shepard didn't want to have anything to do with her, now that he'd gotten what he wanted. He was probably like all the rest; nice until you give it up, and then you don't mean anything to them. You're used up, like a paper towel. She took two from the dispenser and wiped her hands and underarms, crumpled them and threw them in the trash. She remembered the white plastic bag with her things in it and realized she had left it by her stool when she went to the bathroom. Most of the money Gary Shepard had given her, what she had left anyway, was in there.

The trash bag wasn't there. A man in a green minidress and enormous gold hoop earrings and a little hat with a half-veil was sitting on the stool where Rita had been. He wasn't as delicate-looking as Rita's neighbor, whom Rita had actually mistaken for a woman when she first met him. This one had on makeup and a wig, but you could tell he was a man; his arms and legs were muscular and hairy. He had on giant green spike-heeled pumps that just missed matching his dress.

"Did you see a white trash bag here when you sat down?" Rita asked him.

"No, honey," the man said. "The only white trash here is me." He winked at her.

She looked around. The restaurant was busy, and there were only two waitresses; hers turned from a booth and rushed behind the counter, slapped a square of paper on the window to the kitchen and yelled, "Ordering!" in a voice like a drill sargeant's. Rita went around to the end of the counter and waited for her to come back.

"Hey." She grabbed the waitress's arm. "I lost a white trash bag. It was there a minute ago, by my stool, before I went to the bathroom."

"Well, what do you want me to do about it?"

"Did you see anybody take it?"

"Did you ever hear of tipping?"

"What?" Rita said, confused. She was trying hard not to cry. "What?" a sense of panic rose in her.

"I said"— the waitress said each word slowly—"Did— you—ever—hear—of—leaving—a—tip?"

"I'm sorry. But my stuff. That was all I had. My money. I don't have any money." She tried to explain herself to this girl who could care less, who was looking at her now like she was spouting gibberish. Maybe she was; her thoughts were getting more disorganized.

"Sorry about your stuff, but I'm busy." She turned away toward the kitchen.

Rita left the Copper Penny and headed down the street. I should have tucked that money safely away, in the Barker. How stupid was that? Or at the restaurant. I sat there for an hour and all I had to do was reach down and take it and keep it close to me. How am I going to get anywhere if I keep losing ID's and clothes, and letting money just slip away like that. Lost the apartment on Jones Street. The room at the Barker, two more days paid and down the drain. And, oh yeah, I lost my husband.

There is something seriously wrong with me.

It started to rain. She kept walking, down the middle of the sidewalk, not even bothering to stay close to the buildings where an occasional awning offered cover.

Go on. Just go on and mess with me some more. She wasn't sure who she was talking to—God, or fate, or nobody. It just seemed like somebody, or something, wanted to grind her down. No matter what she said or did she was trash. If there was a God, he wasn't going to help her. He had sent the rain to drive her right into the sidewalk pavement, where people would walk over her, men in dress shoes and boots and sneakers, women in suits and sharp heels, until she was flattened to a stain. She didn't deserve any better.

This was her new prayer: Keep it up. I don't care anymore. Hit me with your best shot.

*

The tattooist at Skin Deep lifted his T-shirt to reveal a picture of singer La Toya Jackson on his chest. Her breasts were naked, and where one of her nipples would have been inked, there was the guy's actual nipple in its place. Jimmy admired it aloud, and then the guy pulled his T-shirt down and asked what Jimmy wanted.

"A heart," Jimmy said. He already had a tattoo, a cartoon devil sitting atop a panther on his right shoulder. He'd gotten it years ago in Trenton. At the time, it was just an image he liked, but over the years it had come to represent to him the demon of his anger, the part of him that lost control sometimes. Now he was afraid he might be going back to jail, or even state prison, and he wanted to have something meaningful that they couldn't take away, something that represented a different part of himself.

"Cool," the tattooist said. "Like, ventricles and shit, right? I can do an awesome heart. Maybe with flames."

"I had something simpler in mind. Just, you know, a heart. With a banner. The old-fashioned kind."

The tattooist looked disappointed that he wasn't being asked for something more challenging. He wore black leather cuffs on each thin wrist, and a heavy chain link choker around his neck. "Okay," he shrugged. "You sure?"

"Yeah," Jimmy said. "Left shoulder."

The needle made a pleasant buzzing sound. Like the last time, it didn't really hurt; it was more an irritated feeling, and that feeling passed as his endorphins kicked in. He watched some angelfish flip back and forth in an aquarium on the counter. One swam to the glass and watched him, its mouth working, making kissing shapes. Jimmy looked up to where a few taxidermied ducks hung from the ceiling, twirling on wires.

It didn't take very long. The heart was red, the banner blue. Inside the banner it said *Jimmy & Rita*. The tattooist smeared it with Vaseline, slapped a square bandage over it, and he was done.

"Get some Curél," the tattooist said, handing him a piece of paper that said Caring For Your Tattoo.

Jimmy stepped out of the shop into a downpour. Under

his jacket and shirtsleeve and bandage he could feel the sting of the tattoo. He felt awake for the first time all day.

*

Gary had spent the morning visiting clients in jail. One was a male prostitute and speed freak who did tricks so he could afford to buy drugs. Right now he was in for burglary. His dealer had been busted, and the prostitute had broken into the dealer's apartment, which was full of boosted mountain bikes and fax machines and stereos, and ripped him off and sold a few items on the street. A day later, when he went back for more, the cops were there. He was put in the same cell with his dealer. "Hey, man, what are you doing here?" the dealer had asked. "I got busted breaking into your spot and stealing your stuff," the prostitute told him, whereupon the dealer dropped him as a client. The loss of his drug connection was causing the prostitute more anxiety than any pending charges.

Another client was up for kidnapping a woman prostitute named Violetta. He was already on probation. The client figured he would just get violated, but the DA's office envisioned a bigger party for him and was filing charges. Gary was betting that Violetta wouldn't show in court, though. He had a good laugh with a lawyer friend about the speed freak and his dealer being put in the same cell, and a better laugh with a cop who told Gary how he'd gotten a suspect to confess by convincing him that a copy machine was a lie detector. The cop had the suspect stand next to the machine and put his hand on the glass while the cop ran copies and asked questions. Gary didn't get a chance to call back the number on his pager until an hour or so after it came in, and when he did, a strange male voice answered.

"Lonnie?" the voice said.

"No, it's Gary Shepard. I had this number on my pager."

"Well, it ain't the right number," the voice said, "if you ain't Lonnie."

Gary hung up. He called Annie, who had also paged him.

"Northwestern Securities," Annie said. "Can I—" she was laughing. "Can I help you?" she got out.

"Hey, it's me. What's up?"

"We're laughing at Claudine," Annie said. Annie's boss was a bitch on wheels. Everyone in the office had bonded over hating her. "I was just thinking. Are you doing yams with the turkey?"

"I hadn't thought about it," Gary said. "Probably."

"My mother called this morning and wanted to know what we're having, and she wanted to remind you that she doesn't eat mushrooms, and if you do yams she doesn't want any sugar or honey or butter or anything."

"Check," Gary said. "No mushrooms, plain yams." He was on the phone in the old county jail, on the sixth floor of the Hall. Two sheriff's deputies—one black, one Filipino—were escorting a Chinese gang member in handcuffs. Multiculturalism at its finest.

"So, when will you be home tonight?"

"I've got to be in court right after lunch. Then I've got that surveillance again."

"I'm going to meet Kate at Moose's this afternoon," Annie said. "She's in town on her way to LA for the weekend." Kate and Annie had both gone to the Art Institute. Kate did things with textiles. She had moved to New York and had already been in a couple of group shows in good galleries. Kate was married to an architect and had a baby girl. They were buying a house in Park Slope. Whenever Kate's name came up, Gary's stock with Annie sank.

"Have fun," he said.

"Miss you."

"Miss you, too." He hung up, took the old noisy elevator down to the street, and decided to skip lunch and check in on Rita instead.

✱

She finally went to Marco's, so cold and wet she didn't care about anything but getting inside out of the weather. Marco was small and skinny and as long as she wasn't high, she was pretty sure she could keep him off her if he tried anything. It was too early to get into any of the shelters. And they would fill quickly, once they opened. There were never enough beds. Sometimes people just slept sitting on folding chairs. She rang Marco's buzzer, but there was no answer so she pushed the other three buzzers in his building, one at a time, but no one was home. Or else they wouldn't let her in. She peered through the heavy glass doors into the dim interior of the building, then sat at the top of the grimy marble stairs, where at least she was protected from the rain, and waited. The rain stopped and the sun came out, and she sat on the lowest step to catch the warmth.

Marco showed up finally with a girl in tow. She couldn't have been more than sixteen. Marco's snakeskin jacket was draped over her shoulders.

"Rita!" Marco said, falsely hearty. "What's up, girl?"

"I got kicked out of my hotel."

"Wow, that's too bad," Marco said. "This is Meredith."

"Pleased to meet you," the girl said. She had about ten earrings in each ear, and a tiny steel ball between her lower lip and her chin, and black eyeliner that was smudged underneath her eyes. Her nipples stuck out through her wet tank top. She kept hunching forward, trying to hide them.

"Meredith's from Oregon," Marco said. "She just got to town."

"Listen, Marco, can I crash here awhile?" Rita knew already he was going to turn her down. "Please?" She smiled at him. I hate you, she thought. Someday I am going to kill you.

"Hey, I'm sorry," Marco said, pretending he really was. "I just told Meredith she could crash with me."

"Could I just come in for a while, then?"

Marco put on a face of exaggerated concern. "Bad timing, babe," he said. Meredith was biting her cuticles, looking from Marco to Rita. "I'm sorry," Marco said again.

"I bet you are," Rita said, thinking, fuck you very much. She stood up. "If I were you," she said to Meredith, "I'd go back to Oregon. Asshole," she said to Marco.

"See you, Rita," he said as she walked away.

She headed off blindly. The sun had disappeared again. The wind came up and then the rain was back. She walked close to the buildings, shivering, her arms crossed over her chest. A few people, most of them with umbrellas, were striding purposefully in one direction or another, their heads down and coat collars up. This was a real storm; the sky was dark gray, and the rain poured down endlessly and landed in the puddles it had already made, and cars rolled through the puddles at intersections and sent waves of dirty water spraying over whoever was foolish enough to stand at the curb. Rita passed doorways in which men sat or lay next to piled shopping carts, wrapped in sleeping bags or old blankets, or under newspapers whose sheets blew up at the edges and sometimes lifted away. A small park with graffittied cement benches and a play structure was empty except for a roaming dog. Lights were on in the bars and restaurants. Every-

one who could afford to be inside sat and talked about what-
ever people talked about when they were warm and com-
fortable and not wandering through the rain without even a
quarter to call Gary Shepard, let alone a damn dollar to ride
the damn bus and dry off. She set off walking in the direction
of the Haight, to hang around and try the shelter when it
opened. She hoped there was room for her. There was no
place else to go.

*

As Stan's Cadillac cruised through a wide puddle at Van Ness
and Market, Jimmy looked up blearily, starting awake from
a drunken nap. Through the back and forth of Stan's wind-
shield wipers, he thought he saw Rita, walking fast with her
arms wrapped around her. He and Stan had just left the Blue
Lamp and were on their way to the Paradise Lounge, south
of Market, to shoot some pool. Jimmy had spent all after-
noon at Stan's shop, drinking beers while Stan cursed the
rain for driving away any potential customers. Stan showed
Jimmy a clock he wanted to sell—bullets glued together in a
circle around the clock face. Jimmy had admired it, but he
didn't want to buy it. Stan closed up early, and they went to
eat German food and drink dark beer at Speckmann's, then
for martinis at the Café du Nord. The du Nord was under-
ground so they didn't even know it was raining again until
they emerged onto the street, and Stan roared his Stan roar
and threw out his arms and put his head back. *Aaaaahhhh,*
he yelled, and it made Jimmy happy to see how much pleas-
ure Stan could take in anything, even something like pour-
ing rain, and then jealous and unhappy because he himself
was never like that; or not anymore, at least. His stomach
was bothering him. They had gone to a succession of bars

and smoked a lot of pot, and in one there was a bathroom where the graffitti said CUNT WHORE and FOLLOW YOUR BLISS, AND DOORS WILL OPEN WHERE YOU NEVER KNEW THEY EXISTED; he had gone out to the bar and borrowed a pen and written down the words about bliss carefully on a napkin, going back in to make sure he'd gotten them exactly right. But he'd lost the napkin somewhere, or maybe it was on the floor of Stan's car.

And it looked like Rita up there ahead of them, her shape, her odd gait—she took steps way too big for her—but she was turning, going right, and the tattooed heart on his shoulder was quiet under its bandage—he was too numb to feel it—and Stan continued through the intersection where the light was yellow but had turned red partway across, and she was gone.

*

The rain drove her into a doorway. It was stupid to try to go anywhere in this storm. The Haight was miles away. She longed for a cigarette, for her room at the Barker, for a blanket to wrap herself in. It was just as stupid to stay here, outside with the rain slanting furiously past and the wind sometimes blowing it in toward her, and nobody around to ask for help. She wasn't far from Polk Street; she could go by the Bagel Shop and walk inside and head straight for the bathroom, and maybe they wouldn't try and stop her and tell her the bathroom was for customers only; she could dry off with some paper towels and then maybe bum money from somebody. She stepped back out.

*

"Are you sure you want to go?" Gary said. He was on the phone with Annie again, in a bar called the Mother Lode. He'd tried all afternoon to find Rita. He'd been to the Barker and Miz Brown's and roamed up and down the Tenderloin. Now he had given up looking for her and was trying to find a drag queen named Twanda. Twanda was friends with a queen named Lucille, who was lovers with a man named Bobo, who could corroborate a client's alibi. Or so the client said.

"Hey, it's Friday night and my husband's not around. It'll be fun. It's sunny in LA." Annie's voice on the phone sounded giddy with wine. "It's Kate's show," she said. "Of course I'm going. Right, Katie?" They were in a bar somewhere, a crowded one from the sound of it. The Mother Lode, on the other hand, had barely a handful of customers, each one of them alone, each one of them focused solely on raising his blood alcohol level to meet the strenuous requirements of getting through another evening.

"Go, then. You should go."

"I hope we can take off in this storm. We're going to head for the airport and hope for the best. Take care, sweetie. Defend some bad guys."

"They aren't all bad guys," he reminded her. It was true that he had helped a few less-than-upstanding citizens beat criminal charges. But the deck was heavily stacked against his clients to begin with. He was just balancing the odds a little. He had helped out plenty of poor deserving fuckers. Feckers.

"Whatever," she said vaguely. "Love you."

"Have a good trip."

The bartender said Twanda would be in soon, if she was going to be in at all, so Gary ordered another beer. After that he had a third, with a shot of Jack Daniels. The light in the bar was a miasmic red. The jukebox played Peggy Lee: "Fever," "The Man I Love," "Something Wonderful." A boy in hot pants and bright magenta rubber boots sashayed in, looked at Gary, turned and went back out. A man with a sparse beard and wire-rimmed glasses sat alone at one end of the bar with a bottle of Corona in front of him, squeezing the life out of a lemon slice and having an imaginary conversation with some-one named Gloria. The bartender played dice with a slim man in a white jumpsuit. The man was bald and had on gold hoop earrings and made Gary think of Mr. Clean, the man on the detergent bottle. He didn't care anymore if Twanda came in or not.

*

There was no paper towel dispenser anymore in the bath-room of the Bagel Shop. Instead there was a roll of toweling that stayed in the dispenser, which you had to jerk down one section at a time for the clean part, while the soiled part disappeared back inside. Rita stood under it on tiptoe, awk-wardly drying her hair. She took off her soaked shirt and wrung it out, blotting it with clean toweling, and pulled out toilet paper from the stall and bunched it into big wads to dry her face and arms. She ran hot water into the sink and put her hands in it and held them there, then dried her hands on the toweling, put her shirt back on and walked out. The rain was glittering down past the streetlights outside the big win-dows.

She stopped at a table and quietly asked a man in an Army jacket and a red bandanna headband if he could possi-bly spare a cigarette.

"Sorry, I just have tobacco," the man said. "I roll my own. I'd roll you one, but I'm out of papers."

"How about the price of a cup of tea, then?" Rita said.

"I'd give it to you if I had it, sister. You want a sip of my coffee?" He motioned for her to sit down. "Take a load off." He was about fifty, heavy-set, with long greasy black hair and a brown face full of creases and pockmarks. "I'm Indian Pete," he said. "Here, have some coffee."

Rita sat. She took a couple of sips. It was bitter, but at least it was hot. She pressed her palms against the sides of the mug.

"Hell of an evening," Indian Pete said.

Rita nodded, and took another sip. She knew she needed to think of her next move, but she was too tired. She sat drinking Indian Pete's coffee, while he drummed with his yellowed fingers on the plastic tabletop.

"Hey, Bear!" Indian Pete shouted. "Hey, man."

A huge man in a green poncho came toward them. His gray hair was slicked against his forehead from the rain. His face was perfectly round, like a basketball.

"Got any papers?" Indian Pete said.

"Man, what a night," Bear said. "What a scene I just came from. You know Dan?"

"Dan? I don't know him."

"Dan, the dude who hangs around here? You know Dan," Bear said to Indian Pete.

"Dan," Indian Pete said. "What's he look like?"

"He sold you that shitty weed that time, remember? Dan. You remember Dan."

"I thought that guy's name was Dave," Indian Pete said.

"Dave. I don't know any Dave," Bear said.

"Yeah, you do. You know, *Dave*."

"No, I do not know *Dave*," Bear said.

"Okay, what happened to Dan?"

"He OD'd."

"Wow," Indian Pete said. "Bummer."

"I went by there to score and there were cops all over," Bear said.

"He was an asshole, anyway," Indian Pete said. "Hey, how about buying my friend some tea?" He turned to Rita. "You still want some tea, sister?"

"Damn," Bear said. "I really wanted some smack. I should've gone over there this morning. You know anybody who's holding?" he asked Indian Pete. He put his big hand to his forehead, pushing back his wet hair. "What a night," Bear said.

"Is your friend dead?" Rita said.

"According to my sources," Bear said, "my sources being a couple guys who said they lived in the building, yeah, he's history." He smiled at Rita. "Tea!" he said. "What I need's a drink. You guys want to come up the street? If I can't spend it on dope, I might as well spend it on booze."

"I'm there, brother," Indian Pete said.

They went two doors up to a bar where there were sports pennants all over and a 49ers helmet hanging above the cash register. Bear started reminiscing about playing football in high school and how he almost made it to college on a scholarship to University of New Mexico, but then his grandmother got sick and he went back to the Taos pueblo to take care of her. Indian Pete said he'd never played football or set foot on a reservation, but he did used to like baseball while he was growing up in LA, where everyone thought he was Mexican until he explained he was a proud Native American, so instead of Pedro everybody started calling him Indian Pete. Rita asked him what tribe and he said, "That's for me to know and you to find out." She doubted then that he was Native American at all because he really did look Mexican.

But then she remembered that there were Mexican Indians, too, so maybe he was one of those. Bear and Indian Pete drank shots and beers and bought Rita vodka cranberries.

She went over to the jukebox with money they gave her and played B.B. King and another song that went, "I still got the blues for you," and sat between Bear and Indian Pete while they talked and laughed and made plans to rob a McDonald's in Daly City. The bartender was an old woman, her long gray braids tied with two pink ribbons; the ribbons made Rita sadder. Bear had bought a pack of Camels and they were all smoking. The bartender sat at the far end of the bar and crocheted a tiny sweater she said was for her new-born nephew, and pretty soon there was different music on the jukebox, and Indian Pete said to Rita, "May I have the honor of a dance, sister," and they moved around next to a table and he fondled her ass and whispered in her ear that she could stay with him tonight and he'd be nice to her; his breath stank, and so did his clothes.

The song ended. Rita went to the bathroom. She sat on the graffitied toilet for a long time. When she finally stood up she felt dizzy. She staggered, and grabbed the sanitary napkin disposal on the wall to keep from falling. After she flushed, there was a knock on the door and Bear came in, filling the small room, and she backed against the sink.

"Are you all right?" Bear said. "Just wanted to make sure you didn't fall in." He was smiling. He leaned against the door. "Are you all right?" he said again.

"No," Rita said. "I think I'm going to be sick." She gripped the sink behind her. "I really think I'm going to throw up," she said.

"Poor baby," Bear said.

"I'll be out in a minute," Rita said.

She thought he was going to make her do something. But he held her hair back from her face while she threw up in the sink. When she was done he got her some paper towels.

"Thank you," she said.

"No problem. You want me to leave you alone?"

"Please."

"I'll ask for a glass of water," Bear said.

She rinsed the sink, held some paper towels under the faucet and wiped her face thoroughly. There was no soap in the dispenser. She dug the Holiday Inn shampoo out of her purse and used that to wash her hands and face again, and studied herself for a minute. Jesus. She put on makeup, and lipstick, and combed her hair back with wet fingers.

The bartender was rinsing glasses. A couple of young men with Marine haircuts were sitting at a table with a pitcher of beer in front of them, holding hands on the table.

"Hey, sister," Indian Pete said. "Feeling better?"

Bear held out a glass of water. "Let me tell you something," he said. "We all need help sometimes."

"Sometimes you can't trust anyone," Rita said, drinking the water.

"Then you just got to trust yourself," Bear said.

"Maybe," Rita said.

"You got a place to stay?"

"I wish."

"You can stay with me," Indian Pete said, repeating the offer he'd made on the dance floor.

"I don't think so." She thought she might trust Bear enough, but it turned out he lived with somebody.

"I've got a good woman," Bear said. "But she's jealous as hell. She wouldn't understand, me bringing somebody home."

"You're lucky to have her," Rita told him.

"Just remember," Bear said. "You've always got yourself."

"And me," Indian Pete said. "If you want me, I'll be true."

"I'll just have another drink, if that's okay," Rita said. She didn't care so much now if she had to go back outside, even if she had to walk all night in the rain. She had thought Bear was going to do something to her, and he hadn't. That meant something.

Another good thing might happen, she thought. Even to me.

Bear ordered more drinks. "Keep the faith," he said when the bartender came, and they all raised their glasses.

*

Up to Market Street, right on Market past the Civic Center plaza. In the plaza there were a few bodies under tarps toughing out the weather. A streetcar went by, the faces inside lit by eerie, dirty yellow light. Bear walked her past the plaza and said good night.

"Take care, little sister," he said, and gave her five dollars. "Get something to eat."

There was a crowd outside the Orpheum Theatre: women in shiny dresses and long coats, men in suits and tuxes opening black umbrellas. The lit marquee said LA BOHÈME. Rita pushed through the mob of people on the sidewalk, not caring that some of them stared at her.

Another block. A Carl's Jr. on the corner, red and white inside, a black man in dreadlocks unwrapping a hamburger, another black man with a bandaged left arm sucking through a straw on a gigantic soda. She was cold and wet again, so she went in.

She got some French fries and tea and turned from the

counter, and he was standing there. He had on the corduroy suit and feathered hat again. He held a closed umbrella like a walking stick or a cane. He smiled at her.

"About time I caught up to you," he said, not sounding mean or menacing. Just happy. Happy to see her, his old friend Rita. He tapped the point of the umbrella on the brown-tiled floor and she looked down at his hand on the handle. Burned, deformed. "I've been following you," he said. "And I could have waited outside, but I just got tired of waiting, you know?" He smiled.

She jerked up the cup, meaning to throw the hot tea in his face, but he stepped back and it arced up and splashed on the front of his jacket and on the floor between them. She stood a second, unable to move, and as he reached out his good hand and grabbed her arm she recovered and dropped the cup and fries and pulled out of his grip and turned toward the door, where another customer was entering. She ran for the door and halfway collided with him, dropped her purse, slipped through the door and started running.

She could hardly feel her legs, could no longer feel the rain except as a coldness all over her body. She ran across Gough Street and turned the corner, past a long brick wall, knowing he was coming, just behind her, through the rain pouring down and the wind blowing; the wind was his breath on her neck. He couldn't catch her; if he caught her, he would— She couldn't think it, her mind went cold like the rest of her, and she surged forward. Past a dresser set out on the sidewalk, no drawers in it. A green Dumpster, filled with planks of wood. Blank window of a closed restaurant. Under the freeway, where it was too dark and the concrete pillars rose up into blackness and wet newspapers were plastered against a chain link fence. Her lungs started to hurt. At

the next corner, a woman in a miniskirt stood under a street-
light, holding a Japanese parasol over her head, leaning into
the passenger window of a car. Rita ran to her.

"Help me," she said.

"This is my date, baby," the woman said. Then she looked
over Rita's shoulder and, apparently assessing the situation,
stepped back.

Rita got into the car. "Put up the window," she said. "Go,
go!" She pushed down the lock. The car's heater was on and
the rush of warm air hit her face.

"What's the deal?" the driver said. He was an older man
with wavy silver hair, and his black pants were unzipped and
his penis was out. "Maybe you better—" he said, but then
the man chasing her was at the window, and the driver sud-
denly hit the gas, and they fishtailed forward. She looked
back and saw the man standing there, looking after them.
Then he turned to the woman with the parasol and punched
her in the face.

*

"So how about it?" the driver said after a couple of blocks,
glancing at her. He hadn't tucked himself back in.

"How *about* it?" Rita said. "Are you kidding me? Drop me
off at a gas station. No, not yet," she said, when he slowed at
a Shell station. "Maybe the next one." She sat shaking from
adrenaline, feeling nauseous, alcohol and bar peanuts and
stomach acid rising in her throat.

"What am I, a taxi?" he said.

"Shut up. Just shut up. Or—my pimp will cut you," she
said. That worked.

"Okay," he said. "I don't want any problems. Just let me
know where you need to go."

"Go down Fell Street." She might as well get a ride to the Haight. At a brightly lit Chevron where a couple of motorcycles were filling up, she asked him to let her off. "Can you give me any money?" she said.

"But we didn't do anything," he said, in a whiny voice. "Why should I pay you?" He had at least zipped up.

"Think of it as your good deed for the day." She was angry. She held on to the anger because underneath it was fear, and she had to push that very far down or she would not get through this. How old was this creep, anyway? What was he doing, running around town with his dick out, picking up women?

"This isn't fair." Reluctantly he took out his wallet. "Here's five dollars," he said. "Not that you deserve it."

"Go home to your wife." She got out and slammed the door.

At the Holiday Inn, Gary Shepard had given her a special number, her own personal code so he would know it was Rita calling his pager. She remembered the code, but she had lost the piece of paper with his pager number on it. She went inside the gas station and bought some animal crackers and ate them sitting on the curb, protected by an overhang, and tried to remember the number. She knew the prefix, but what was the rest? 5473. 5743. 5347. The first time she dialed it was the wrong one, but the second combination worked, and he called her right back.

"I was looking for you," he said.

She tried to tell him where she was, but as soon as she started talking the crying started, and the words fell apart. This was it. It was all coming up and she was not going to be able to hold it together; she was going to lose it right here and the cops would come and she had no ID and they would put her in jail or take her back to the Tenderloin where the

man with the claw hand was waiting for her; or maybe he
had followed her here and any minute now he was going to
swoop down on her and carry her off. Gary Shepard was on
the other end saying, "It's okay, slow down, tell me where
you are," and she could not get out a single word.

A man in a red windbreaker came out of the food mart car-
rying a Diet Pepsi, a little white dog in a studded collar leashed
to him, and looked at Rita. "Are you all right, honey?" he said.
The dog sniffed at her shoes. It was one of those little snuffly
ones with tight, dirty-white curls all over it.

She shook her head. She wanted to give him the phone,
but her body didn't seem to be obeying her brain.

He came over to her. "Do you need help?"

She shook her head again. No. Meaning, *I am beyond help.*

Then she managed to make her arm move and handed
him the phone and collapsed on the curb. She put her knees
up and her head in her arms and sobbed. The dog tried to
worm its way in to sit on her lap.

"Bippy, stop!" the man said sternly to the dog. "Hello?" he
said, and then he gave Gary Shepard the information he
needed, and hung up the phone.

"He's coming, honey," the man said, and dragged the dog
off to a minivan at one of the pumps and drove off.

5. She sat on the closed toilet lid, the way she always did when her mother took a bath, and talked to her. Her mother's breasts were white and had such big flat nipples. Rita studied them covertly, not wanting to embarrass her mother but fascinated by how huge they were. It was very hot in the bathroom, steam rising from the tub, and the mirror that opened into the medicine chest where her mother kept her pills was misted over and perspiring. Rita began sweating. Then she yelled at her mother for not opening the window above the sink, like her mother always told her to. Her mother sat up in the tub and wept. She was a weeping saint. Blood poured from her hands.

She woke up naked and feverish in Gary Shepard's bed. He wasn't there.

She didn't remember anything after getting into his car at the gas station.

There was no light in the room, but the door was open to another room where a lamp was on. It was quiet. No scratching in the walls, no footsteps or screaming or sudden crashes followed by cursing, no tinkling bell from the birdcage next door. Her pillow was sweaty. She raked her hair back and tried to sit up, but she was too weak. There was a weight on her chest and she was paralyzed. She felt in a panic that something was draining the life out of her body; sweat was coming out of her everywhere. She would lie there growing weaker until she was a shell. She had seen her mother's body pass in an instant from something that had a person in it to a great emptiness. Her mother's soul had gone, and what was left was a thing that immediately began to lose its resemblance to the person Rita had feared and loved.

The bed was king-sized, a comforter on it that she'd pushed away in her sleep.

Gary Shepard came to the door. She couldn't see his face, his body was backlit. He was a huge shadow, a destroying angel coming toward her in the eerie silence.

"How do you feel?" he said.

"Not so good," she said.

He brought her some pills and a glass of water.

"I can't sit up," she said.

She felt his arm behind her shoulders, raising her up enough to swallow the pills and water.

"Do you want a light on?"

"No."

"Just sleep then," he said. "I'll be here."

*

In the morning, the sun came through a window next to the bed and laid a row of perfect rectangles on the braided rug on the floor. The walls were peach-colored. On an old-fashioned oak dresser, a pitcher held a bunch of dried blue flowers. There was a photograph of Gary Shepard next to the flowers, a black-and-white close-up of his face, half-turned away from the camera, his eyes looking off into a blurry distance. An overweight cat wandered in, meowed loudly, and jumped on the end of the bed, then lay down on the pillow next to her. Rita stroked its head and ears and listened to the sounds from the kitchen. She smelled sausages and coffee. The cat made short dissatisfied sounds and finally settled into purring, curled into a circle, its head tucked in.

She went into the bathroom off the bedroom and took a hot shower. Hooks on the back of the door held a red silk kimono, a white terry cloth robe, and a pale blue cotton one that had Marriott stitched on the right breast. She put on the white one. She studied the cosmetics on the counter next to the sink, a mascara wand and purple eye shadow in a round container and two lipsticks and an eyelash curler, a jar of Noxzema, a tube of foundation she desperately wanted to use. She didn't touch any of it. A memory flickered, her mother saying, *Here, honey, I'll show you. Now blot your lips on this. Don't you look pretty. You're pretty as a princess, Rita, you could be in a movie one day.* Rita had spun around in her black velvet dress with the white lace on the sleeves and collar that scratched her a little, wearing her mother's blush and lipstick. *I'm going to be a movie star and live in a big house with you, Mommy, and we'll have a big car, too.* Her mother caught her up and hugged her and she smelled the familiar baby powder and cigarettes and gin scent of her. She wiped a circle on the steamed mirror and looked at herself, at her hateful birthmark and stunned eyes and the discolored skin around her mouth where the bruise hadn't yet healed. She had to stop looking at herself all the time, it was too depressing. She found some toothpaste and squeezed some on her finger and rubbed it on her teeth, then put her mouth to the faucet to rinse.

Gary Shepard set out eggs scrambled with cheese and jalapeño peppers, sausages and sourdough toast and a silver jelly caddy with three jars in it, like a restaurant; Rita ate three pieces of toast so she could taste each kind, blackberry and strawberry and orange. After breakfast they sat on slatted wooden chairs at a round table out on the deck and smoked his cigarettes. There were wind chimes, long silver tubes, clanking together prettily in the breeze. The air smelled clean from all the rain. The backyard was a long narrow rectangle that sloped away down the hill, bordered by an uneven wood fence. The yard was overgrown with weeds. Rita imagined a row of tomato plants (it might be a little too foggy for them here, but she could get the kind that would tolerate that), a couple of rows of corn, zucchini squash, snap peas, artichokes. Rosemary and thyme, and mint so she could make her own mint tea. For flowers, she would put in lots of calla lilies along the side of the yard. They were so pure and nakedly white and fresh. In Golden Gate Park, she sometimes expected to see fairies hovering around them.

"I shouldn't be here," she said.

Gary Shepard had cleared the dishes and was rinsing them at the sink and putting them in the dishwasher. He had on black jeans and no shirt. His back and shoulders were tanned. There was a tuft of dark hair at the small of his back. "Yes, you should," he said over his shoulder.

"Where's your wife?"

"Don't worry about it." He came over and stood behind her chair and she leaned her head back. "Do you want to talk about what happened last night? You said someone was trying to kill you."

She remembered sitting on his couch, crying. She hadn't told him anything else, she was too upset. Every time she'd tried, she started crying again. She was sick of crying. She knew your body was mostly water, and she figured she must have nearly emptied out the reservoir in there by now.

"The man I saw in the Barker," she said. "He saw me, too. I was looking through the crack in the bathroom door and he looked right at me. Then he was hanging around the neighborhood. I saw him in the adult bookstore. And last night he must have seen me at the Bagel Shop or coming out of the bar. He chased me and I ran and got in a guy's car, and if I hadn't I'd probably be dead right now."

"You should have told me earlier that he could ID you."

He was rubbing her shoulders. She felt like a plant being watered. She wanted to relax into the pressure of his hands, to be as simple and brainless as a plant, but her thoughts were taking over. Maybe he saw me at the Bagel Shop and waited outside all that time while I was there and then in the bar. He followed me and Bear. He followed me into the Carl's Jr. because he was tired of waiting. Tired of fooling around with someone who could recognize him as the man who had dragged a woman's dead body out of a closet late at night.

"I'll take care of it," Gary Shepard said. "Don't worry about him anymore."

"Right." She wanted to believe him, because he sounded so sure.

His hands moved to her face, his thumbs lightly passing over her closed eyelids. He slid his palms down under her robe to hold her breasts. She didn't feel desire but she wasn't repulsed, either. His hands were warm and he smelled sharp, like smoke, and he was wearing some cologne she hadn't smelled on him before, light and pleasant. He was above her taking long slow deep breaths and her head was resting back against his belly, where the breathing started and rose up and washed down over her like a wave of fullness and contentment. He led her to the bedroom and pulled off his jeans, and she lay back in the white robe. He opened the drawer in the bedside table for a condom. She watched him unwrap it and put it on. Time to disappear. She closed her eyes. He unbelted her robe, pulling the strip of terry cloth free of its loops and taking her wrists in his hands and raising them above her on the pillow, knotting them loosely together.

"Is this all right?" he said. He moved to kneel over her and she felt his legs pressing against her hipbones on either side. He gently took her tied wrists in his left hand and held them against the pillow. Then he parted her legs and was inside of her, moving slowly, watching her face.

"It's all right," she said, opening her eyes for an instant. A talking doll whose string he'd pulled, giving the answer he wanted. Sometimes, if she blinked her eyes fast, they actually made a little clicking sound, like a doll's eyes would. Jimmy was the only one who had ever noticed that.

She could see how it excited Gary Shepard to do this. He was different than he'd been in the Holiday Inn. Even though he was looking at her, she felt like he didn't see her. Maybe he was getting off on bringing a prostitute home, fucking her in the bed where he slept with his wife. Probably his wife wouldn't let him tie her wrists together. She turned her face aside.

He laid his body down on top of hers. His mouth was close to her ear, talking to her. *Sweet girl,* he was saying. *Sweet baby.*

While he moved inside her and whispered to her in the king-sized bed, Rita looked at a framed poster on the wall that said, The Doors of Eau Claire. There were thirty doors in all. She counted them. Thirty photographs of pretty doors with iron knockers or holiday wreaths, with glowing lamps or stained glass or red brick on each side, doors that looked like they led to churches instead of houses. They were houses she would never see, doors that would never open. She knew that, but Gary Shepard didn't. He was kissing her neck and groaning above her while she tried each door, put her hand on a crystal knob or brass handle and twisted and tugged and pulled as hard as she could, and every one of them was locked up tight.

*

On Saturday morning, Jimmy called in sick to work again. Yesterday, he'd talked to Jorge, one of the dishwashers he was friendly with. But today his boss got on the phone.

"What's going on, James?" Walter said.

"I'm sorry," Jimmy said. "It's my stomach. It's still really bothering me." He could hear the familiar sounds of the Piazza di Spagna's kitchen behind Walter—the rock station on the radio, a clatter of dishes, a tray of glasses being set on the long steel counter—and he longed to be working. But the cops might go there. He imagined again the diners watching as he was dragged away in handcuffs, saw the disappointment on Walter's face.

"We need you here," Walter said. "You know I need to know I can count on you. Especially on a Saturday."

"Yes, sir," Jimmy said. "I'm sure I'll be okay by Tuesday." Sunday was Jimmy's day off, and the restaurant was closed Mondays. "I'm sure I'll be okay by then."

"Make sure you are," Walter said, and hung up.

"Right," Jimmy said to a dead line. He put down the phone and lit a cigarette. He drank some coffee, did some pushups and crunches, and skipped rope. He took an eighth of an ounce of pot he'd gotten from Stan and flushed it down the toilet, Baggie and all.

If Robin had filed a police report, the cops would quickly discover that Jimmy was on probation. They'd get his address from his probation officer. An arrest warrant would be issued. It was all so logical, so inevitable. It was going to happen, because he had done what he'd done, and because guys like him didn't get a break. It had seemed like a break, moving up to waiter, when the Salvadorans and Mexicans he worked with had been there longer and were still stuck in the kitchen or bussing dishes. Stuck there forever, unless they improved their English. It had seemed like a break, but he should have known it was only something to make him relax his guard.

He took a long shower, dressed in clean jeans and a T-shirt, and sat on his couch with his D harp, playing along with Little Walter on "Just Your Fool." He had played with all the greats. All the harp players who were dead and gone or who, one way or another, he would never play with in real life. He felt calm, no longer nervous or panicked. His head was clear. He was as ready as he was going to get.

*

"What about family?" Gary said. "Is there anyone who could help you out?"

"I guess I wouldn't be here if there was, would I?" Rita said. "I mean, in my situation," she said. "Not here this very minute."

They were smoking in bed. He was lying back on the pillows, the ashtray on his bare stomach. Rita had belted herself into the robe again and was sitting cross-legged, facing him. She lifted both arms up to stretch, and the sleeves of the robe slipped down. He saw the red pinprick of a needle mark, in the center of a small mottled bruise in the crook of her left arm.

"Where are your parents?" he said.

"My dad kind of came and went. When I was twelve he went for good. We got a couple postcards from Las Vegas. My mother's dead, killed when I was thirteen." She took a drag and blew smoke rings at the ceiling. "Then Social Services was gonna put me in foster care, so I ran away. But I got beat up, so I came back and bounced around to a few messed up so-called families, and I left the last one when I was seventeen, and I've been here ever since."

Rita delivered this information in a flat voice. Gary couldn't help thinking of how Annie dramatized every little thing that happened to her—some obnoxious Muni passenger who'd made a nasty remark on her way to work could send her into a tirade. For Annie, every slight was a grievous wound, and Gary was supposed to nurse every one of them or he was an insensitive bastard.

"Poor baby," he said.

She made a face. "Oh, please."

"You've had a tough life."

"You should be on a talk show," she said. "You're a regular Montel Williams."

"When did you use last?"

"That day I met you—Wednesday. That afternoon. But that's not going to happen anymore."

"Where did you get the dope?"

"Questions, questions," she said. "Haven't you got enough answers yet?"

"I want to know."

"A guy I know named Marco. He's an asshole, though."

Gary felt jealous, imagining Rita with some scumbag dope dealer named Marco. Some lowlife who gave her drugs and then probably screwed her.

"I'm done with that," she said. "All it does is get in my way."

The phone rang in the kitchen. There were two lines, one in Gary's office for work, and the other for personal calls and Annie's Tarot readings. The machine picked up and Annie's voice said, "Hi, it's Annie and Gary. If you're calling for a reading, please call back on Tuesday or Thursday between eight and eleven. Wait for the long, annoying beep and then leave us a message."

Then Annie's voice again. "Hi, honey. We're at the Doubletree in Santa Monica, on Fourth Street. It's under Kate's name if you want to call, but we probably won't be here. We're going to the beach. It's beautiful here. Hope you're okay. I miss you." She gave the phone number of the hotel and hung up.

Gary looked at Rita, then looked away. "Sorry about that," he said.

"Hey," she said. "No big deal." She got off the bed and went out through the kitchen and onto the deck.

Gary put on his jeans and went outside to stand beside her. He put his arm around her and pulled her toward him. She resisted, then let him hold her.

"I better get going," she said.

"Don't," Gary said. "Stay. Stay here with me this weekend. We'll figure something out." He didn't know what. Maybe he could help her get a place, a place where he could come and see her. Annie wouldn't have to know. Maybe he should leave Annie. His life with her was stale. Boring and middle class and safe. Rita was trembling against him, maybe crying. She needs me, he thought. She needs me and I can take care of her.

She was laughing. "*We'll* figure something out?"

"Just stay with me," Gary said. "Stay. Okay?"

"Got any beer?" she said.

*

Jimmy sat handcuffed in the back of a squad car. He talked to the two cops in the front about where you could get the best burritos. He told them he liked El Toro on Seventeenth and Valencia or Pancho Villa on Sixteenth, which was owned by the same people. One cop said, "Yeah, those are good burritos. El Toro's right by the station, but I like La Cumbre better," and the other cop said, "My wife says I have to stop eating so many burritos." Outside there was bright sunlight on everything, bouncing off the windshields of parked cars, glittering on the bits of broken glass on the sidewalks and the windows of used furniture and clothing stores and cafés, and it hurt Jimmy's eyes so he sank back and looked from one cop to the other, through the glass at the back of the driver's head and through the wire screen at the profile of the second cop.

The driver had been the one who'd showed him the warrant and told him it had emanated from the DV unit. The other one had asked Jimmy, "What did you do, slap your girlfriend? Don't you know that after O.J., nobody gets a pass on this shit anymore?"

"Christ, I'm glad it's not raining again," the driver said. The window was open, his left arm resting on the car door, right hand relaxed on the wheel. Like he was taking his family to the beach.

"Supposed to be more on the way," his partner said. "Hard to believe."

"My sister's getting married day after Thanksgiving," the driver said. "They're going to have it outdoors, on a dock. I think they're nuts. It's bound to rain. Where are you going for turkey?"

"My mother's, in Daly City. I bought her a big flat-screen

TV for her birthday last month, just so I could watch the Lions beat the Bears."

"That's where my money is."

They had stopped talking to Jimmy and he was glad to be forgotten by them. He was lucky they were nice cops and not assholes; they were doing their job, being police officers, and he was doing his job of being taken into custody, being a good suspect—for that's what he was, he reminded himself, not a criminal, not a fuckup—though of course he was, or why would he be here instead of at work, saying, *Hello, I'm James, can I get you something from the bar?* He was going to jail because he wasn't really a waiter, he was someone who hit women. He had hit Robin. Once, a long time ago, he had almost hit Rita, too. She had locked him out of their apartment on Jones Street, and he had kicked in the door and broken the chain lock, and dragged her to the bed, and then he realized what he was doing and stopped and broke down crying. That was one reason he left; he felt he was out of control, that it was somehow Rita's fault, that she made him do things like that.

Mentally Jimmy apologized. *I'm sorry, Rita. It was me and not you, I see that now. I'm sorry, Robin. I am one sorry son of a bitch,* Jimmy said to himself, *and what am I going to do about it?* He didn't know any lawyers. He knew the drill; he'd be provided an attorney. They'd take him down to County Jail #9 for booking. They'd take his property and feed him into the machine that was the criminal justice system just like last time. He didn't want to think any further ahead, to remember what it had been like last time.

He looked out the window. There were all the free people walking around on a Saturday afternoon, oblivious to how lucky they were. Even if they were drunk or napping on the sidewalk. Or trying to sell a lone bunch of crummy flowers to every car that stopped at the light, like that guy on the median strip. That guy was lucky to be walking around on a nice day when the rain had let up, peering into rolled-up windows at drivers who sat stone-faced staring straight ahead or who flicked their eyes at him once and then looked away. The squad car stopped next to the man, and he leaned down, right into the open window, and said, "Hey, I don't need to beg, I sell flowers," like he was affronted, as though the cops had insulted him in some way even though they hadn't said anything. Jimmy avoided his eyes.

Mission Station was the first stop. Jimmy sat around with a couple of other guys, similarly cuffed, on a stainless steel bench, ignored by everyone else, exchanging a few words with his fellow suspects. One was a boy in wire-rimmed glasses with black skin, mottled with pinkish-white patches, who kept talking about how his mother was going to kill him. "I mean it, man," he said. "My mama, she crazy. She say she goin' to shoot me. She a crackhead, she got no idea what she doin' anymore. I'm better off here where she can't get to me." A cop came and took Jimmy to a desk and filled out some paperwork. A police van arrived, and Jimmy and the black kid and a couple of guys who were busy talking to each other in Spanish were led into it. There were two long padded benches, one on either side of the van. Jimmy sat next to the black kid, facing the other two prisoners.

"Hey, I hear they got Stairmasters at that new jail," one of them said. "You think that's true?" he asked Jimmy. "That new jail's supposed to be tits, man. I hope we get to go there."

"I don't know," Jimmy said. The new jail was supposedly a lot better than the one at 850 Bryant, where he'd been held last time before being sent to San Bruno. Who cared if they had a Stairmaster. He took slow deep breaths. He kept getting jostled into the kid next to him by the motion of the van. There were no windows in back, and he tried to see through the screen up front past the cop driving and through the windshield, but he couldn't tell what street they were on now. Not that it mattered anymore; they were in the machine. It was going to grind them up to nothing or else spit them out, and there was nothing they could do about any of it but wait.

Breathe and wait. I'm a waiter. He couldn't help laughing aloud.

"What's so funny," the guy who had spoken to Jimmy said. He had a girl's mouth, soft and full. His left eye had a clot of red in the white part.

"Nothing," Jimmy said.

"You think I'm funny?" the guy said aggressively and then laughed. "Hey, man, did you ever see that movie, the one where the Mafia guy goes, 'Do you think I'm funny?'— and he scares the shit out of everybody? Then later he shoots at this dude's feet and makes him dance. I think he fucking kills him, I can't remember. That was a funny movie."

"No," Jimmy said, and nobody said anything the rest of the way.

✱

By late in the afternoon the sky had changed again, after filling with dark clouds that looked like they were going to dump more rain. Now it was sunny once more. Rita closed the blinds of Gary Shepard's living room window and looked over the books lining the shelves. Gary had gone out. He'd told her to stay put, not to answer the phone—as if she ever would— and that he'd be back by dinnertime. He had kissed her good-bye on the forehead, holding both her hands in his.

Who's Who in Nazi Germany, she read. Another one called

Inside the Third Reich. They seemed to have a lot of information on Nazis. Also books with *blood* in their titles: *Bloodletters and Badmen. In Cold Blood. Wise Blood.* There were a number of big oversized books of photographs; she pulled a few down and passed some time studying them. One she especially liked was by a woman who took a lot of pictures of her kids. The kids were nude in several of the pictures. There were some that made Rita uncomfortable—a shot of one of the little girls posing next to a dead deer on the tailgate of a truck, or the boy, injured, with a close-up of his stitches. But in several they glowed like angels who had fallen starlike to earth and been caught standing in the reedy grass by a pond, or floating on their backs in the water, or sprawled stomach-down on a front porch playing a board game. Looking at them was like having a gorgeous dream. Maybe someday she and Jimmy could have children as beautiful as that. After she had flipped through a couple of other books, she liked the first one even better; the others were full of ugliness, retarded people playing dress-up and junkies getting off and whores sprawling on beds in dingy rooms, the kind of thing she had seen plenty of and didn't want to have to look at anymore.

When she got restless she went to the kitchen and opened another beer and wandered around the house. Gary Shepard's office had a computer and more books and a weird sculpture on the wall, a gigantic blue-green shape that looked kind of like the torso of a pregnant woman. On his desk, there was a picture of him and a woman who must be his wife, standing close together on a little arched bridge and squinting into bright sun. Annie Shepard was dark haired and pretty, wearing a long yellow dress with pale blue roses on it. Rita found the dress in the bedroom closet, on a padded hanger. There were lots of dresses and soft blouses and two leather jackets, one tan and one black, and three shelves crammed with shoes. Rita tried on the dress. It was too long and loose for her, but at least she liked how she looked in the full-length mirror on the back of the closet door.

She went downstairs and discovered the darkroom in the basement and looked at some pictures clothespinned to a line stretched across one corner. There was an unpleasant chemical smell in the darkroom, so she didn't take time to look at them all closely. Two were of Gary Shepard: In one, he was lounging on the couch with his arms over his head, gazing seriously into the camera, and in the other, he lay on his back on the floor with his hands folded on his bare chest, flower petals scattered over him, two petals covering his eyes. That one gave her the creeps. She hurried back upstairs, lifting the dress so it wouldn't get dirty.

She took one of the cigarettes from the pack he'd left on the kitchen table and walked to the living room window again, wishing for her own Marlboro Lights. She wanted to go out to a store and buy some, but she didn't know how far away the store was and she didn't have a key to get back into the house. She peeked through the slats at the small neat yard where a set of pink plastic flamingoes, one large one flanked by three smaller ones, were staked in the ground. A little boy stood straddling a scooter in the driveway across the cul-de-sac, then pushed off and rode away. In the other driveway a tall woman in shorts and a halter top hosed down a car. It made Rita want to be outside, running under a sprinkler. Naked like the children in the photography book, young enough that it didn't matter. You could just run, feeling the air and heat and then the cold shock of the water on your skin, making you shiver, and your hair hung down your back and stuck to it but you hardly felt it, you were running through the water again and laughing and the soft slick blades of grass stuck to your feet.

She returned to the kitchen. A wooden puppet, a peasant woman in a green dress with long flowing black hair, hung from the ceiling beside a wooden spice rack of small clear bottles. On the counter next to the refrigerator was a wrought-iron wine rack, half-full. It made her think of Terrance with his cupboards of wine and gin and vodka. *Never run dry* had been Terrance's main motto. *You do not fucking know me* was another and *Fuck this shit* was yet one more.

Stuck to the refrigerator with a magnet in the shape of a miniature coffeemaker was a photo of Gary Shepard and his wife at a restaurant, both of them dressed up, champagne glasses in their hands, their faces red and shiny. Smaller magnets with words on them were all over the refrigerator, some of them pushed together.

open desire

celebrate change

smoke your fool life out

steaming heart animal

She made *voices needle stars* and *water dance.* She opened the freezer door and found a quart of Skyy Vodka lying on its side on the shelf in the door, mixed it with some Snapple Diet Lemonade, then settled on the couch in the living room and turned on the TV.

*

Gary got back around eight with two Safeway bags of groceries. Rita was asleep, curled on the couch under a brown and white afghan Annie's mother had made. The TV was on.

He put the bags on the kitchen counter, then sat on the coffee table and watched her sleep. Even in sleep she didn't look relaxed. Her face jerked slightly, her mouth moved like she was trying to form words. He thought of what he'd said to her earlier: *I'll take care of it.* Like he could protect her. The show *Cops* was on the TV behind him; someone was going on and on about their cow being shot. Then a Microsoft commercial. He took the remote from the floor and clicked the TV off. Rita's drink was next to the remote, half-empty, and he picked it up and drank the rest.

A few hours earlier he had been looking at photographs of a fifteen-year-old black girl with colorful beads in her braids, wearing jeans with a flower embroidered on one knee, part of her head blown away. A new case, one more thing he couldn't talk to Annie about. What would Annie say, how would she explain that girl's body with her Tarot card wisdom? That bullshit couldn't help her. But neither could he. He held Rita's glass in his hands, wanting to throw it across the room, to hear the satisfying smash it would make against the wall. He wanted to wake Rita and shake her. Tell her to get her life together, to lay off the drugs and drinking and get a job, any job that didn't involve prostitution.

He thought of the money he'd given her that day at Miz Brown's and then at the Holiday Inn, saw himself handing it to her, saw other men like himself reaching for their wallets, flipping them open, taking out a few bills they'd gotten from the ATM for this purpose—married men, lonely men, predatory men who were attracted to a small girl with creamy skin and intense blue eyes, men who wanted to touch her breasts and feel her small hipbones in their hands as they positioned her body beneath them.

He got up abruptly and went back to the kitchen to unload the food.

*

Processing. Ink roller sliding across your fingertips. Standing in front of a piece of white cardboard for your mug shot. Front view, side view, step down. Medical screening. The cell, a bunch of guys who stank, a steel toilet that stank more. Noise and drunk men and sick men and eyes that challenged you or studied you or slid away. Three phone calls. One to Chumley, one to Stan, one to Chelsea, the bartender at Piazza di Spagna. Just in case anyone knew a lawyer. Chelsea said she might know a friend of a friend, and Jimmy said, "Please don't tell Walter." Chelsea had said in a surprised voice, "What are you doing in jail?" and Jimmy had felt ashamed. "You don't belong in jail," Chelsea had said, and he was grateful that someone who knew him, even as little as she knew him, would think that. All day he said to himself, *You don't belong here.* By nighttime, he almost believed it, but he wasn't sure anyone else would.

*

Gary Shepard had barbequed steaks. There were thin-sliced potatoes, and a salad with orange flower petals in it that he assured Rita were okay to eat—she loved that, eating flowers—and a bottle of red wine. There were two very long, cream-colored candles in holders that had fish etched into them, swimming around the base and up through wavy lines of water; a slim vase that matched the candle holders was on the table, too, with more flowers—star-lilies—that Gary had bought. She poured them wine while he opened a cigar box on the table and took out a carved stone pipe and Baggie of pot. He loaded the pipe and they passed it back and forth. Sometimes in the summers, before her father had left, he would grill out on the cement patio of the house in Reno. Charred meat and smoke. When her mother died, Rita had tried to find him, calling Las Vegas Information long-distance, but none of the John Jacksons or J. Jacksons she found turned out to be him. He hadn't come to the funeral. She had held that against him, even though she realized he probably didn't even know about it.

Over dinner, Gary Shepard told Rita stories, like the one about the cops passing off a copy machine as a lie detector, and described what it was like at the courts and how the dyke DA's and PD's wore men's suits and suspenders. He talked about the wine they were drinking and how you could go up north of San Francisco and drive around to the wineries.

"Maybe we can go there sometime," he said. "We could rent bicycles, and ride between the wineries. We'd have a great time."

"Bicycles," Rita said. What was all this *we* shit about? There was no *we*. The only *we* was her and Jimmy.

"Or, we could just drive around," he said.

"What would be the point of that exactly?"

"Wine-tasting."

"We're tasting some right now."

"Do you like this wine?"

She shrugged. "Sure," she said. She liked vodka better, but whatever. "It's fine," she said.

He refilled the pipe and they smoked some more and she started to relax a bit. She felt good and warm and stoned; every so often she would look at the dark corners of the kitchen, where the candlelight didn't quite go, and feel afraid, and turn back to Gary Shepard's reassuring face smiling at her and his big body that would protect her from whatever was trying to gather itself together in the corners and become real. She nodded and smiled and listened, enjoying how funny he was even about stuff she knew wasn't funny, like the junkie couple named Mabel and Abel—well, that part was funny— who lost their kid after a dependency hearing.

"Mabel ended up hooking along the Capp Street corridor, a bad place for anybody to end up but especially a white girl. When a white girl lands there, death is knocking on her door," he said, but somehow made it sound like a joke; and Rita laughed imagining Death, a frail skeleton with a sickle in its hand, knocking on the door of messed-up Mabel with her herpes and gonorrhea and her lost children, Mabel who weighed over two hundred pounds, which was really funny since now she had started shooting speed, and nobody could be fat doing that.

But when she stopped laughing she thought about where a white girl could end up and she saw herself with Death standing over her, huge and black and hairy, smiling and showing his fangs, ready to tear her apart.

They finished the wine and started on a second bottle. Blues played on the stereo in the living room. It began raining again, and the wet smell of the air came in the open door from the deck, and she went out into it and lifted her face up, tasting the small needling drops on her tongue, her eyes closed, and said aloud, "This is the life, man, this is the utter life."

Then she thought of Jimmy and pretended she could turn around and look into the kitchen where the candles flickered and beyond them to the living room where the music was playing, and she would see Jimmy sitting back on the couch, playing his harmonica along with the stereo, wearing a dark gray T-shirt with a bleach stain on one sleeve. He would look up at her and she would tell him, *That was beautiful Jimmy, I love your music.* He would pretend it didn't mean anything that she said it, but she knew he needed more than anything to hear it and so she said again, "I love your music."

And Gary Shepard answered, "I'm glad you like it, this is Paul Butterfield, have you ever heard of him?"

"Well, yeah," she said. "Don't you think I know anything?"

"He played in the sixties and seventies. A lot of people your age probably don't know who he was. It's cool that you do."

"Okay then," she said. "Glad we got that straight."

And Jimmy looked at her from the couch and said, *I guess you don't want me anymore now you've got your new man with his nice house and candle holders and Paul Butterfield playing, well good-bye, wife, the hell with you anyway.* She stared out at all the nails of rain rushing angrily down to stab the grass and earth.

"Come inside," Gary Shepard said.

She turned, and Jimmy had gotten up from the couch and walked out, slamming the door.

*

It was impossible to sleep soundly with the jail smells of alcohol and body odor and anxiety, and guys snoring worse than Jimmy's old man used to, which was pretty bad, and a few late-night poker players slapping down cards and calling games like Three-Toed Pete and Low Spade in the Hole; Jimmy drifted in and out of waking. He was back in San Bruno, writing letters to Rita that he'd never mail, telling her about what it was like inside. He had mailed one, actually, to their old hotel, but if she got it she never wrote him back.

Dear Rita,

Maybe your surprised to hear from me. Let me explain what has happened and then I hope you can forgive me. You probably thought I was an asshole not to come back to our hotel but I got picked up by the cops with Chumley and now I am in jail in San Bruno. Every day I kick myself for being so stupid. Sometimes I can't get out of my own way, this was one of those times. I hope you get this and can come see me and still want to because I miss you like crazy, girl. No matter what has come between us I always hold you in my heart and think of you. You are beautiful and my love for you is forever.

Rita, here is what I was thinking about today, remember that time we went to the beach and some girl talked to us about the bird holding the scarf in its mouth flying over the mountain and wearing it down, talking about reencarnation or something? That's what the days are like here. It seems endless like I'll never get out. I remember those canned mageritas we drank, pretty good for store bought. Also I thought about that blue piece of fabric you hung over the bars on our hotel room window. I guess I think about it because that was the last place I saw you and what I remember isn't the bad, but the true things between us and I know you were trying to make it nice where ever we were, I guess it didn't really hit me till now. This place gives you a lot of time to think.

Anyways, Rita, I hope you get this and can write me back and come see me soon.

Loving you big time for all time,
Jimmy

In the dream, he kept getting interrupted and having to begin each letter over because he wanted to get every word right. He pressed the pen into the paper and tore it. There was a clock on the wall of his cell, and he started pulling out the bullets that were glued around it in a circle, putting them in his pockets in case he needed them. They got heavier and heavier, and he fell to his knees and crawled around, then had to lie down and curl up to catch his breath. They were playing Low Spade in the Hole. He had the two of spades and was going to win a shitload of cigarettes but he was betting bullets, not cigarettes, and a guard was dropping the bullets one by one into a manila envelope with his name on it. He took the envelope and put it in the closet of his apartment, next to the square cardboard box with his mother's ashes. On top of the box was a smaller box, a hard box with a black velvet shell. His wedding ring was inside, like a corpse in a coffin. He picked up the ring and was about to slip it back on his finger, but Stan was there and he was afraid Stan would take it and melt it down, so he threw it out the window where it broke into a million pieces on the street like mercury in a thermometer, little gold squiggles running off in all directions.

Then it was Sunday morning, and he was still locked up. A few guys' names were called, but not many, and everyone settled in for another day inside the machine and tried to ignore the grinding that sounded exactly like mechanical jaws working, or maybe it was their own jaws, their teeth scraping over each other, wearing themselves down.

*

In the house in Reno, before Rita's father left, there were always donuts on Sundays. By the time Rita got up (but not her mother—she slept late and then stayed in her room and watched TV), the flat, white rectangular box was on the kitchen table and her father had gone to work selling for Golden West Photography. He worked evenings and Sundays when people were likely to be home (he never went to the welfare families in the projects like some of the less scrupulous salesmen); once he sold the coupons for ninety-nine cents or $2.99 or even $4.99, depending on the neighborhood, the photographers would come through with their lights and portable backdrops. The young couple or their baby or the whole family would sit in front of the swirled gray paper rolled down behind them and smile, saying *cheeeese*. When the slides were done the proof-passers would come back with the slides and try to shame or browbeat them into buying thirty or a hundred dollars worth of photographs in all sizes. Sometimes Rita's father would take the pictures, if the regular photographer was sick, and sometimes he would work as a proof-passer, too, but he wasn't sleazy enough (he explained to Rita) to try to get money from the ones who clearly couldn't afford it.

He took pictures of Rita, and she sat still under the lights with her back very straight and kept her mouth closed because she didn't like her teeth. She had been riding her bike standing up and peddling with Claire sitting on the seat; when they hit a bump she fell forward and chipped a front tooth on the handlebars. Her mother had filed it too far down, right to the root, and the nerve throbbed and she was in terrible pain until finally Claire's mother took her to have it pulled, and the new one didn't grow in for a long time. Her father would coax her and try to make her laugh but in all the pictures she only smiled with her mouth closed, a tight, strained smile; she always looked worried.

Somehow her father was always disappointed in her. She tried to smile for him and to keep the house clean and make sure her mother took her pills on time and the right ones and not too many, but still her father when he was home would sigh and look around with a sad expression before saying, *I have to go out, I can't stay here,* and leave for the bar to drink with his friends. Late Saturday night after the bar closed, he would stop at the all-night donut shop and bring home the glazed and chocolate and white-powdered donuts that would be there sweet and fresh the next morning; she could have as many of whatever kind she wanted and get a big glass of milk if there was milk, then head to Claire's and go with her family to the ten o'clock Mass at Our Lady of Sorrows. Rita liked Sunday mornings because she remembered being happy then, and she disliked them, too, because after her father left, there were no more donuts on Sundays, and then she and her mother moved to San Jose, away from Claire and her family, and there was no more church, either.

Gary Shepard was making omelets. The radio was on—a woman singing with a guitar, her voice high and nasal. She was followed by a skit about some cowboys named Dusty and Curly talking about not wanting to be cowboys anymore. Rita went out to the deck for a smoke. Gary Shepard had gone out earlier and brought her back two packs. The tangled vegetation of the backyard was wet from the previous night's rain, and the sky was an ugly gray, promising more; the sky was full of bad promises. The leaves of bushes along the edge of the fence shook in the wind. The topmost branches of a giant Monterey pine in the next yard nodded back and forth in a way that seemed friendly one minute and ominous the next.

Gary Shepard whistled in the kitchen while the radio went on with another drama, about a detective named Guy Noir. The smell of eggs and herbs came to her on little gusts of wind. She was barefoot in the blue Marriott robe. She shifted from foot to foot on the damp cold boards of the deck, staring at the sky and willing the dull clouds to part, willing a face to be there the way it had been once, a stern but somehow kind face looking down, seeing her shivering below, here on the sorrowful earth. Where are you. You were there when I was little, where are you now? I feel you sometimes but I need to see you. It's Sunday, so I might as well pray.

She heard a woman's voice behind her and turned. She recognized Annie Shepard from the photographs. Her hair was longer than in any of the pictures; it fell past her shoulders, thin and straight and nearly black. She was taller than Rita had imagined, standing at the entrance to the kitchen, wearing jeans and a red sweater the color of old blood. Dried blood on a sheet or on somebody's sleeve after shooting up. Rust-colored. Evidence of something that had happened. Annie looked at Rita uncomprehendingly.

"Who are *you?*" Annie said. "Gary—?" She wasn't getting the situation yet. Rita watched her face move from confusion into the glimmerings of what might be happening, watched her suddenly hit on what she was looking at here.

Rita pulled the robe tighter around her and pressed back against the deck railing. There were no stairs from the deck to the yard, no way out except through the kitchen. She stayed where she was.

"What—" Annie said. "I don't believe what I'm seeing," she said.

"Annie," Gary Shepard said. He was standing by the stove, holding the spatula aloft. His voice was flat, like he was saying her name for the first time, like someone who was learning to read but couldn't yet connect the letters on the page to the words he knew.

Rita waited for him to say, *I can explain everything,* the way men did on TV when this kind of thing happened. But he didn't say anything else. He moved toward Annie, knocking into the handle of the skillet on the stove. The skillet slid off the burner and bounced on the floor, splashing out some of the omelet. Rita watched its motion as it rocked around on its circumference, settling gradually, like a hubcap that had rolled loose. He stood in front of his wife while she hit him. He held the spatula, dripping with egg, up over one shoulder—like he was either keeping it from her reach or keeping it handy as a weapon.

Rita watched her register the flowers on the table, the bottles of wine from last night still sitting there. "No, no," Annie said, her voice changing. "No, no, no. I'm not seeing this." She put her hand over her eyes, still blindly hitting him with one fist, crying and leaning into him at the same time she was pushing him away.

Gary Shepard stood silent, his head down. Rita crouched down on the deck. She was still holding her cigarette. She dragged the burning tip against the side of the railing to put it out, and dropped it over the edge into the bushes. Annie Shepard was screaming again, telling her husband how much she hated him. It was a TV show, it wasn't happening. It wasn't happening even when Annie started toward Rita, screaming, "Get out of my house, get out get out get out." And Rita went quickly past her and Gary Shepard followed, as Annie drove them both to the front door. Then Rita and Gary Shepard were outside on the front stoop, and he had turned and was pushing against the door that Annie was trying to close from inside the house.

"I have to get my car keys," he said. It was the only thing he'd said the whole time.

"Fuck you!" was Annie's response. "Who *are* you! I hate you. I hate you. I fucking hate you."

He managed to shove the door open and went in, leaving it ajar. Rita sat down on the steps. She stared at the plastic flamingo babies grouped around their mother, the family pink and red and delicately balanced on one leg. The cat streaked out the open door and across the yard. Rita was amazed it could run that fast, it was so fat. Its loose flesh went swinging side to side beneath it as it ran. Inside the house Gary Shepard and his wife were talking—that is, he was talking and she was yelling. Something heavy crashed against a wall. They went on and on. Rita wanted to get up and leave, but she sat there, numb. She wasn't here. It wasn't happening.

Finally, he came out. "Get in the car," he said.

"Yeah, get in the car!" Annie yelled behind him. "Get in the fucking car and get out of my life. You goddamned son of a bitch." She'd stopped crying. Her dark eyes were ringed with black, from eyeliner or mascara, and her hair hung limp in her face, and she was pulling at the right sleeve of her sweater with her left hand, grabbing the fabric and letting go.

"How could you do this," she said. "How could you do this to me? To *us*."

Rita felt her own invisibility, her nonexistence.

"What is *wrong* with you?" Annie said to her husband.

Annie stood in the doorway while they went to the car. Gary Shepard got in the driver's side and leaned across the passenger seat to unlock the door for Rita. It seemed to take a long time; she stood there with her back burning, feeling his wife's eyes on her now that she didn't have to look at Rita's face, didn't have to acknowledge her as an actual person. Annie didn't say anything else, just stood there breathing hard. Rita got in and hunched down in her seat and looked at a wrinkled Starbucks napkin on the floor as he backed the car out of the driveway. She didn't want to be driving off with Gary Shepard, wearing nothing but his wife's bathrobe, but getting her own clothes didn't appear to be an option right now.

There was a little *ping* on the windshield, and Rita thought at first Annie that must have thrown a rock at them, but as they turned and headed down the street she realized it must have been Annie's wedding ring.

✳

Gary Shepard drove to a Kwik & Convenient store. While he was inside, Rita watched the wind push plastic drink lids and candy wrappers around the parking lot. He came back out just as the rain—would it ever stop?—began in earnest. He got in the car, opened a pack of Camel Lights for himself, and passed a pack of Marlboro Lights to her. They sat in the car smoking, and she looked through the blur of the rain at the store signs, like they meant something more than they did. Super Lotto. Budweiser. Fresh Coffee. Check Cashing. Copies 5 Cents. He smoked two cigarettes in a row before starting the car. She cracked the window to let out the smoke. The chill and the rain slipped in.

"Where are we going?" she asked after a few minutes.

He didn't answer. She settled back while the streets floated past. Few people were out, and the ones who were moved quickly, hunched against the weather.

"C'mere," he said, reaching his arm across the seat.

She slid toward him. She didn't want to be held. But more than that, she didn't want to be outside, dealing with the rain. She put her head on his shoulder. He held her so tightly she almost couldn't breathe. The windshield wipers swept back and forth, going nowhere.

I'm never going to find you, Jimmy, am I? The wipers went *yes-no, yes-no, yes-no.*

Rita sat up straighter. She felt a rising panic, trapped next to Gary Shepard, the rain coming down. She had to stay with him. She couldn't go back to the Barker. She didn't want to go back to the Tenderloin ever again. She hated the familiar streets, the bars and liquor stores and the few spindly trees that managed to grow where one small square of sidewalk had been taken out, and the shitty hotels with the signs saying All Rooms Must Be Paid In Advance—No Exceptions, and Not Responsible for Personal Property, the people passing through them like ragged stinking ghosts. She hated all of them. She hated being one of them. And somewhere among them was a man who likely wanted to kill her. Gary Shepard was her only ticket right now. So wherever the bus was going, she had better stay on it.

He was parking the car. He'd driven them out to the Sunset, to a hotel—not a Tenderloin hotel, at least, but not a nice one either, not like the Holiday Inn. She pulled the robe more tightly around her as they entered the lobby, feeling ashamed to be out in public without any clothes, even here where nobody was paying any attention; two old men sat in matching green armchairs in front of a TV and didn't even glance their way. Gary Shepard paid and the tiny Hispanic-looking woman behind the counter led them upstairs, along a hall that had a carpet of huge threadbare roses, to a room she unlocked for them before handing over the key. The woman was so skinny she was skeletal, her legs and arms like sticks, like a starving woman Rita had seen in a newspaper photo. Her black hair was pulled back tight. She was a grinning skull, looking at them.

"Have a nice day," she said.

Rita followed Gary Shepard into the room and sat on the bed. It had a thin green blanket, a pillow without a pillowcase. There was a chest of drawers, painted white, with a big smiley face sticker on the bottom drawer. A brown plastic water pitcher sat on top of the dresser next to a Wisk detergent box. A TV was bolted to the wall in one corner, a remote connected to it by a dangling cord so you could use it to control the TV, but not walk off with either one. Next to a sink, a square mirror leaned against the wall below where it had once hung—Rita could see the nail hole in a little crater of white plaster.

"I'm sorry it isn't nicer," he said. "This is the best I can do right now. The credit cards are in Annie's name, except for one, and that's maxed out. She's probably already called to take me off the accounts."

"Okay," she said. It was a room, anyway.

Gary Shepard seemed to feel the need to explain himself. "I just took out a couple hundred bucks at the convenience store. That's about all that was in the checking account."

"Do you have a savings account?" she said. How could someone like Gary Shepard not have any money? He had a nice car, a house, a good job. He was one of the normal people, the people who had it all figured out.

"In Annie's name, too. I've never been able to save a dime."

"That makes two of us. So this is it. Well, it'll do."

"It's only for a couple of nights. I can get paid on Wednesday, before Thanksgiving. Or I'll borrow some dough. I'm sorry, Rita." He came over to sit next to her on the bed. "This is a hell of a way to start."

But we're not starting anything. She let him put his arm around her, and felt immediately claustrophobic. "What's in the bag?" she said, sliding away from him.

He'd bought some things at the Kwik & Convenient. She reached for the bag. Six-pack of Beck's, church key, a couple of cellophane-wrapped sandwiches. Also a pint of Jack Daniel's. She popped open two beers. "What are you going to do?" she said.

"I don't know. Things weren't working between me and Annie."

"And what exactly were you doing about it?"

"Things were just wrong." He looked toward the nail hole on the wall, like the wrong things between him and his wife were going to materialize there.

They drank their beers down quickly and he opened two more. Rita was starting to feel better, letting the alcohol round out the edges. The rain was loud outside, sounding like it was falling into an empty pail just beyond the one window. The glare of the overhead bulb was softened by a white paper shade, decorated with a drawing of green bamboo, that someone had left.

"You have to do something," she told him.

"What?"

"What we were talking about before. You and your wife. You can't just sit back. You have to work things out. Plus it's almost Thanksgiving." Then she felt foolish, giving him advice. What do I know about it? Well, I tried. With Jimmy. I still want to try. It's not me who walked away from things.

But then she wasn't sure that was true.

"Maybe I don't want to work things out," he said. "Maybe I just married the wrong person."

"Well, you must've married her for a reason."

"Probably the wrong reason."

"Til death do us part," she said. "You made a commitment."

"I don't want to talk about it."

"Fine, don't."

"Fine. I won't."

She opened a third beer and lit a cigarette. Gary Shepard had been smoking steadily the whole time, ever since the Kwik & Convenient. She wondered if he was feeling sick. *I would*, she thought. They could start on the Jack Daniel's next. She hoped he could get enough money to keep them both drunk for a while.

＊

She couldn't sleep. They'd finished all the alcohol Gary Shepard had bought. He'd gone out and gotten some more, and they watched the TV, which only got a handful of fuzzy channels, and passed out. She got up and turned it off, then lay curled away from Gary Shepard, who was snoring. Every so often she gave him a little push, so that he mumbled and turned over on his side and quieted, but soon he would flop onto his back again, his mouth open, and let loose a steady series of clogged, noisy breaths. He lay there like a huge fallen animal. She didn't know him at all. The loneliness inside her was a hole she kept trying to climb out of, but she was falling further in.

There doesn't seem to be any place for me in this world.

She saw herself gone from it. Not in a cheap hotel bed lying beside some stranger, not walking through the streets being looked at by other strangers who wanted to take something from her, something they thought she had. Not anywhere in the world. Subtracted from it. Gone in a puff of smoke, it's magic, ladies and gentlemen, she's disappeared. What difference would it make? If Jimmy still loved her he would have found her by now. He had probably moved on and found some other girl to love. A girl who grew up normal, with a father who worked in an office and a mother who packed her lunches for school. That girl had finished high school, instead of running off just before graduation, and she never lashed out hitting and kicking when she and Jimmy were making love, thinking for a minute he was someone else and trying to fight him off. That girl never had to get high sometimes just to make it through her day.

She lay with her eyes open in the dark. She could see in the dark like a cat. She could see the dim bulk of the dresser and the door with a little crack of weak light at the bottom of it and the balled cellophane from the sandwiches they'd eaten and the empty Jack Daniel's bottle lying on its side. She could see Annie Shepard, standing in the front yard while they drove away. Gary Shepard didn't seem to want to go back to her, this wife he had vowed to cherish. People were disposable. You could use them up and throw them away. Annie's robe lay next to the bed, a rumpled cast-off shadow.

Now I don't have anything—no clothes, no ID, nothing. Gone, vanished, dead, who would care? Nobody. No body. She was saying it to herself, over and over, in the empty spaces between Gary Shepard's labored breaths.

6. When she woke up, she saw that Gary Shepard had brought hot tea in a Syrofoam cup for her, and some clothing—a long dress made of patches of different-colored velvet, like a hippie outfit, and some flat back slippers, the kind you could find all over Chinatown. He'd cleaned up the mess and folded Annie Shepard's robe on a corner of the bed.

Rita turned her back to him and dressed. "How do I look? Stupid, I bet."

"You look fantastic," he said.

She reached for the tea he'd set on the night table. "Right," she said. "I look like the Summer of Love." She hadn't fallen asleep until nearly dawn, weak light sifting in through the rusted wire mesh and thin curtains over the window, and she was groggy and hung over. The warmth and caffeine of the tea cleared her head a little. She breathed in the steam from the cup.

"C'mere," he said, reaching to take her tea from her.

"Can I just drink this in peace?" she said. "Jesus."

"Sorry. I thought maybe—"

Last night she had let him. He had woken from his god-awful snoring, gone to pee in the sink, come back to bed, and reached for her. They were drunk, she was tired, he was crying. Those were good enough reasons last night, but this morning those reasons had vanished. "No," she said.

He was unshaven, his eyes rimmed red. Some kind of rash

had broken out on his face and neck. He looked like something had run him over and then backed up over him again to make sure. He slid his palm over his face, down his chin, and went to the sink to wash. "Want some breakfast?"

"I want a Bloody Mary."

"That's exactly the breakfast I had in mind. I know a place near the Hall. Then we can go over and look through some photographs." He splashed water on his face, ran his hand through his hair, lifted up the front of his T-shirt and used it to dry himself. "I've got a friend in General Works who'll let us take a look through her books."

"Like on TV, you mean?"

"This guy who's after you—if he has a record, maybe we'll get lucky. We'll see if he has a name."

"Oh, he has a name," Rita said. He was the Bogeyman. He was coming for her. She could feel him looking, searching the streets and alleys, going into hotel lobbies and creeping up the stairs, quietly prying open locked doors as she drank her tea down, trying with its heat to flush out the cold knowledge of him.

*

It was Monday. On the outside, people were getting dressed, the radio or TV on for company. Women were putting on makeup, leaning over the bathroom sink to get closer to the mirror. Men brushed their teeth in the shower and stepped out into the steam, onto soft rugs. Jimmy could see them behind his closed lids—the straights, the suits, looking forward to their day, thinking about their careers and their stock investments. He hated them. Right now he wished he were one of them, living on, say, the twenty-seventh floor of some highrise. Twenty floors higher, that is, than the seventh floor of 850 Bryant. He might as well wish he were on Mars with that machine NASA had just sent there to roll around and collect space rocks. Reluctantly he opened his eyes, and immediately had to avoid making eye contact with a dwarf-sized skinhead, the only other white guy in the cell, who was staring at him fixedly with an expression of malice on his acne-pitted face.

He was in C block. C-3, to be exact, with six other guys. No one was discussing their stock holdings. Somebody was coughing blood into the toilet. Two of his cellmates were involved in a disagreement over culinary matters.

"You get a relish tray with dinner at that restaurant," one said.

"No way, you don't get a relish tray."

"Yeah, you do. The whole ball of wax."

"Well, I never got a relish tray."

"You gotta ask for the whole meal. 'Full course,' you gotta say."

"I tell you, they don't have a relish tray."

"Fuck you, you don't know anything."

"Fuck you."

"Fuck you, too."

Jimmy drifted back to sleep. When he woke up again his skin was crawling. His arms itched terribly. He crossed them and scratched surreptitiously. He sat up and stared at his orange canvas shoes. Everybody was in orange sweats, like some kind of team.

"Man, this sucks," somebody said, echoing everyone's sentiment.

"It ain't as bad as Ad Seg," somebody else said.

"What's Adds Egg?"

"You're kidding. You never heard of Ad Seg? Administrative Segregation. They're locked down twenty-three hours of every day. Only get out for about twenty minutes, and usually everybody heads for the phone. It's a bitch, man. I wouldn't want to be there."

"Well, I don't want to be here. I want to be at home with my old lady, putting my feet up on the coffee table and having myself a beer."

Jimmy longed for the six-pack in the fridge in his apartment. And for the space and privacy of his one room, where the walls were thin but you could put on music and mostly ignore the other lives around you, the cooking smells and kids yelling and toilets flushing on all sides. Now his private space had shrunk to a few inches around his body; he would have to try and protect that. Maybe they'd let him go home soon. Maybe at the arraignment the DA's office would dismiss the whole thing and offer him an apology for keeping such an upstanding citizen locked up with the lowlifes and scumbags. *Mr. James D'Angelo*, the judge would say—*am I pronouncing that right, sir? Mr. D'Angelo, the court wishes to offer you its sincere apologies for any inconvenience you might have experienced. Please accept our best wishes for a happy and productive rest of your life as a law-abiding member of society. Now get the fuck out of here and don't darken our door again.*

*

A few floors down from C block, Rita was looking through booking photos in a cubicle in the General Works Bureau. She was pleasantly buzzed; she'd had two Bloody Marys. Gary Shepard had drunk three, at a bar decorated for Thanksgiving with a plastic turkey dangling above the cash register and a couple of black cardboard Pilgrim hats tacked to the wall above the booth they sat in. The two men at the bar were also drinking their breakfast.

"They're defense attorneys," Gary Shepard had said. "This is a popular spot for lawyers. Off-duty cops, too." The bartender comped their first two Bloody Marys, and when Gary Shepard tried to pay for his third the bartender waved him away. "Forget it, Shepard," she said, and Rita thought she seemed a little drunk, too. It made for a festive atmosphere at that hour of the morning.

"Any luck?" he said, looking over Rita's shoulder.

"Don't you think I'd tell you if I saw him?" She'd been through three books so far.

"Touchy," he said mildly. "Be right back." He left the cubicle and returned with a can of Diet Pepsi and two croissants wrapped in bright green napkins. He settled into a swivel chair opposite the metal desk where Rita sat.

"No donuts," he said.

She looked at him. "What?"

"You know, cops and donuts? In San Francisco they eat croissants."

"Oh."

"Little joke."

"Ha, ha." She'd barely spoken to him all morning. She couldn't help it; he got on her nerves. After the sex last night he'd gone right back to snoring while she lay there sleepless, listening to the different rhythms of their breathing, to a car pulling out of the parking lot with a dragging muffler, to the dark, tormented voices in her head. Then him trying to have sex with her again this morning after giving her the tea, and her telling him no, and him looking so hurt. Now he was making stupid jokes. If she had some junk she would be running it up her arm right now, no question about it.

"There sure are a lot of criminals in the world," she said. It was depressing, looking at face after face caught by the camera. Maybe it was because usually, in photographs, people smiled. No one was smiling here. If they didn't look scared or mean, they looked drugged, like they were looking at you from underwater. Like they had already drowned.

"I need a cigarette." She used a napkin to mark her place and closed the book she'd been looking through.

"We've got to go outside," Gary Shepard said. There was a sign above the desk that read Smoke a Cigarette, Go to Prison. A clean ashtray sat on the desk, holding down a single piece of paper—some kind of form. ACKNOWLEDGMENT OF DISCOVERY, Rita read. PEOPLE V. _____. COURT NO. _____. The ashtray was bright blue with a green island and a palm tree at one end, Hawaii in gold letters against the blue.

Outside, the sky was the same blue as the ashtray. They sat on the steps together and smoked. A policewoman—Gary Shepard's friend—stood a few feet away from them, just finishing her own cigarette. She dropped it, stepped on it with her boot, and then picked up the flattened butt and threw it toward a nearby trash receptacle; it landed about halfway.

"I saw that, Jackie," Gary Shepard called to her.

"Don't you just feel like a pariah?" the policewoman said. "I hate this town. Find anything interesting?"

"Not yet."

"Don't take all day," she said. She walked back inside, giving Rita a quick look. Rita wondered if she was a dyke. She had short brown hair and wore pale pink lipstick. She looked like a man in makeup.

"What's a pariah?" Rita said.

"A member of an oppressed social caste in India."

"Oh." She shifted restlessly, blinking her eyes. It was too

bright. She needed sunglasses. She needed to lie down already. She thought maybe she could sleep for a few days, or a week.

"In other words, an outcast," Gary Shepard said. "Anybody who's despised, put down, by other people."

"In other words, I got it," Rita said. "Christ. I got it from the first thing you said."

They finished their cigarettes in silence. Rita took the butts and threw them in the trash can. She picked up the policewoman's and threw it in, too. They went back inside, past the line of people waiting to go through the metal detectors—Gary Shepard walked her in under the Exit sign and waved casually at the cop sitting at a table—and she resumed looking at the faces of men who had screwed up, done bad things, made some grave error in judgment. Some of them were evil, she was sure. But after a while they all looked the same. There were clearly too many bad people in the world. She tried to force herself to concentrate. She didn't want to miss him. He was out there somewhere, walking around, violent thoughts of her filling his head.

"Oh, God," she said. Her pulse started pounding in her forehead.

"Did you find him?" Gary Shepard came around to her side of the desk to look.

"It's Jimmy. It's my old man." She touched the small face in the photograph with her index finger. Jimmy looking at her. Jimmy looking away.

Jimmy.

"Does this mean he's in jail? Why's he in here?" She felt like he was physically there, trapped in the page, and she was seeing him through little windows. She touched his profile again.

"Hard to say. This just shows that he was booked."

"Well, how do we find out?" She grabbed one of his wrists

in both her hands and pulled at him. "What do we do now? Help me out here."

Gary Shepard appeared to be considering. "I'll ask Jackie," he said. "We can go to 475 and pull a copy of his Mugshot Profile and take a look."

"Where's that at? What street is it?"

"*Room* 475," he said.

"Okay," Rita said. "You do that." Suddenly she needed to get away from him, from this place. She needed privacy. She did not need Gary Shepard's face, this cubicle, these square fluorescent ceiling tiles. "Go look," she said. "Is there a bathroom around here somewhere?"

"Down the hall and hang a left. Tell me his full name, date of birth. His social if you know it."

"James John D'Angelo. October 27, 1966. I don't know his social." It sounded to her like they were talking about someone else, someone possibly not even real. "I'm going to the bathroom, then," she said.

The bathroom had four stalls of gray marble. She entered the far one, put down the toilet lid and sat on it, hunching forward. She looked at the floor, small black and white tiles, a few broken ones so she could see the cement underneath. A plastic tampon wrapper lay there like a shed skin. She was shaking. She rubbed her palms rapidly up and down her arms, trying to stop.

She wiped her sweating underarms with some toilet paper, stood up and opened the lid and dropped it in. Please Do Not Flush Tampons, a sign next to the handle said, but the lettering was sloppy; Rita misread it the first time. Please Do Not Rush Tampons. She unlocked the stall door, went to one of the sinks and splashed water on her face. She gripped the edge of the sink until she finally stopped shaking, but she could feel her heart still going a million miles an hour.

*

James John D'Angelo's Mugshot Profile informed Gary that Mr. D'Angelo had been taken into custody on July 6, at 2:37 A.M. Under his photo was the code 212(B). He'd been charged with Robbery, Second Degree. Rita's husband was a thief. At least he apparently hadn't been an armed one; that would have been First Degree and a year or two in state prison. Depending on what he'd been convicted of, he could still be incarcerated. On the other hand, he might be out by now.

On his way back to General Works, Gary saw Selina, a junkie who'd been a witness in a case he had worked on. She'd spent her life trying, and mostly failing, to fend off guys intent on taking her pants down. The last time he'd seen her, she'd said, "I'm looking for a career change." It was clear she hadn't yet found a new line of work. She sat on a wooden bench near the jury room, nodding out.

"Selina," Gary said.

"Whoa," she said, trying to focus, not really seeing him.

He went back to Jackie's cubicle, but Rita wasn't back from the bathroom yet.

He waited. He picked up a framed photograph sitting on the desk: a smiling black woman holding a toddler. Jackie's girlfriend and her daughter. The toddler was much lighter than her mother. Her hair was in neat cornrows, like the dead teenager he'd seen photos of the day before. The girl wore a T-shirt embossed with a cartoon Dalmatian. Gary studied every detail of the picture, obsessively, as though there was something in it he had to figure out. Jackie's girlfriend wore a slim gold watch. Gary tried to read the time on the watch; he thought if he had a magnifying glass he probably could. He stared at the tiny watch face in the photograph, then set it back down.

He could check the jail list, to see if Jimmy was there. That was the first place to look for criminals, if you were looking. And it made your job easier—you didn't need to hit the streets and deal with all the crazies. If Jimmy was in jail, Gary could find him with a phone call.

Rita pushed open the door, and he stood up. There were croissant flakes on his pants and he brushed them off, feeling foolish.

"So what did you find out?" she said.

"He was arrested in July."

"I knew it."

"You knew?"

"I mean, I get it. Why I couldn't find him. Why he didn't come back to our hotel. You have to help me find him." She had picked up a croissant and was eating it hungrily, walking back and forth in front of him, talking with her mouth full.

"What if he doesn't want to be found?"

"It's not like he's hiding or anything," Rita said. She looked at the rest of the croissant in her hand, shoved it in her mouth and came over to the desk and picked up her soda and started chugging it. She looked like she might grab the ashtray next.

"How do you know he's not hiding?"

She looked at him like he was unutterably stupid.

"That's what you do, right? You can find all kinds of people," she said, and resumed pacing. "All—kinds—of—people," she said, like a chant.

"Not always," he said. "Sometimes I can't." He tried to sound like it would be a big disappointment to him if he couldn't help her. He went over and put his arms around her from behind, to stop her pacing. She stood stiffly, looking down.

"Look, of course I'll see what I can do." He didn't want to

help her find her ex-husband. Husband. Whatever. Who was he, anyway? Some loser with a record. There were thousands just like him all over the city, in jail and out of it, their lives contaminated—that was the word that came to mind, contaminated, as in stained, polluted, dirtied—with drugs and guns and get-rich-quick schemes that went nowhere, with arguments and elaborate revenge scenarios that got enacted, or didn't, against people just like themselves. He thought of the Mission gangs, Norteños in their red colors, Sureños in blue. Just so they could tell each other apart. Otherwise, how would you know who was your brother, and who was your enemy? This shit's so obvious, he thought. Amazing that they never get it. And she's hung up on some guy who's probably forgotten all about her.

"Thank you," Rita said. She moved away from him and did a little turn in front of the desk. "This is great. I'm going to find Jimmy. It's about time. It's *really* about *time*. How do we do it? Where do we start?"

"Let's start with lunch," Gary said. "It might take a while."

"But you'll do it. You'll find him."

"He might have left town. He might have left the state."

"Well, even if he has," Rita said, "you could still find him, right? That's your job, right?"

"Maybe," Gary said. "I'll try, Rita."

"Try hard," she said.

She looked so happy. That was what he'd wanted, to make her happy. But now he felt like he might be a little in love with her. It wasn't the good kind of love. It was the jealous, selfish kind, that wanted her all for himself. To hell with what she wanted. He could help her by being with her, he could make her life better.

He glanced at the photos of James D'Angelo. Fuck you, pal, he said to them and closed the book.

*

The judge at the arraignment in Department 12, a court-room at the end of the hall on the first floor of the San Francisco Hall of Justice, was a tired-looking older black woman with straightened hair. She did not apologize to Mr. D'Angelo for the terrible mixup that had led to his unjust incarceration. She asked if Mr. D'Angelo could afford counsel; Mr. D'Angelo allowed that he could not. He was assigned a public defender, but the public defender informed the judge that her office had defended Mr. D'Angelo previously, so it might be best if this went to the Conflicts Council. There was a wait while the conflicts attorney was sent for, and then the judge waived a formal reading of the charges, and Jimmy's new attorney entered a plea of not guilty. Then it was the next guy's turn.

Jimmy's attorney was rail-thin and looked to be about the same age as Jimmy. He had a bone-crushing handshake, probably something he had practiced to seem confident, but his eyes betrayed him. They darted all over the interview room when he talked, his glance lighting everywhere but on Jimmy's face, like a wild animal that was trapped and looking for a way out. He wore a curly brown hairpiece. You almost couldn't tell it was one, so it was probably expensive.

"The DA's coming down heavy on crimes against women," the attorney told him. "We'll have to hope for a good judge."

"I didn't try to rape her," Jimmy said. "I hardly knew her."

The attorney laughed, like Jimmy had made a joke. There was a pale smear of mustard at the corner of his mouth. He'd probably just had a hot dog; his breath smelled of relish and Altoids. "Right," he said. "Mint?" he offered, opening the tin and taking one for himself.

Jimmy declined, and watched him do it three more times while they talked, taking the tin out of his leather briefcase, removing a mint, putting the tin back. Sucking on the mint and then chewing it, talking the whole time, then five minutes later taking out the tin again. It was making Jimmy sick. He tried to overcome his dislike for the guy, since he was stuck with him, but he couldn't muster up any warm feelings. This guy had probably never been in jail in his life, probably never even had an unpaid parking ticket. Jimmy looked at the walls of the room, to avoid seeing any more of the attorney's ritual with the mints, but there was nothing to look at. The attorney's words hung in the air: attempted rape. Felony assault. Lucky they didn't tack on GBI. Great Bodily Injury, dude. That could add three years to your sentence. Lucky for you.

Yeah, I feel lucky, Jimmy thought bitterly.

Finally the attorney stood, snapped his briefcase shut and offered Jimmy his hand, sliding his eyes at the table and then the floor. Jimmy felt himself being squeezed again. Wrung out.

"Nice to meet you," the attorney said. "Stay cool."

"Yeah," Jimmy said, trying to pull his hand back. "Thanks. You, too." What a clown.

"Right on," his attorney said.

*

Gary took Rita to a Cambodian restaurant. The teenaged waitress was chatty. She had just come from Cambodia, where she had lived on a farm. She loved America, she loved Whoppers, she loved all the American movie stars.

"I like Tab Hunter," she said.

"Tab who?" Rita said. "Only Tab I know is a soft drink.

Remember Tab?" she said to Gary. "Do they still have Tab? It tasted like shit."

The waitress frowned at the word *shit* and went to get them beers.

Afterward they went to a few bars and got slightly loaded. "Get me out of this hippie dress," Rita moaned. "I'd like to," Gary said, but she gave him a dirty look. They went to the Goodwill, where Rita picked up some clothing. Then another bar where they knew him and would give him credit. He'd tried to call Sanchez at the Medical Examiner's Office to borrow some money, but Sanchez was still in Mexico for his anniversary.

He figured he could stall Rita about finding her husband for at least a couple of weeks, telling her he was checking different possibilities. Then he'd tell her he'd exhausted all his leads and just couldn't find him. Sorry, I'm not God. It was a lame excuse—hey, I'm only human. But he couldn't think of a better one. Excuse me for living, he thought blackly, mentally facing a stern, disapproving Annie, then a crying Annie—Annie miserable and hurt, curled on their bed, hating him.

They ended up in North Beach at The Saloon on Grant Street. Johnny Nitro and the Doorslammers were playing. It was packed, the crowd at the bar three deep, people pushing their way through the crush of dancers to get to the bathrooms at the back. Rita had on a jeans skirt and a black tank top. She was dancing, then crying and crying.

"You'd better not have anymore," Gary said, though he was more than a little drunk himself. He reached for his glass and knocked it over.

The crowd thinned out, suddenly, as though everyone was responding to some secret signal. A group of women exited, their arms around each other, laughing in near-hysteria. Some leather-jacketed men followed them and sat gunning the engines of their motorcycles out front before taking off.

The music stopped. Johnny Nitro walked offstage and went to stand at one end of the bar. The other guys in the band went outside. Rita had gone outside, too. Gary went after her, moving slowly.

It was after eleven now. The earlier feel of the streets—an energy made up of the anticipation of couples on their way to dinner and bars and cafés, of young men in twos and threes sauntering toward the remaining strip clubs on Broadway, of raw-voiced street singers hoping for a few dollars to be tossed into a guitar case—the feeling had changed. It was a Monday night, and people had headed home to the suburbs or other parts of the city. Gary passed a trio of hulking boys in letter jackets who pressed back against a building as he went by. "When I heard that story about her penny-tossing night," one of them said, "I almost crapped." Rita was slightly ahead of him, walking fast with her arms crossed and her head down, with that funny loose walk she had—taking steps too big for her, almost loping along; her legs were white blurs. There was a blues bar at Grant and Green, and from its doorway came a wave of buzzy amplified bass guitar and the reek of beer and urine. On the far corner a blond teenaged boy in suspenders slouched against a streetlight, playing something vaguely French-sounding on an accordion.

Rita turned down Green Street, and Gary hurried around the corner to keep her in sight. The fish he'd eaten for lunch rose up in his throat for a moment, sour with bile, and he swallowed it, hardly noticing the taste. He was feeling lighter all of a sudden, riding on the adrenaline rush of fear that she was going to disappear, that he'd be left drunk in North

Beach with no place to go. He couldn't go home. He couldn't go back to that hotel room in the Sunset alone; it was too sad and ugly without her in it.

"Rita," he called. "Hey. Wait up." He tried to keep the panic from his voice.

She sped up; she was practically running. A deer headed for the woods. The one time he'd gone hunting with his father they had gotten up before dawn, opening the refrigerator for a paper bag of sandwiches his mother had made for them. Cold light on the red and white squares of the kitchen floor. The quiet click as he closed the front door. Slipping outside into the chilly darkness, and then the warmth of the car heater while his father drove them north. The deer had stepped out right in front of him; he'd just stood and watched it until it caught his scent and ran off. He couldn't pull the trigger.

But his father had; and had made him watch as he opened it up with his hunting knife.

He felt sick again.

He ran after her, stumbling down the hill into Washington Square Park. She sat on a bench with her feet drawn up. He dropped onto the far end, blood pounding in his head.

"Go away," she said.

She put her head in her arms and rocked a little on the bench. A couple walked by, their heads close together, the woman's arm around the man's shoulder. A man dragged a miniature poodle on a long leash, waited while it squatted to shit, and went off without scooping it from the path. Then it was empty. There were a few lights along the path, and the church was lit up, but they were in shadow under the trees.

"Go away," she repeated. "Go far away and leave me alone."

"No. I don't want to."

"Just go," she said, "Or I will." She didn't move, though. She'd stopped rocking.

"I love you." He didn't know if he meant it or not.

"Oh, please stop with that shit," she said, sounding tired.

"It'll be all right. I'm getting some money tomorrow. Or soon. From a buddy of mine." He needed to keep talking. If he kept talking, she'd stay, and he wouldn't pass out. His adrenaline had drained away. He could feel his brain stubbornly trying to shut itself down, to pass through a black doorway into a room where there was nothing but silence and soft, inviting sleep. He started to move toward her, but she flinched, so he stayed where he was. "It'll be all right," he said again. Everything's going to work out. But he was thinking that, not saying it aloud, and then he was lying on his back on the bench, saying (or thinking), Rita? Are you still there? and the trees were black above him, looking down at him with pity, slowly shaking their heads.

*

Four men had attacked a drug-dealing couple on the corner of Eddy and Taylor. While the male dealer lay on the ground with a gun held to his head, one of the attackers put his hand down the woman's sweatpants and said, "Give me everything you've got in your pussy." Then they broke her jaw. In the Witness Statement, the male dealer had said of the attacker, *He entered her sweatpants near the region of her vagina area. Then he began feeling around, like it was the beginning of intimacy.*

On another day, Gary would have been amused by the literary style of this particular witness. He would have repeated the statement to a few attorneys and cops who would similarly appreciate it and who might have stories of their own to recount, stories most people would find sad or sickening or offensive. Today it wasn't funny.

He'd woken up alone on the bench in Washington Square Park early in the morning, his clothes damp, fog dripping from the trees. Now he had a bad hangover, despite the Bloody Mary he'd drunk earlier to take the edge off; he didn't want to risk drinking more than that because he had to be in court. After court, he had to find a crack whore named Baltimore in reference to an assault case. He was sick of assault cases. He was sick of crack whores, too. "Crack tosses," they were called. "Toss-ups." Lately, the new term that some of the white cops used privately for black defendants was "Triple-A's"—African-American Assholes. The courts were a joke. Justice was a joke. Usually the joke was funny, but right now he'd lost his sense of humor.

He made it through the court hearing and then went to get another drink. In the Hotel Coronado on Ellis Street, he interviewed Baltimore, who was growing a goatee, and who offered to give him a blow job for twenty dollars. He declined. He called Sanchez, who was finally back, and borrowed three hundred dollars and went back to the hotel in the Sunset with some takeout shrimp chow mein and a fresh bottle of Jack Daniel's and waited, hoping Rita would show up.

He lay on the hotel bed in his boxer shorts. Annie had bought them for him. He had failed Annie. Rita, apparently, would rather be on the streets than anywhere near him. No wonder so many people in rooms like this did nothing but live from one drink or needle shot or crack hit to the next. They were sick of the whole deal. It wasn't funny. He picked up the bottle from the floor and poured about four more fingers into his glass. He thought of Annie, sitting with her Chardonnay night after night. Of Baltimore saying, *Well, if you don't want your dick sucked, how about loaning me five dollars so I can get a drink?* Of the men he'd seen that morning, rolling up their bedrolls on the church steps, heading over to Columbus or Broadway to beg enough change for a bottle.

He remembered a man he and Annie had seen on their honeymoon in Italy. They'd gone to Harry's Bar in Venice one night and eaten an obscenely rich, obscenely overpriced dinner; afterward, on the street, they watched a well-dressed man stagger from the bar to an expensive hotel across the way, so drunk he lurched crazily around on rubbery legs like someone with a bad case of palsy. It was funny to Gary because the man was so pathetic, but Annie had been upset.

Annie was right. It wasn't funny.

Gary raised his glass and looked through it at the ceiling light, the bulb trapped inside the paper shade that dangled from the ceiling, drowning in amber fluid.

"Here's to us," he said. "Drinkers of the world unite."

*

Rita spent Tuesday on Haight Street and in Golden Gate Park after riding the buses most of the night. Charles was in the park, without his dog. "I spent the night at Civic Center Plaza," he said. "When I woke up, Sally was gone. I don't know what I'm gonna do. I don't know why I'm living." Charles told her the city was doing a special trash pickup that night out in the Sunset. Ordinarily he would go, but he was too depressed. He was drunker than she'd ever seen him, and didn't offer her a taste from his bottle.

At dusk, she walked past the old Kezar Stadium to Ninth and Irving and caught the streetcar. The fog had come in from the ocean and was hovering a few feet above the houses. Her skin and hair felt clammy, and when she found a Raiders sweatshirt she put it on right away. A whole army of people was already there, silently picking through boxes and trash bags set out by the curbs. People with shopping carts and dollies and vans and pickups, hauling away old mattresses and dressers and sewing machines or just carrying what they could. Lamps and books, cassette tapes and stuffed animals and good sheets and blankets. Clothing of all sizes. She found a red backpack that only had the outside zipper broken, and stuffed in a pair of jeans and a couple of T-shirts. She found a hardback copy of *Little Women* that had belonged to the San Francisco Library—inside the front cover was a sticker that said DATE DUE and ended at February 3, 1995—and flipped through it.

Her mother had read her some of that book aloud, years ago, but somewhere along the line she'd stopped. This one had black-and-white drawings and a few color illustrations with captions. In one, the girls and their mother sang around the piano. The caption read, *The girls never grew too old for that lullaby.* A few pages later she read, *The young pair took their places under the arch,* below a picture of one of the girls in a long wedding dress, standing with her husband-to-be before the preacher.

Rita and Jimmy had gone to City Hall and had a woman justice of the peace. "Marriage is not a commitment to be entered into lightly," the woman had said in her nasally New York voice. She looked at them, Rita thought, as though they had been caught shoplifting. Rita wore a beige dress. Later that night, they went to a party a friend of Jimmy's threw for them. She remembered going out to sit by herself on the deck where the keg was. She wanted to be alone for a while with her happiness. She kicked off her shoes and sat on the railing and looked at the moon, and put her bare feet in the ice around the keg.

A ring around the moon meant bad weather was coming. There had been a ring that night. But bad weather was always coming. You just had to ride it out.

She slipped the book into the front pocket of the backpack and headed back to a streetcar stop on Taraval. Tonight she wanted a bed. But not Gary Shepard's bed. He had said he was her friend, but he didn't mean it. He'd said he would help her find Jimmy, but she knew he was lying. He was like the rest of them; he wanted what he wanted, and the hell with her. Well, she would sleep in her own bed, paid for by her own self. She didn't need anyone to take care of her. I've done all right until now, haven't I? she thought. Yeah, right, she answered herself. You've done a brilliant job with your life. Ha ha ha, I crack myself up sometimes I'm so funny.

The streetcar stop was near a Taco Bell. She was hungry for a burrito, but she only had enough for the fare if she was going to get a room. She rode back toward downtown, wondering if maybe Jimmy was living out by the ocean or nearby in Daly City or if he was even in the Bay Area anymore. She wondered if she was traveling toward him or away or doing anything but going around in circles.

Give me a sign, she thought, looking out the window. I'm talking to you, are you listening up there? Do you care? I'm not praying here, I'm just asking a question.

Lit-up Chinese restaurants. A florist shop, closed and dark. Houses with TVs on in the living rooms and cars in the driveways. Woolworth's, which was closing—big SALE signs all over the windows. Bar neon: Joxer Daly's, The Philosopher's Club. Then the bright arch of the West Portal tunnel.

Probably no one will remember that Woolworth's when

it's gone. Something else will be there. Everything changes, and how the hell are you supposed to keep up? There has to be something to hold on to.

She looked down at her hands, locked together in her lap.

The car stopped at West Portal Station, taking on a few more people. Then it lurched off into the dark, going underground, taking her she didn't know where.

*

He wasn't in jail anymore. He was standing in front of a door, and Rita was opening it, then shutting it almost all the way to slide the chain off, and then she was standing there in jeans and a white scoop-neck T-shirt, wearing a thin gold cross at the end of a delicate chain, the cross glittery against her skin. He could smell her vanilla oil and the balsam scent of the conditioner she used. He had brought her a sunflower, it drooped toward her and she laughed. He pulled her to him and they danced, forward-step-drag-together, like his mother had showed him when he was a kid. *Jimmy*, Rita said. Then she turned and crumpled to the floor and only her clothes were there, like the movie on TV last week; a comet passed close to the earth and everyone went outside to see it and they turned to dust. He picked up the cross and closed it in his hand. When he woke up he was lying on his back and his fist was clenched beside him on the bunk, and he opened his hand slowly but of course there was nothing.

*

She stood under a streetlight in a jeans skirt and a little gold jacket and some slightly tight heels she had found in the stuff left out in the Sunset, and she waited. That's all you ever had to do, wait for them. They were like dogs. They sniffed you out, whether you wanted them to or not. Their heads were full of pictures from dirty magazines or movies, and there was a feeling in the center of them connected to that, down deep in their balls somewhere, and it drove them to find you wherever you were, walking down the street minding your own business, but your jeans were tight and they focused on your ass in front of them. Or you were wait-ing for a bus, lost in your own thoughts and dreams and sad-ness, but your sweater stretched over your breasts and they saw some porn actress squeezing her breasts together with her mouth open saying, *Oh yeah, give it to me,* and that's what you were to them, a pair of breasts and a mouth saying the thing that would relieve that feeling in them. Or else you deliberately stood a certain way or wore a certain outfit, it didn't take much, and they were calling out disrespectful shit to you or watching and waiting politely for their chance to drag you off somewhere.

A car stopped, a white Toyota with three white guys who were about her own age, all of them looking scared and pleased with themselves to be talking to a prostitute; the one in the back, who had fat cheeks and ears that stuck out, stared at Rita, practically drooling. She got in next to him. They were middle-class boys; she could get this over with and walk away with a good chunk of cash. The one next to her was high on something, coke or speed from the way he was jittering back and forth; he put his hand on her knee, touching it tentatively and staring at her to see what she'd do. The two in front were arguing about which motel was cheapest and closest. The car smelled of pot and French fries and cologne.

Rita looked out the window. I'm going nowhere in a hurry, she thought. There's got to be something. Give me a sign.

The boy next to her inched his hand up her thigh, under her skirt, and she pushed it away and told him to fuck himself.

*

Afterward, they refused to take her anywhere. They were in the Days Inn on Lombard Street. They were all snorting coke and had gotten too high to drive. They offered to let her stay there, but she wanted to get away from them.

At the front desk, she asked about another room, but the clerk said the motel was full. The woman looked at her with what Rita knew was feigned kindness. Rita could see the woman hated her. Earlier, when they'd all gotten the room, the woman had flicked her eyes at Rita, a cold look Rita could see was still there, just beneath the surface of the woman's cheery demeanor. "Sorry, honey," the woman said. "We're full up. You'd better go somewhere else."

She hurried out, ashamed. There were other hotels along the street, a hotel every few feet, but she couldn't bring herself to go in, afraid the next clerk would look at her the same way. She walked down Lombard toward North Beach, the red backpack over one shoulder. A car occasionally honked or slowed, a face peered out at her, blurred by glass, twisted by curiosity or lust; sometimes they called to her. The heels were hurting her feet so she put them in the backpack and took out the shoes Gary Shepard had gotten her and kept walking. In North Beach, she bought a slice of pizza and a pint of Jose Cuervo, figuring that would get her high faster than anything, and went to sit in a doorway.

A man who looked like Jimmy walked by—same height, same black hair, but a leather jacket that was beat up, not anything Jimmy would wear; Jimmy didn't like clothes that were worn out. The man was drinking something from a paper cup through a straw, walking slowly, peering at each establishment along the street as though trying to memorize it. She watched him pass a strip joint, a girl in long blond pigtails and a silver dress trying to convince him to come in, telling him he didn't have to pay the two-drink minimum because it was almost closing time, but he should come in anyway, just come and watch the dancing. Rita wanted to run after him, even though he wasn't Jimmy. She wanted to make him Jimmy, to pretend for five minutes that she'd found him.

But I'm not even looking, she told herself sadly.

How do you find anybody? she thought. It was an accident we met in the first place. That party my neighbor gave, that I almost didn't go to. How Jimmy came right up to me by the kitchen table and asked if I wanted a beer and asked my name. And after that we were together, and pretty soon he was there every night and I rubbed his head so he could fall asleep. Every night. And now he's so gone it's like he was never here. So what's the point. What's the point of loving anybody or trying to do anything right in this messed-up world. And if God made it, he's pretty messed up, too.

She stood up and the girl at the strip place glanced at her. Rita was sick of people looking at her, the men in cars, the boys in the Days Inn staring and staring when she took off her clothes. *Her body's all right*, one of them said. The desk clerk with her neat gray hair and an ugly gray silk bow at her throat. *You go on, now.*

From the doorway, decorated with photos of strippers, the girl said with her eyes, *You're pitiful. You're not worth anything. I'm standing here dressed up and made up and I'm beautiful and I have a job and I'm doing it, and you're on the street with your pint bottle and your greasy dripping pizza.*

She finished the slice and downed the tequila until she felt sufficiently drunk, then took another big swallow before standing up. She started walking again, down Columbus, then through the Financial District. She was tired but she couldn't stop walking, she didn't want to stop because stopping meant thinking how she'd failed at everything, at finding Jimmy and at having some kind of decent life and being somebody. She walked, and the night air was clear and fresh, and the wind pushed her hair off her face a little, and it was quiet among all the tall buildings where nobody was working—only the janitors vacuuming the carpets and emptying trash baskets somewhere inside, behind the lit glass windows, getting everything ready for the workers who would come in the morning. She would walk until she was too tired to walk anymore and then she would lie down and give up finally—why had she even tried?—and whatever happened would happen, she didn't care anymore. She stopped on the sidewalk and drank some more.

A van slowed beside her; she didn't even look. Then someone was behind her. An arm locked around her throat, cutting off the air. She dropped the bottle, heard it hit the sidewalk, but it didn't break. She tried to fight him, but she was dizzy, and he was much bigger than she was. She was trying to scream, but his hand was over her mouth, and the side door of the van was sliding open for her, and it seemed like a dream she was having—the kind of dream where you can't move and you scream inside but nothing comes out of your mouth—and then the door closed, and she saw the other one, sitting in the driver's seat and turning to look at her. His face was familiar, and she almost laughed because Death wasn't the way she always pictured him; he wasn't in flowing black robes with a skeleton face at all, he was wearing a stupid corduroy jacket and big glasses that were bifocals, magnifying his eyes so he resembled a fly, a big-eyed ugly fly who looked at her and smiled and told her, "Hello."

＊

Gary jerked awake in the middle of the night to sirens whining past—a fire truck, then an ambulance. Then another. He looked into the darkness, confused, automatically reaching out an arm for Annie. Then he realized where he was, and couldn't fall asleep the rest of the night. There were no more sirens. He thought maybe he could hear the ocean, but then again it might be a fan somewhere. When it started getting light, he went out and found a coffee shop and drank down three cups, blacker and progressively more bitter, and scanned the headlines of Wednesday's *Chronicle* without seeing them.

It came to him that he had wrecked his life as surely as any of his clients had wrecked theirs. He'd committed the same crime, of not looking in the mirror to see who he was, just going blindly toward something he thought he wanted, something that was going to magically change his circumstances without his ever dealing with them. It was easier to blow up your life than to sit down and try to figure it out. That was the lesson he should have learned from the streets, through seeing it happen over and over.

He thought of Annie waking up in their bed alone, getting ready for work, putting on what she called her Front Desk Appearance. Taking the bus to the Financial District every morning, the same routine day after day, so there would be some steady money coming in and they didn't have to rely on his constantly shifting caseload. Doing her Tarot cards. He thought of her waiting dinner or leaving it on the stove for him or just eating frozen pizza and drinking wine, sitting up in front of the TV, and he got for the first time that Annie was in real pain, and that she had loved him, and that he had a lot of shit from which to redeem himself in terms of their marriage. If they still had a marriage. He didn't even know if he wanted it. At least Rita had known what she wanted, even if she didn't know how to get it.

He went to the pay phone by the bathroom and called County Jail #9. It didn't take long to find James D'Angelo, charged just two days ago with assault and attempted rape. He'd been booked on Saturday, too recently for that info to have made it into his Mugshot Profile when Gary looked. But now here he was conveniently back in custody. How considerate of him, Gary thought, to get rearrested so I could find him easily. He asked where the inmate was housed. He knew Jimmy's attorney—not a bad guy, but definitely B team. He called him at his office.

"Tommy Boy. It's Shepard. Listen, I heard about a case you just caught. James D'Angelo. You got an investigator?"

"No," said Tommy. "Not at this juncture."

"Let me do this," Gary said. "I know the people involved. I don't care if you pay me on this one."

"I'll get you an order. You want the case, no problem, I'll get you the case."

"Thanks, T.B."

"Right on, Shepard."

"You keep saying that," Gary said, "you're gonna start growing an Afro."

"Very funny." Tommy was sensitive about wearing a hair-piece.

He got the rundown on Jimmy's case. Jimmy had done three months in San Bruno for the robbery. He had admitted to Tommy that he'd hit Robin but said he hadn't tried to rape her. There were other people to contact: a guy named Stan and Robin's friend Patricia.

"This guy, D'Angelo," Gary said. "What's he do? He got an address? A job?"

"Works at a restaurant south of Market. Trendy place. Piazza di Spagna. Waiting, bussing tables. One of those. No, waiter I think."

"My wife knows it." That was the restaurant Annie had wanted to go to the night he had taken Rita to the Holiday Inn.

"I heard it's good," Tommy said.

"What do you know, you think Pizza Hut's good. Listen, I'm on this. Catch you later."

"Right on."

"Thanks, bro." Gary hung up. He got the address of Stan's store and decided to drop by. He called Robin at work, told her who he was and that he needed to talk to her. She agreed to meet him that afternoon in a bar in the Financial District. When he hung up he felt like things were rolling in the right direction. Turning from the phone he saw some graffiti, printed neatly in large letters on the green tile wall near the Men's Room: I AM THE VINDICATOR OF THE DAMNED. He laughed. It was funny again.

*

Light hit the smoked windows of the van and turned to a gray dust that filtered in, tiny particles on a broad beam of light that diffused and gradually disappeared in the shadowy interior. She was lying on her side, naked, looking at a telephone—a tan plastic cradle and handset. The van had other junk tossed back there: a dusty clock radio, a Folgers coffee

can on its side, a half-full bag of Kingsford Charcoal Bri-
quettes. The silver duct tape that had been used to cover her
mouth and bind her wrists behind her was sitting on the
white plastic tray of a baby seat—the kind that rolled, so the
baby could sit inside it and use its feet to propel itself across a
room. Last night, as they drove, it had rolled across the van
with every turn, bumping against her. The phone's cord was
tight around her ankles. Her feet were numb, dead, heavy.
She could reach them with her hands by arching her back,
but her hands had been taped so she couldn't use her fingers
to untie the cord. There was a quilt underneath her, but it
was worn thin, and through it she felt the ridged metal of the
van floor against her hip. Earlier, when she'd awakened,
she'd had to pee. It had dried on her legs; the quilt was still
damp. The smell of her own urine, sharp and familiar, was
somehow comforting.

They had hardly touched her. They hadn't fucked her.
Yet. She knew the one with the corduroy jacket was proba-
bly going to. That and worse. The other one, the one who
had grabbed her, the same one who'd helped the driver that
night at the Barker, had gotten out of the van the night
before; he and the driver had had an argument.

"Cut her clothes off," the driver had said.

"Ah, come on," the other one said. "I could hardly cut the
duct tape. This is stupid." He waved a pair of child's scissors
in the air—small ones with blunt ends and a yellow duck
head for the handle, so that the scissors were its beak.

"What happened to the real scissors?" he said.

"I don't know," the driver said, "You had them last. Don't
you have a knife or something?"

"What do I want to carry a knife for? What if I get
searched sometime?"

"Less than six inches is legal."

"Yeah, but it tells them you're a certain type of person, know what I mean?"

"Just cut her clothes off."

"No, man, I ain't gonna do it. This whole thing sucks."

"You want to be paid, cut her clothes off." The driver's voice was mild, logical.

"How can you treat her like this?" the other one said. "I thought she was your girlfriend."

"Was," the driver said, "is the operative word here. We've got some issues to work out."

"You're not gonna hurt her." Rita could hear the doubt in his voice.

"I know what you're thinking," the driver said. Logical. Not threatening, not threatening at all. "I told you, I didn't even know it was a body until we got there. All the guy told me was, 'pick up some stuff from the hotel and take it down to Hunters Point.' That's what we did, right?"

"Yeah, but it was a dead girl. And now, Jesus. This is like kidnapping or something."

"This is between me and her," the driver said. "Isn't it, baby?" he said, turning around to look at her. "I'm sorry, honey," he said. "This is the only way I could get you to listen. We're going to work it out. You'll see."

The driver started singing along with the radio, which was tuned to an oldies station. "My Girl" was followed by "Chapel of Love," which he took the high harmony on. She lay rigid and kept her eyes closed and listened to his voice.

"This is wrong," the one in the passenger seat said. "I don't know what she did to you, man, but this is wrong. I ain't gonna cut her clothes off. Besides these scissors ain't sharp enough. She's got on a denim skirt."

"Maybe you should stay out of my business," the driver said.

"Hey, you're the one that asked me along."

"Well, now I'm asking you to leave."

"Fine. I'm leaving. Let me out."

"Fine. I'll call you."

"Fuck you, don't call me. I'm through with this kind of shit. I don't *want* it, I don't *need* it."

The van pulled over and he got out and slammed the door. The driver leaned over and locked it. He drove on, singing to more oldies: "Michelle" by the Beatles, and "Cherish" by she didn't know who, but it was the same band that had done "Along Comes Mary"—oh, yeah, The Association. Her mother used to play their album. And "Spooky" by she really had no idea. It must be the love song hour or something. Every so often, the driver turned and looked at her. All she saw was the streetlights bouncing off his glasses. She was glad she couldn't see his eyes or his messed-up hand.

They finally stopped somewhere, and he got out and came back with a long kitchen knife, and, while he cut through the thin gold jacket and tank top and skirt (he slid the knife under her waistband and pulled the blade toward him, having to saw a little at the waistband) and her panties and gently removed her shoes, he talked to her like she really was his girlfriend, like they had had a falling out and now he was going to make it all up to her and they would be just fine. "Hey, sweetheart," he said. "Everything's going to be all right now," he said. "Don't worry, I'll be back soon." Then he took her right nipple between his thumb and forefinger and squeezed it so hard she nearly passed out.

Now it was dawn. She lay listening to the noise of birds

welcoming the day; there were a lot of them, calling to each other, answering back. "Chapel of Love" played over and over in her head. The birds knew. Knew what? The birds didn't know anything. They were chirping away while she lay there helpless, they were singing and thinking about the worms they'd get and how they'd fly around all day in the blue sky. What day was it, anyway? She thought back. Sunday she'd been at Gary Shepard's house. Monday she saw the picture of Jimmy, and thought for a while that Gary was going to help her find him. Monday was the bright spot. Tuesday it got darker, and Tuesday night darker still. Today was Wednesday, the day before Thanksgiving. The day the dead bird gets carved up and eaten. She realized she was cold, and had been shivering; now she started shaking. *Today's the day, we'll say I do. And we'll never be lonely anymore.*

*

It took less than half an hour to handle Robin. Gary had gone by Stan's shop already, and once Stan understood that Gary wasn't a cop, he'd been happy to discuss all the legal and illegal drugs they had been consuming. Stan had even given his drug legalization speech, which Gary assured him was an incisive critique of the state of the current administration's policy.

"I'm only here to find out what went on that night," Gary told Robin, after they'd gotten drinks—a Cosmopolitan for her, a Beck's for him—and ordered some fried calamari and pizzeta. "He said he didn't try to rape you. You know, it will be a big hit if he goes down for these charges. Do you really hate him that much?" He had his ace in hole—he could explain to her that the details of that night would come out in court, from the coke she'd snorted to other times she'd left bars with guys (he didn't know that for sure, but he had a feeling her friend Patricia would confirm it). He could have gone there, but he didn't even need to.

"I know the DA," Gary told her. "We can go and tell him what really happened, and all this can go away. You won't need to go to court. After all, you were clearly victimized. You were hit in the face." Gary acknowledged that Jimmy had done an awful thing, hitting Robin. But he also happened to know how terribly sorry Jimmy was about the whole episode. Jimmy had said that after he was free, he wanted to personally apologize for what he had done. By the time Gary finished bullshitting, Robin was apologizing for ever filing the police report, and their appetizers hadn't even arrived yet.

"It's all right," Gary had said. "Hey, we all make mistakes. You thought you were doing the right thing."

"The thing is," Robin said. "I liked him. I really liked him."

"He's a good guy," Gary said. "I met him. I talked to him." Or anyway I will, he thought. "He really liked you, too," Gary said.

"Maybe you could give him my phone number," Robin said.

"No problem," Gary said.

Now he was back at 850 Bryant, waiting in an ugly room with a table and two chairs. My home away from home, he thought. Maybe my only home anymore. He didn't want to believe that. He hadn't called Annie yet, but he knew he had to, soon. The longer he waited, the worse it was going to get.

A guard brought Jimmy in. Gary could see why women would like him. Dark Italian good looks, a lean body, and that brooding expression that said, *I'm troubled. I'm filled with sorrows. I'm dangerous and sensitive, and the world has treated me badly.* Women loved that shit.

"Jimmy," Gary said, and stood up to shake his hand across the table. "I'm Gary Shepard."

"Hey," Jimmy said. "You a lawyer or something?"

"I'm an investigator," Gary told him. "And this is your lucky day."

*

Her arms hurt. She rolled around, trying to ease the ache in her back and shoulders, her right hip; everything hurt. More than anything she wanted to be able to open her mouth; she worked and worked her jaw, trying to loosen the tape. Her tongue felt enormous, it seemed like it would choke her. She kept having to swallow and feeling panicked that her saliva was going to fill up her mouth and throat and somehow drown her. She thrashed around frantically, and then lay still, breathing fast through her nose.

The passenger door of the van opened, and he got in. He wore a pair of tan pants and a pale blue knit shirt like golfers on TV wore. He kneeled over her and put his hands on either side of her head and then his face was close to hers, so close she could see every pore in his skin. He smelled like garlic and motor oil and he wore a retainer; she could see the thin silver wire across his front teeth, and it gave him a slight lisp when he spoke.

"This was all a mistake," he said.

Mistake. There weren't any words of her own in her brain; there was only fear, a steady dull hammering at the back of her skull, and the words he was saying. *All a mistake. This. Mistake.*

"I didn't mean to kill her." He smiled, and she looked into his mouth, at the cloudy pink plastic of the retainer sticking to the roof of his mouth, exuding its own smell of germs and saliva and decay.

Kill her, Rita thought.

"She just made me so mad!" he cried, rocking back and sitting on Rita's thighs. Her hands were trapped beneath her, and the sudden weight caused a searing shock in her wrists. She shifted under him and succeeded in easing the pain a little.

"It has to be corrected," he said.

Corrected. It has to be, has to be, has to be. Her life was a mistake, and he was going to correct it, finally. She had prayed for a sign, and God had sent this man to her. God was merciful and just, and his punishments were just. She had let her mother die at the hands of Karl Hauptmann, and God was finally getting around to punishing her.

His palms were on her breasts, rubbing them rhythmically. He was above her with his eyes closed and he was going to punish her now not only for her mother but for her entire life, for being a whore, for losing Jimmy, her husband, when she was supposed to cleave to him always. God knew all about her. God has his eye on the sparrow. The birds know.

She peed herself again.

"You know how sometimes, you do something you didn't mean to, but then it seems like you were headed for it all along? You know?" He seemed eager to hear Rita's opinion; he opened his eyes and looked at her intently. "Like it's your destiny or something."

He was on his knees again, rubbing himself against her where she had wet herself. She could feel him half-hard through the softness of his pants; his hands were soft, like his pants. God was gentle, looking down at her through the clouds; she closed her eyes and saw him, as she had when she was little, lying on the grass; God loved her, didn't he? *Jesus, loves me, this I know.* When did I know that? A long time ago. Then he stopped because I was bad. He went away, everyone went away. Now he's come back to give me what I deserve. God's will.

Now drops were falling on her face, big cold drops of his sweat hitting her closed eyes and cheeks and forehead. His dick had gone completely soft, his soft hands were around her neck, she was sinking into black pillows.

"Oh, hell," he said, "I can't."

She opened her eyes. He was looking at her sadly, with a pleading expression, like a little boy who'd just had a special toy taken away from him and was begging for it back.

"I have to be hard," he explained.

Rita nodded. *Hard.* Not soft. She understood, she showed him with her eyes that she understood. She couldn't do anything that would anger him. She had to please him, and maybe he would only fuck her up, maybe he wouldn't kill her.

"It's just no good otherwise." He climbed off her and sat beside her. "It's the drinking," he said. "I had, let's see. Three beers and then some vodka tonics. I thought I'd need to drink a little, you know? But it's a fine line. Now look," he said. "My pecker won't work."

He sighed. "You have nice tits," he said. "A little small, but nicely formed. I'm definitely going to fuck you first. Definitely."

Rita looked at him. God had decided she was not worth saving, not even worth teaching a lesson, getting fucked up and then let go. She hated God but he was all powerful.

"So here's what I'll do," he said. "I'll take a little nap. Then

I'll have two, maybe three vodkas. That should be about right. Then I'll come back. Turn over," he said.

Rita rolled over, away from him. She felt him check the tape around her hands, then the phone cord.

"I'll come back," he promised her.

Come back. She was alone. And it had started to rain again, for real this time; a few drops thwanged on the van's metal roof, then it came down hard and loud for several minutes. She smelled wet earth. She remembered watering her father's garden, water on the broad flat leaves of the zucchini plants, on the snap peas (she would always break some off to eat); the tomato plants sagged with fat tomatoes, and there was a little row of herbs that was her own to take care of: bunches of basil, thyme, the chamomile that she didn't pick that grew large and sprouted yellow flowers.

I'll come back. She listened hard to the rain. It stopped suddenly and the silence seemed louder than the rain had been, and she could tell the sun had come back out because some of it found its way in even through the windows.

She closed her eyes and saw Karl Hauptmann. He had yanked her jeans down and pushed inside of her, her underwear still on. He moved the fabric aside, the little bit of cotton cloth protecting her. The underwear said *Monday* in red script. She had a pair for each day of the week. He had held his hand over her mouth and she had tried to scream, to kick. She tried to bite him, but he pushed the heel of his palm against her mouth and closed her nose with his thumb and forefinger so she couldn't breathe. She nearly passed out before he let her have any air. There was nothing she could do.

Nothing I could do.

She saw Karl with his buck knife, that was usually on his belt in a leather sheath, and the quick movement he must have used. After he ran out she went into the bedroom and there was her mother and the blood everywhere; she wadded up the top sheet and held it to the wound but the blood wouldn't stop, it soaked through the sheet; how could there be so much blood? Her mother looked at her wildly, clutched at her own throat and at Rita, making horrible sounds, and Rita was crying saying, *Mom, Mom*, and outside an ambulance wailed, but it wasn't coming their way; it receded into the distance. She didn't know if she should run for help. She was afraid to leave her mother, to stop the pressure on the wound. And then her mother's body relaxed and her eyes were still open, two holes taking in the daylight that seeped around the edges of the curtains. And Rita was supposed to find forgiveness in her heart for Karl Hauptmann but she could not, and never would, forgive him.

She struggled up onto her knees and looked around the van, at her red backpack with the broken zipper and the stuff around it, the baby seat and bag of briquettes and some old clothes and greasy rags, at a tiny spider crawling over the Folgers can to the rim where the red handle of a pair of scissors stuck out.

*

Jimmy's apartment building smelled like tomatoes cooking; the guy in the wheelchair who lived downstairs was probably making spaghetti, or rather, the friend who took care of him was. It smelled better than Piazza di Spagna. It smelled amazing, and his room, with its small kitchen and bed against one wall where photos of Muddy Waters and Little Walter and John Lee Hooker were framed in a row, looked cozy and inviting. He wanted to sit on his couch, crack open a beer and not do a thing but be in his own place, enjoying the luxury of it. Instead he showered and dressed in a white shirt and pressed black pants and went in to work.

Walter was sitting at one end of the bar having a bagel dog from Noah's for lunch and reading the *Examiner*. When he saw Jimmy, he folded the newspaper neatly and set it on the bar and picked up a wineglass he'd been drinking from. There was nothing but water in it; Walter had been dry for years.

"James," Walter said. "We had given up all hope."

"I was in jail," Jimmy said. "Otherwise I would have been here."

"Well, that's a hell of an excuse," Walter said. "Whatever happened to 'my grandmother died'?"

"I'm sorry. But I want you to know, I didn't blow you off. There wasn't anything I could do."

"Why didn't you tell me until now?"

"I was afraid you'd fire me. Look, I've been a good worker. I—"

"What were you in jail for?" Walter interrupted.

"Um, assault," Jimmy said. "But the charges got dismissed." He decided not to mention the rest of it. The word *rape* would not sound good to Walter's ears.

"Then you didn't do anything."

Jimmy didn't know what to say. Of course, he had done something. He knew what he'd done. "No," he said. "I guess not."

"Don't ever go into the restaurant business," Walter said. "Too many headaches. Too much responsibility. Where does the time go? I used to be like you. Young and full of myself. Rebellious."

"Yes, sir," Jimmy said uncertainly, wondering if that was really how he came off. Rebellion was the furthest thing from his mind.

"Well," Walter said, "You'd better get in the kitchen because our slacker friend Rufino didn't make it in today. You don't mind washing dishes, do you? Can you stay?"

"No problem," Jimmy said. "I can stay."

✳

Rita managed to use the sharp ends of the scissors to stab the tape that bound her hands by getting the scissors upright and backing up onto them a few times. When she could use her fingers, she pulled the tape off her mouth as fast as she could, one quick rip that made her gasp in pain, then took long deep breaths, drinking in the air. She cut the telephone cord. The scissors were sharp. Beautiful scissors. Beautiful sharp scissors.

Thank you. Thank you, you won't be sorry. I can be better. Do you hear me?—and though nothing happened she felt a flutter in her stomach; that was good enough for now.

She opened the backpack and pulled out a T-shirt. She could put her jeans on later. She drew the backpack over her shoulders. Her feet started tingling painfully, the nerves waking up, and she rubbed them until she felt she could walk on them. Holding the scissors before her, she crept up front into the space between the driver and passenger seats and peered carefully over the rim of the window.

The van was pulled up beside a one-story, pink house with three steps and a wooden railing leading up to a small porch area and the front door. There was an identical house on the other side, only painted gray. Up and down the street, the same design happened over and over—three steps to the door, and to the right or sometimes to the left of it, the only variation, a big picture window. On the stairs of the pink house were some potted cactuses. A couple of yards over, a little girl squatted in the grass studying something Rita couldn't see, her thumb planted in her mouth. Otherwise, no one was around.

She crawled over the driver's seat and pushed the door handle down slowly. Locked. She reached up and unlocked it, her fingers slippery with sweat, then pushed down on the handle again. The door made a loud, frightening click and swung open. She hoped she'd guessed right, that he was in the pink house on the other side of the van, and not the gray one she was facing. She jumped out and ran.

*

She had guessed wrong. He came running out of the gray house, yelling "Hey! hey!" and started after her. She didn't know where she was; nothing looked familiar. She ran down the sidewalk under some scrawny trees, carrying the jeans rolled under one arm, the backpack rhythmically hitting between her shoulder blades. She veered toward one of the houses and scrambled over a low fence into someone's back yard, and shrugged out of the backpack. There was a bicycle on its side, a sandbox with a blue bucket in it, some yellow flowers spread low to the ground that she trampled through, heading for the back fence. It was higher, but there was a metal shed she could climb on to get over. She heard a dog barking and when she got on the roof of the shed she saw it on the other side, lunging on its chain, staked to a post in the yard. It looked like a cross between a Doberman and a pit bull, black and squat and angry, pacing back and forth in a shallow muddy ditch worn into the sparse grass of the yard, looking up at her. There wasn't any place else to go. If she ran fast enough she could get away from it; the chain wasn't long. She turned and the man was coming toward her, his hair messed up and no glasses, looking almost ridiculous, almost funny; he didn't have any shoes or socks on. He climbed. "Hey," he said. "Hey," and got hold of her ankle.

*

Gary looked for her around Polk Street and the Tenderloin. Finally, he went back to the hotel, but she wasn't there, either. He let himself into the room, lay on the bed with his hands behind his head, and looked around helplessly. There was nothing to tell him who he was. No shelves of books, no prints on the wall, nothing. He felt an overwhelming sadness that there was no trace of him in this crummy room, that it refused his presence so completely. It wasn't a place where he belonged.

He got up and opened the window and stood there smoking, looking out at the parking lot and a large puddle where a couple of birds were washing themselves. The puddle was oil-slicked and shiny, and he wondered what it was in the composition of grease that made it scatter colors like a rainbow. A seagull glided down toward the puddle and the smaller birds flew off, until it lifted away and they hopped and skittered back. Past the parking lot were the flat tar-and-gravel roofs of some houses, and then the ocean, looking gray and riled up after all the weather, whitecaps as far as he could see. He flicked the end of the cigarette through the bars on the window and watched it drop to the asphalt below, then went over to the mirror leaning against the wall and, after pushing the nail in farther, hung it carefully from its wire. He wrote out the address Jimmy had given him on the back of one of his business cards and wrote JIMMY above it, then looked around trying to decide where to put it. Finally, he made the bed and put the card in the center of the pillow. On the back of a second card he wrote, CALL ME.

He stopped by the front desk and paid for another night, making sure the woman understood that Rita might come back, that she wouldn't have a key and might need to be let in. Then he went home to try and talk to Annie.

*

Jimmy scrubbed bowls and plates and silverware and turned glasses upside down on the yellow brush and fed everything into the big metal dishwasher, then turned it on so it was a grinding, sloshing beast that nearly drowned out the sound of the radio on the counter. He didn't mind that he was back to washing dishes or that someone had switched the radio from nineties rock to seventies disco or that his good pants had already gotten a small grease stain on them despite his blue apron. He felt his body churning with energy. His sleeves were rolled up and he was sweating profusely. He had to keep dipping his head to one shoulder or the other to wipe the sweat from his eyes.

"Look at you," Jorge said. "Slow down, man, you'll make us all look bad."

"I feel good!" Jimmy yelled, doing a James Brown imitation over the noise of the radio.

"Yeah, well slow down before you break something," Jorge said. "You gonna drop something, moving so fast."

"No way," Jimmy said. "Nothing gets broken from now on."

*

Rita felt herself being dragged down off the shed, through the wet leaves on its roof, over the sharp edge. She tried to find something to hold on to. There was nothing to grab but more leaves and sticks and mud. She kicked at the man but he had gotten hold of her with both his hands; he pulled her and fell back into the yard and she fell down on top of him, and threw a hand out to break her fall, and pain shot up her right arm. The dog was going crazy yelping and barking, its nails scrabbling against the fence on the other side, its chain clanking. Good. Maybe its owner would come. Maybe the people in the house would look out their window.

He had her around the waist now and was hoisting her up. She flailed at him. He punched her and she felt bone ring against bone, his knuckles hitting her just below her left eye.

No.

I don't want to die I don't want to die I don't want to die please God. Though I walk through the valley of the shadow—

He got her slung over his shoulder and started out of the yard. There was a little gate, she saw it as it swung closed, after they went through it, heard the click of the latch. There was a yellow flower. A spider web on a corner of the house with a scattering of tiny insects in it, hardly a meal, the whole thing shuddering in the wind. She was fighting to keep her head up and scream as soon as she caught her breath. She struggled again, and he gripped her tightly, heading back toward his house, cutting through the yards; where was the little girl who had been outside in the grass, where was anyone? The neighborhood was empty. There was no one. And it was sunny, how could it be sunny? No one should die when the sun was coming through the leaves throwing patterns on the grass, and a squirrel was running across a lawn and nearby there was a freeway, she could hear the trucks and cars passing with people in them, there were people everywhere but here, it seemed.

And then there was a police car coming around the corner, its lights swirling, coming for her, for she was worth saving after all, and the car halted abruptly at the curb and a cop got out, a brawny black cop wearing a uniform and a nightstick and a gun, and the Bogeyman stopped and then he simply dropped her; he let her go.

*

Annie wasn't home. Usually she would be back from work by now; maybe she was out taking pictures. Or getting divorce papers drawn up. Gary walked around their house, looking at the things they'd accumulated together. The pottery they'd shopped for in Mexico. A green glass serving bowl they'd been given as a wedding present. The Harry's Bar cookbook from Venice that they'd never used except to make Bellinis one night; afterward they'd danced around the house, the music blasting. Annie had chosen the peach color of the walls; Gary had painted them, painstakingly taping along the molding and floorboards. They had picked out the expensive couch together, the only one that would do, with the deep cushions he had loved sinking into after a long day.

She'd taken all his clothes out of their closet and piled them on the floor of his office. He went into their bedroom. She'd left the bed unmade. The T-shirt she'd slept in was lying on the floor. There was an empty wineglass on the night table, an empty bottle partway under the bed. He picked them up and took them into the kitchen.

The kitchen table had been left the way it was when Annie walked in Sunday morning—evidence of his offense. He put her glass in the sink, dropped all the wine bottles in the recycling bin on the deck, put the candles away. He wrote her a note and left it on the table, under a pepper grinder. *Annie, I'm sorry. I don't know if we can make each other happy but I want to try. Please call me. I'm so sorry I hurt you.* It was inadequate; it was the best he could do. He drove back to the office to take care of some paperwork, but all he did was smoke cigarettes and drink a can of Rainier Ale from the office fridge.

Then Rita called him from Mission Station, and asked him to come right away.

⁎

"What about the other guy?" Gary said.

They were in a room in Mission Station that smelled like Chinese food and brownies; the brownies were sitting on the desk, half unwrapped from their tinfoil. He watched her eat two of them. She'd given her statement to the police already. They had the guy who had grabbed her in custody. It was Gary's considered opinion that he wasn't going to be back on the streets anytime soon.

"The other guy," Rita said. She described the one who had argued with the driver, the one who hadn't wanted to cut her clothes off. His short spiky gray hair. How he smelled like cigarettes and pot.

"Anything else?" Gary said. "Tattoos, scars, anything unusual?"

"Well, he wore rings. Like three or four on the same hand. And he did have a tattoo on his arm. A peacock."

Gary laughed.

"What's so funny," Rita said.

"It's Stan. The guy I interviewed this morning at his jewelry store. Beautiful. Six degrees of separation. It's more like two."

"He was actually kind of nice."

"For a kidnapper."

"He just thought I was the other man's girlfriend."

"I'm sure he's a terrific guy."

"It wasn't his fault."

"Of course not," Gary said. "It never is."

He stood behind her chair and put his hands on her shoulders, and thought of how she'd leaned her head back against him, in his kitchen. He felt a physical pain in his chest. They were literal, he realized, those things people said about the heart; it really did ache. It felt like it could fracture and crack open.

"I found Jimmy," he said.

She inhaled sharply, exhaled a quick, high "Ah—" a sound she had also made when they made love. Had sex. Whatever it was to her, he didn't know.

"I have his address." He didn't tell her the rest. He had only told Jimmy that he knew Rita, that she wanted to find him. He'd told him that much in case Jimmy reacted with indifference or told Gary that he didn't want to see Rita. But Jimmy had smiled. Had said, "Rita. Tell her where I am. Tell her to come on over."

"He's living here in the Mission," Gary said. He turned to the desk and tore off a ruled piece of yellow paper from a pad, wrote down the address, and handed it to her. "I left it for you at the hotel, too," he said, "in case you went back there. It's paid for tonight if you need a place."

She read the address and then folded it and put it in the pocket of her jeans. "Thank you," she said. "You're a good man."

He looked at the pen he still held in his hands and set it back in a white coffee mug with other pens and markers in it. He picked up a brownie and took a bite though he wasn't hungry. "It's my job," he said.

He was done.

★

She walked a block down Twenty-second Street and then ran for the 14 Mission bus that started to pull away from the curb right as she got there. She banged on the doors, and the bus stopped, and the driver—a pretty woman with long dark permed hair, streaked with magenta—opened them and smiled at her, even though Rita knew she looked like hell. Her neck was bruised, she had a black eye, her arms were scratched up. She had cleaned up the best she could in the bathroom at the police station.

"Thank you for stopping," Rita said.

"No problem, honey," the driver said. "I hope you're leaving him for good."

"Something like that," she said.

★

Piazza di Spagna closed from three to five thirty P.M., between lunch and dinner. It always took time to clean up, and then there were invariably a few people who lingered over their lunches so you had to wait for the plates and silverware and glasses to make it back to the kitchen. The radio blasted, and everyone was focused and happy because they were almost done and looking forward to heading home for their own dinner or stopping by a bar somewhere. Then Walter had asked Jimmy to stay and help set up for dinner, and Jimmy almost had to work another shift because a bus boy was late, but at six thirty the bus boy showed and he was finally able to leave.

He had a feeling she was there already. He got off the bus at the flower stand and bought a big sunflower. The woman who sold it to him was an old Latina with a face like cracked

leather. "Very beautiful!" she said as she wrapped some
green tissue paper around the stem, and he said, "Yes, very
beautiful," and it was, it was the brightest thing on the street
as he walked the two blocks toward his building.

*

She'd found a thrift store and picked up a long-sleeved silk
shirt for three dollars. Turquoise, expensive, not even a
sweat stain on it. It was amazing what people gave away.
She found a big leather purse and in a drugstore she bought
foundation and lipstick and eyeliner and put them on with
the help of a small rectangle of mirror on a rack of sun-
glasses. Then she bought a pair of sunglasses since the area
around her eye had started to swell.

If she kept the sunglasses on and no one looked too
closely, you couldn't even tell.

She found his building, went up the hall stairs, and
knocked on the door of his apartment. He wasn't home yet.
As she was going back down, the door of another apartment
opened, and a man in a wheelchair rolled partway into the
hall.

"You looking for Jimmy?" he said.

"I am," Rita said. "Do you know what time he'll be back?"

"No. You can come in and wait for him if you want."

Music was playing in the apartment behind him, and
someone was washing dishes. A male voice was singing
along with Elton John, doing the song for Princess Diana,
who had died in August. Rita had been at Terrance's then.
Terrance had shed many tears for Princess Diana.

"Thank you. But I guess I'll wait outside." She wondered
if he had AIDS, like the man from the Blue Door who had

been Jimmy's friend. He didn't look like he was wasting away, though. He had strong, sunburned arms and a massive chest under a sweatshirt with the sleeves cut off. He had a tattoo on his forearm that read, HOW DO YOU LIKE YOUR BLUE-EYED BOY, MR. DEATH?

"Suit yourself," he said.

She went outside to wait on the steps. She watched the late light burning on the windows of buildings across the street.

She sat for two hours, getting more and more hungry. She'd eaten nothing all day but those brownies at the police station. It felt like no time at all because soon he was going to come walking down the street and she would say, *Hello, Jimmy,* very quietly and not at all like she had been waiting to see him, just a soft Hello to let him know she was there if he wanted her.

And if he didn't, she would manage, somehow.

She was thirsty, too, but she didn't want to risk leaving for even a few minutes to get a beer, in case he came back. People went in and out of the bar across the street. The fruit stand on the corner closed. She watched a couple of men roll the big wooden bins inside, then let down a corrugated metal door over the entrance.

Tomorrow I'll shop there. If they're open on Thanksgiving. Well, maybe the day after. I'll get some mangoes and make them the way Jimmy likes them, with some lime and hot pepper.

The thought of mangoes made her thirsty again.

Maybe I'll just stop into that bar over there and have a quick one.

But she stayed where she was. It was evening, and shadows were filling the street; the dark was coming. But it was

KIM ADDONIZIO

only ordinary darkness. The streetlights came on all together. Lights began flaring in windows up and down the block, where people were returning to families or friends, looking forward to the holiday; soon they would give thanks, grateful to spend a few hours with those they had chosen or been given to love, those they had gathered around them to help them live.

acknowledgments

Gratitude: to V, for his stories and his generous assistance with the details of matters legal and illegal. To Leo Litwak, Sally Arteseros, and William Vollmann for feedback. To Larry Fondation, who said that survival is a form of hope. To Susan Browne for reminding me of the importance of the pain-body. I am also grateful to everyone at Simon & Schuster, especially my editor, Marysue Rucci, who deserves every superlative I can think of. And to my agent, Rob McQuilkin, for his belief in this book and in me.

about the author

Kim Addonizio's critically acclaimed debut novel, *Little Beauties*, was described by Oprah's *O Magazine* as "a wonderfully optimistic, quirky testament to the power of chance encounters." An award-winning poet and fiction writer, Addonizio was a National Book Award Finalist in 2000. Her work has appeared widely in journals and anthologies, including The *Mississippi Review, The Paris Review*, and many others. She has received a Guggenheim Fellowship, two NEA grants, and a Pushcart Prize. Addonizio lives in Oakland, California. www.kimaddonizio.com